PASSION'S VOICE

Selena was reaching for the cut-off switch when she heard Mark's voice. She wanted to shut off the com unit but her hand betrayed her.

"Selena, this is Mark."

Selena could only stare at the unit, her mouth too dry to speak, afraid that her voice would betray her as had her hand.

"I know you don't want to talk to me, Selena. Just listen and say 'yes' when I'm finished. I'm not going to give you a list of reasons—"

Belatedly, Selena's hand followed her command. Quiet came to the tent, but not to Selena's mind. As though her hand had never moved Mark's voice continued in her mind.

But you can't reach me.

Mark's reply was gentle and tinged with laughter. *Selena, darling Golden Eyes. Many possibilities exist that you've never dreamed of. Come to me; we have so much to learn and share and enjoy.*

Selena wanted to cry Yes, but it was strangled by old fear and recent hurt. She tried to shut out Mark, to hurl him from her mind, but he was far stronger. Suddenly she was alone with only the ghost of his last words to disturb her. *I've been stupid, Selena. I thought it was rejection you feared, but it's love.* Rich with anger and sorrow, his words echoed through the frightened pathways of her mind.

Also By This Author

Writing as Ann Maxwell

Shadow and Silk*
The Ruby
The Secret Sisters
The Diamond Tiger
Fire Dancer
Dancer's Luck
Dancer's Illusion
Timeshadow Rider
The Jaws of Menx
Name of a Shadow
The Singer Enigma
Dead God Dancing
Change

Writing as Elizabeth Lowell

*Winter Fire
Autumn Lover
Only Love
Only You
Only Mine
Only His
Untamed
Forbidden
Enchanted
A Woman Without Lies
Forget Me Not
Lover in the Rough
Tell Me No Lies
*Desert Rain

*forthcoming

EVERYBODY LOVES ANN MAXWELL!

WRITERS LOVE ANN MAXWELL!

"Ann Maxwell's voice is one of the most powerful and compelling in the romance genre. She writes intense stories, and her readers are equally intense in their response. She has contributed much to the definition of the modern romance novel."

—*New York Times* bestselling author Jayne Ann Krentz

"No one has a voice like Ann Maxwell. She is stellar!"

—Stella Cameron, author of *Sheer Pleasures*

"Ann Maxwell may be *the* most talented, evocative writer in the genre. I pick up her books for more than pleasure. I pick them up to be inspired."

—Suzanne Forster, author of *Blush*

CRITICS LOVE ANN MAXWELL!

". . . Weaves together past and present, tosses in tidbits about archeology without impairing the story's non-stop action or putting a crimp in the romance. Maxwell's control of her material and unabashed willingness to entertain make this book a success."

—*Publishers Weekly* on *The Secret Sisters*

"Only Ann Maxwell could have brought this story to such explosive life. . . . An unforgettable sensory experience, this splendorous tale of adventure is everything a reader could wish and much, much more."

—*Rave Reviews* on *The Secret Sisters*

YOU'LL LOVE ANN MAXWELL, TOO!

ANN MAXWELL

CHANGE

PINNACLE BOOKS
KENSINGTON PUBLISHING CORP.

PINNACLE BOOKS are published by

Kensington Publishing Corp.
850 Third Avenue
New York, NY 10022

Pinnacle and the P logo Reg. U.S. Pat. & TM Off.

First Pinnacle Printing: August, 1996

Printed in the United States of America

10 9 8 7 6 5 4 3 2 1

I

"Selena Christian, stand and face the court."

With neither haste nor reluctance, Selena rose from her chair at the defense table and faced the court. It was the third week of her trial, and her lawyer was sweating with eagerness to be rid of her. Contempt for him, and for the curious, seething mass of spectators straightened her shoulders. Her golden eyes flashed in the sudden blaze of light as holo crews switched on their machines to record every twitch for posterity.

Treason, sedition, conspiracy, the list of charges seemed as endless as a dark street on a lonely night. When she heard the word "witchcraft" she barely suppressed a laugh. Were she a witch, she would have conjured herself the hell out of here, leaving a trail of snakes and mice. Her so-called lawyer would be no trick; Molls was already two-thirds mouse. The rest was pure rat.

And the prosecutor. . . . An unpleasant smile distorted Selena's lips. For a searing instant she craved the malevolent powers implied in the charges. Then Mark Curien would suffer as few men had.

As though sensing her hostility, the prosecutor turned his attention to her. His face and body gave away nothing when he looked at her. His eyes did not linger on her lustrous dark hair or the finely turned curves of her body, nor did they approve of her tautly restrained energy as they once had. Now, it was as though a computer had scanned her and said, yes, this human is Selena Christian.

"Sit down, Selena," whispered her lawyer urgently. "And don't stare at anyone, especially Mr. Curien."

Selena leaned away from Molls, but sat down as directed. "Does it matter?" she said very softly. "I'm dead whether I stare or shut my eyes."

"You ought to know. You helped Curien write the death warrant."

Anger tightened Selena's hands into claws. "Let go, little man. I've had enough shrill from you. We agree that Curien is a snake and I'm a bird-mind; now let it be. I'm paying the charge."

"On the contrary," he whispered. "The Minority is paying. We would have had the Humanistos where it grows close. They would have been powerless, humiliated, defeated. World Government would have been rid of them. But no; you had to . . ."

Selena's look shut off Molls' invective just as the judge called for the first in the daily parade of witnesses. Without interest, Selena recognized the government agent who had arrested her. He identified her for the court.

His voice reminded her of that night—how many months ago?—when she took the payoff to Nado's drop. Nado, long may he writhe, was an Ear. If any parans were around and using their talents, he'd find them. And if the parans weren't registered, Nado blackmailed them. Not too much. He left you enough to survive, if you didn't mind starving.

Nado, of course, was registered. He was a citizen in good standing, an Ear, a combination bloodhound and judas goat and a useful tool of the government—or anyone else who could afford him.

Selena wondered briefly if Nado had been caught, then dismissed it as irrelevant. He probably was short or owed a favor, and she was payment.

The government man stepped down, to be replaced by the other person who had assisted at the arrest.

As the Good Earther took the stand, Selena didn't bother to conceal her contempt. The sect was not nearly so powerful as it had been ten years ago. Green cowls and jumpsuits, pyrite cubes and saltwater were losing their hold over the average mind. Even little children get bored with too many fairy tales, no matter how terrifying.

Again she heard the insipid Good Earth incantation:

> *The salt and water*
> *Of this Good Earth*
> *Restrain the Devil*
> *And his curse.*
>
> *The Blessed Cube*
> *Shields pure minds*
> *To keep the Faithful*
> *From Demonkind.*

At least this time she hadn't gotten a face full of saltwater. In fact, she thought she had heard a few snickers from the spectators.

Apparently the exorcist had heard laughter, too. He glared at the crowd, kissed his pyrite talisman perfunctorily, and declared himself ready to answer questions.

Selena listened to the exorcist's catalogue of paran bestialities for a few minutes, then withdrew into herself. It was the same old shrill which had hunted and killed her parents and made her life a high-wire act strung between the poles of secrecy for survival and hunger for human contact. Haunting memories of warm arms and laughter, of kisses that healed cuts and long talks that stretched her mind: the past had made the present intolerable. It would have been better if her parents had hated her. Then she would accept hatred as normal, rather than be tormented by loneliness.

Selena moved her shoulders impatiently. The past was dead; as soon as this farce ended she would be dead, too. Everything else was shrill. She'd had plenty of practice at being alone. If the novelty of being close to another person had flipped her off the high wire, then she'd pay the charge—and not ask whether the flame was worth the candle.

But was it?

In bittersweet torment the last months flooded her thoughts. The terrifying night of her arrest, being dragged and kicked and kicking back, lashing out against her captors and the stuporous drug invading her mind and body until even terror slept.

The first cell was small, painted Good Earth green, stinking with old sweat. The drug wore off slowly, but fear didn't wake. Fear is born of hope and her mind had completed the equation burned into her childhood: capture equals death. One pole of life was gone; the hope of survival lay toppled; the high-wire act ended.

Only loneliness remained.

Barely had she grasped this when the cell door opened, framing the green jumpsuit of a Good Earth acolyte—or assistant. The Good Earth was both sect and administrative corps of the Humanistos party.

But this was no administrator. He was too young and drops of fear rode his forehead. His speech was an incoherent mixture of incantation and questions. The only thing she understood was his fear of her and his hatred.

When his questions went unanswered, he swung his talisman at her. She saw the golden arc of pyrite and felt a flash of pain across her cheek.

And she did not move. She, who had fought over scraps in the gutter, who knew the ways of hand-killing, she let a frightened acolyte flay her with a pyrite talisman.

She didn't turn away, but stared at him with unreadable yellow eyes. She heard him scream "Devil!", saw his hand raised for a second blow, green sleeve falling away from a thin and trembling arm. Then faint surprise when the glittering chain stayed suspended, its arc diminishing into stillness.

A different voice spoke, a voice of richness and power, warmth and anger. "Meditate upon the devils within you, acolyte. They will kill you sooner than she."

Long brown fingers uncurled from the acolyte's wrist, freeing him. He left with a hurried bow, closing the door quietly.

Although the new man was dressed in Good Earth green, he wore the loose shirt and cowl which distinguished high officials of the Humanistos party. The cowl partially concealed unruly chestnut hair, made a mystery of olive green eyes, deepened lines which curved his lips into a reassuring smile. Not until his hand gently touched her cheek did her old reflexes return.

When she flinched away he said softly, "I won't hurt you, Selena Christian. I just want to see how badly that idiot cut you."

When his hand again touched her, she didn't move. She watched his eyes wordlessly while he examined the cut.

"Not deep. Clean. Should heal quickly. Unless you want to see a doctor . . . ?"

She made no response.

"Does it hurt?"

Nothing.

"Do you understand that I won't hurt you?"

Silence.

Perplexed, the man returned her unwavering look, trying to reach behind the golden eyes. Then he seemed to realize that she wasn't staring at him, she was staring through him.

He smoothed her tangled hair away from the cut cheek.

"Can you walk?"

Wordlessly, Selena stood and walked past him. She turned at the closed door, wavered, and would have fallen had he not caught and held her.

His strange green eyes were so close. She had not been so close to anyone, ever. Fear struggled in her: to be close was to invite betrayal and death.

Then she laughed weakly, startling him. "You can't hurt me," she whispered. "No one can. I'm dead." Her laughter muted to tears, then soared again to laughter. "I'm free! All those horrible years. No more running; no more fear."

With a trembling sigh she murmured "Free!" and became a dead weight in his arms.

When she wakened again, she was in a different room. Sunlight slanting between window bars told her it was either early morning or late afternoon. With a start she realized her old clothes were gone. In their place a green robe wrapped around her.

Good Earth green. Her lips curled, then flattened. It didn't matter. What did matter was that the robe was clean and warm and softer than anything she had ever owned. She rubbed her palm appreciatively over the fabric. With the drug out of her system her senses were again acute.

She waited for the old habitual fear to come. When it didn't, she relaxed and enjoyed the simple sensual pleasure of fine cloth soothing and caressing her skin. A small smile rose to her lips and stayed, blurring old lines of suspicion and fear.

"I hope you're feeling as good as you look, Selena."

Startled, she stood to face the intruder.

"I didn't have a chance to tell you my name yesterday. I'm Mark Curien."

Selena nodded and sat again on the bed. Even now, fear didn't return. Only this strange acquiesence.

"Am I drugged?"

"No. Why?"

She looked at him intently, believed, and said, "I'm learning the truth of the old saying, 'Without hope, without fear.'" Her soft laughter filled the room. "How much time do I have, Goodman Curien, before I die?"

"I am not a Good Earther, Selena. Call me Mark. And are you so sure we want your death?"

"I'm a Branlow mutant. Every known Branlow is either dead or 'missing.' The Good Earthers saw to that."

"Humanistos are not Earthers."

Wordlessly Selena held out the skirt of her green robe.

He sighed. "Earthers have rich patrons throughout the world. Old money. The oldest. But they lost much of their following after the Revolution. Humanistos had many followers, but little money. We joined. Earthers pay the cargo, but Humanistos control the power."

Selena made no comment. The permutations and manipulations of political power held little interest for her. For whatever reason, at the hands of whatever political group, her high wire had broken.

"Why are you here?" she said finally.

"I will assist at your trial. To do that, I'll need to know more about you."

"I'm a Branlow mutant. What more is there to know?"

"Being a mutant, even a mutant with paranormal powers, is no offense." He ignored her bitter laughter and continued. "If you had registered as a paranormal you would be free. But unregistered, you violate the Alien Conspiracy Acts."

"And if I registered, I could walk out free," she said sardonically.

"No. It's too late for that. The trial will decide whether you used your talents illegally. If you're innocent of conspiracy, you'll be fined for not registering and given your freedom. If you're guilty, then you may, indeed, die."

"Alien contact," she said contemptuously. "What

shrill. The Rynlon were given an outshift years ago, thanks to your Earthers. I couldn't conspire with them if I wanted to."

"Do you want to?"

"No," she said irritably, "but there is something I want to do."

"Yes?"

"Eat."

Mark looked chagrined. "I forgot. I left orders that no one was to come near your room."

He activated the intercom and ordered breakfast for two. Within minutes a discreet knock announced the arrival of food.

As Mark set out the dishes, an odd shyness came over Selena. She hadn't eaten with anyone for longer than she cared to remember.

"If you're worried about drugs," said Mark casually, "I'll trade food with you."

Selena shook her head and sat down across from him. The table was so small she could feel the warmth of his legs through her thin robe, smell the clean scent of his skin, count the bronze hairs which rippled and shone with each movement of his arm. An old, amorphous desire rose in her—to be close, to touch, a little girl's longing honed by a woman's sensuality.

"Selena? What is it?"

She looked at his face, so near, seeming to care, and sudden anger pumped through her. "What is it? I'm a pariah, a paran, a freak. I haven't eaten with or been touched by anyone since I was ten. And there you sit, eating with me, touching me—"

"Are you afraid?"

"Damn you! No! But even freaks," she said harshly, "have the same feelings as normals."

Mark calmly put down his fork. "If by freaks you mean paranormals, you're partly right. Parans do have the same needs as normals, with this difference: parans need more intensely. Their response to every type of stimulus is exaggerated. Lower pain threshold, pleasure threshold, hunger, thirst, sexuality, every 'normal' feeling is magnified. In addition, the paran must cope with a constant, involuntary tide of information and emotion from the people around him. The sensory load on the brain is staggering. Some cannot take it and retreat into insanity. The parans who survive mentally intact invariably have superior intelligence. Intelligence, after all, is the ability to assimilate data from which new data can be made. This intelligence, however, does not guarantee emotional tranquility. It merely guarantees that when a paran acts impulsively—which is often—he knows very well the varieties of fool he is.

"Parans are all too human, Selena. Now eat your breakfast."

Selena looked at him wonderingly. "You're not afraid of me. I don't even disgust you."

Mark's low laugh seemed to tingle across her arms. "You don't seem to realize how attractive you are, Selena." He looked at her curiously. "Surely other men have noticed."

Selena's mouth became a hard line. "The first thing my parents taught me was that human contact outside the family would lead to betrayal and death."

"And after your parents died?"

She picked up her fork. "I survived."

Selena pressed against the hard plastic chair, stretching the muscles of her back. Molls' cross-examination of the Earther had proved the obvious: fanaticism and insantiy coexisted in the Good Earth sect. The next witness, a doctor, was describing exactly which qualities set Branlows apart from normal. She half-listened to the present, half-remembered the past, drifting on currents of fact and emotion.

". . . little difference between a Branlow infant and a normal baby. At first, we assumed that all yellow-eyed infants were Branlows. However, that proved not to be the case. The allele for yellow-eyes has become as common as that for green eyes. It is merely one of the more obvious of the thousands of mutations which have been recorded. I'm sure that the Court is aware of the 'epidemic' of mutations which began in the twenty-first century and has continued unabated. Thus, while all known Branlows have yellow eyes, less than .001 percent of yellow-eyed people are Branlows. The Branlow mutation itself is rare. Less than .0000032 percent of all live births are Branlows."

"Dr. Sayre," interrupted Mark, "are you sure that the defendant is a Branlow mutant?"

"Quite sure. Molecular scanning is very precise. Although Selena Christian carries an ident card which states that she is one of the thousands of yellow-eyed normals, there is no doubt that her genes are those of a Branlow mutant."

Selena suppressed a desire to announce that the card had cost her parents half a year's income, and that they had bought it from a Humanistos forger. Mark knew it; she'd told him months ago. She had told him many other things, too.

She had been a fool.

How easy, even pleasurable, he had made it. For weeks she saw no one else, nothing to undermine the near-giddiness of finally being accepted by another person. Even when he told her that some of their conversations would be taped, even then she had felt no warning. What do the almost-dead have to fear? Those hundred dreamlike days of mutal exploration, of growing certainty that he took as much pleasure in her friendship as she took in his.

God, how the touch of human kindness burned! It was a bright flame in the center of the universe which consumed and renewed her. And she still didn't know when it began. Perhaps the day she tested his statement that parans didn't disgust him. They had tacitly evolved a routine of formal questions for the tape followed by informal conversation.

Often the questions were the same, apparently as a safeguard against lying. The day had begun routinely enough.

"Repeaters again, Selena. I know you're not lying, but His Eminence likes to be sure."

Selena said nothing, content to admire Mark's grace as he quickly set up the machine.

"Ready?" he asked.

She nodded.

"Is Selena Christian your true name?"

"It was the custom of my mother's people to give girls just one name. When the girl contracts for a relationship, she takes the man's family name. In time my parents realized that no man would ever want me, so they temporized and called me Selena of the Spirit. After they were murdered, I took the name Christian."

"How were you different from other children your age?"

"I never was around any children of my own age. By the time I was old enough to have friends, it was too dangerous. My parents made it quite clear that the only way to keep a secret is to share it with no one. No one."

"And you were the secret."

"Yes."

"It's hard to believe that you had no friends after your parents died. Especially when you became a woman."

Selena sighed. They had been over this one many times. His Eminence must still be hopeful of uncovering other parans through her. She spoke at the machine. "No person or friendship is worth dying for."

"Your parents died for you."

"They had each other. For all I know they still do."

"That's all their sacrifice meant to you?"

"I loved them and then I was left behind. Even if I were normal I wouldn't love again. There is nothing worse than being left behind."

"Yet," he said, reaching out and touching her face, "you show no reluctance, no fear . . ."

Selena laughed, but there was little joy in the sound. "No, I'm not afraid of your friendship, Mark. Even should I love you," she said deliberately, "I'll be dead long before your love could hurt me."

When he would have protested, she said, "No. I believe everything you say, except that I'll live."

"You want to die," he said bluntly.

Selena drew in her breath swiftly. "I could have died many times. I fought to live. I gave up everything to survive."

"You gave up too much. You left yourself no reason to live."

"That's enough," she blazed. "When you've lived my life you can criticize it. Until then your opinions aren't worth a cold turd."

Mark's eyes narrowed, but all he said was, "I guess I should be grateful for your belief. It permits you to be a woman for the first—and last—time in your life."

"Next question," she said coldly.

Silence stretched, then Mark said, "All right, Selena, we'll do it your way. For now."

"Now is all there is."

Mark ignored her words and resumed questioning. "A few days ago you mentioned that you're unusually adept with animals. Is it a paran talent?"

"If rather precise empathy is paranormal, yes."

"How did you use this empathy?"

"To make friends."

"But never with people?"

"No."

"Why?"

"I didn't need it with my parents."

"After your parents died, didn't you use this gift?"

"Never."

"Not even to make life less lonely?"

Selena looked at him with rising irritation. "I said never and I meant it. You can't trust people, so what good are friends."

"All people aren't like Nado, Selena."

"No. The rest are so scared of parans they don't know whether to throw up or go get a mob. If you're lucky, they just puke."

"How old were you when the Revolution began?"

"Fifteen."

"And you were sixteen when you came to the Humanistos school?"

"Nineteen."

Mark raised his eyebrows. "Why did you lie about your age?"

"I looked more like fourteen than nineteen. Sixteen seemed like a good compromise."

"How old are you now?"

"Twenty-six."

"How much do you know about the specific characteristics of the Branlow mutation?"

"Other than we're slow to mature physically, not much. I don't subscribe to the Earther's shrill about shape-changing and mind-stealing and perversions too disgusting to talk about."

"Every religion has its demonology," he answered calmly. "But what of such paranormal abilities as mindspeech?"

She made a wry face. "More shrill."

"You're either lying or you aren't a Branlow. Most of the known paran mutations are capable of mindspeech after the onset of puberty. Branlows are among the earliest users of mindspeech—generally in their third year."

Selena stared at him in disbelief. "Then I'm not a Branlow mutant?"

Mark put his hand on her cheek and absently moved

his thumb over the high ridge of cheekbone as he thought over her question.

"Did you ever try mindspeech?" he said finally.

"I . . . once, maybe." Selena closed her eyes as she searched for the memory. "I was very young and I'd hurt myself. I wanted my mother. I didn't cry out to her, but she came anyway. She was afraid—and furious. She punished me by leaving me alone for a long time. I never tried mindspeech again with a person."

She opened her eyes to find his only inches away.

"Did you ever want to try mindspeech?" he said.

"No."

"Not even in your dreams?"

"Yes. No. I . . . don't want to talk about it." Then, perversely she wanted very much to talk about it, to see his horror when he heard, and the fear of parans which he denied.

"Yes," she said, "I've used mindspeech in my dreams, but not with humans. And," sarcastically, "not as a conspiracy. I don't even know if the planet exists, or if I made it up to keep me company."

"You're not making sense."

Selena smiled strangely, never looking away from his eyes. "For as long as I can remember I've dreamed of a strange, desolate planet inhabited by even stranger creatures."

"You're sure it wasn't Earth?"

"The life form was too alien."

"Describe it."

"Large beings, cat-like in agility and speed. They have a kind of society based on either telepathy or empathy."

"And you felt you were on another planet with these, ah, cats?"

"Not physically. I was simply an observer. I couldn't mind-speak with them."

"Did you try?"

"Yes."

"Was each dream alike?"

"Not exactly. At times they radiated—well, intense benevolence. At other times they were mentally joined in great joy. And sometimes . . . sometimes . . ."

"Go on."

"Sometimes I felt whole families die, crushed by the shifting mantle of their own planet." Tears starred her eyes. "It was horrible." She shook her head to drive the memory away. "I can't describe it."

"How often have you dreamed of these beings?"

"Many times. I don't know exactly."

"Have you ever dreamed of other alien life?"

"No." She waited tensely for him to show disgust at her confession. As if he knew her thoughts he smiled gently, approvingly.

Suddenly she felt she must see his face without the green cowl blurring his features. With trembling hands she slid the cowl onto Mark's shoulders, to look into a face whose past had left deep lines of pain across a full forehead. But the pain was balanced by the light which made his eyes crystal pools of green, and his lips smiled when her hair fell against them. His arms tightened around her until she felt the supple heat of his body beneath the heavy green robe.

She didn't remember how long he held her that first time, only that she wanted to be yet closer to him. She was drunk with the glory of being desirable to someone who knew she was a paran, someone who . . .

Selena choked the memories, but they refused to die. It had been a lie, a game. She writhed with humiliation at the thought of how he must have seen her—a pitifully eager, revoltingly responsive paran. He had touched her, yes, but never completely, saying that it would be unfair. But after she was free, then . . .

One day Mark didn't come to her room. Two days. Three. By the fifth day she was nearly frantic; months of companionship had left her ill-prepared to resume loneliness.

Then a day which was even worse than her capture.

"Miss Selena Christian?"

The unfamiliar voice startled her. She nodded stiffly.

"I'm Robert Molls, your lawyer. I'll defend you against the Humanistos' accusations of treason, sedition, and witchcraft."

"Defend me? But . . ."

"Now don't worry, Miss Christian. You have an excellent chance for acquittal. People are finally beginning to question the wisdom of the persecution which followed the Good Earth Rebellion. We hope to make your trial a watershed in public opinion. There's a real opportunity . . ."

"What happened to Mark—Mr. Curien? He was to defend me."

"Mark Curien?" said the lawyer incredulously.

Selena nodded.

"Mark Curien is the prosecuting attorney. You haven't talked with him, have you?"

"He can't be. He said he was going to help me."

"Then you have talked with him," the lawyer sighed. "What exactly did he say about helping you?"

"He said that he was to assist at my trial. For the last three months we've . . . Do you mean that I really had a chance to survive the trial, that he . . ." Words failed as Selena realized the extent of his betrayal.

Robert Molls opened his briefcase, cursing the credulity of young women. "Oh yes. He'll assist you at the trial. Right into the flame chamber."

Selena had no response. She could only stare and hope Robert Molls was an apparition that would disappear with the breakfast tray.

The lawyer sighed again and patted her shoulder. "Don't take it too hard. If you didn't say too much we'll still have a chance. And we will be heard. The Minority Leader has demanded a public trial in hopes of dispelling the baseless fear of paranormal mental abilities."

"But the Humanistos—"

"—will fight to prevent enlightenment," finished Mr. Molls. "However, if you follow my directions, we'll have a good chance. Now, this will be our strategy . . ."

"A few questions first, Mr. Molls," said Selena. "The government arrested me. Why should it suddenly defend me?"

"You're learning suspicion a little late, aren't you?"

Selena lifted her slender chin and glared at him.

"Ummm, yes. Tell me, Selena—may I call you Selena? Tell me then, how much do you know about the Good Earth Rebellion?"

"Very little. But I do know it's called a revolution, not a rebellion."

The lawyer smiled. "A revolution is, politically and realistically speaking, a movement which succeeds in permanently changing the structure of government. As the Humanistos seem to be losing effective political power, I prefer to call their machinations a rebellion."

"Rebellion or revolution," snapped Selena, "I'm still in prison."

"True. And undoubtedly what little you do know about the world is highly slanted by Humanisto propagandists."

Selena shrugged.

"Selena," said Molls, "I'll answer your questions only if you listen. You wanted to know why I—a government lawyer—am defending you. While I'm not as attractive as young Curien, I can do you a lot more good. Now listen and let your brain, rather than your gonads, decide whom to trust."

Selena smacked her hands together. She disliked the little man. He was so sure she'd fallen for Curien. So sure she'd been stupid. And so right.

"Try to forget your vanity long enough to behave sensibly. Believe me, Selena, death is more final than injured pride."

Selena sat down and put her head in her hands. Black

hair cascaded over her face and lay shining across her knees. She wanted to cry but had lost the ability years ago.

The Humanistos, the Majority party, hadn't the power to kill her without a trial, so Mark had been kind and warm and—she'd walked into the trap of his olive green eyes. Now the Minority party suddenly was offering help. What did the Minority really want? What was their trap?

Selena lifted her head. "Mr. Molls, tell me about politics."

The lawyer looked into her jewel-hard eyes and felt a wave of cold move over him. Perhaps telling her would be a mistake. But he cleared his throat and began.

"Fifteen years ago, Earth was contacted by an alien race, the Rynlon, through a combination of telepathy and speech. The newly evolved United World Government was initially strengthened as people were basically more scared by the Rynlon than delighted by the contact. But an Extraterrestrial Embassy was created and relations continued with few incidents.

"Unfortunately, as time passed, a feeling of inferiority—and therefore hatred—grew among the masses. It had been taken for granted by humanity that we would one day inherit the cosmos by right of natural and spiritual superiority. To be preceded in this was unthinkable. So men stopped thinking."

Mr. Molls paused and glanced at Selena's intent yellow eyes. He cleared his throat again and resumed talking.

"The masses became obsessed with being untainted by anything different or 'alien.' Paranormal mental powers in particular became the mark of the alien. Under the careful guidance of the Good Earth Sect, fear and frustration became a political movement.

"Within eight years after first contact, the millions of

Earther converts rose up and demanded that all alien contact cease as it was ugly, unnatural, and evil. It was election time, so World Government hastened to send the Rynlon packing. For six months there was relative peace on Earth.

"But peace was not helpful in recruiting membership for the Earthers. They finally joined with the Humanistos and Tien began his climb for power. After he consolidated his hold over Earthers and 'Nistos, he began a new campaign to rouse even more followers on the pretext that the Rynlon were not out of contact with Earth. Oh, no. All those paranormals who had assisted in the initial contact were still working with the Rynlon; the Devil was still on Earth.

"The frightened people rose again and demanded the surrender of all the unlucky celebrities who had aided in contact with the Rynlon. A minor bureaucrat stole the government records pertaining to paranormals and presented them to the Humanistos. Dominic Tien then had the sine qua non of power: an elusive, dangerous enemy to give plausibility to his repressive demands. And the hunt for thousands of paranormals would provide cohesion and catharsis for the foreseeable future."

Molls paused. Selena's attention had not once drifted during his discourse.

"Go on, Professor. You haven't told me why the government wants me free."

"Well, during the Good Earth Rebellion, known paranormals either died or disappeared. The Earthers, and later the 'Nistos, fed on fear. They had to have their devils—or some other equally powerful tool. By now, Tien was close to having the Majority Party. He pushed through certain reforms, such as secret police to track down paranormals and special courts to try them. The Humanistos police, who were nearly all Earthers, became quite powerful. In recent years, anyone disagreeing with the 'Nistos stood a good chance of being tried as an alien in the 'Nistos' courts. Certain key assassinations occurred, with the dead Minority officials being replaced by Humanistos. But some of the people have begun to get restless. Tien's 'alien arrests' are more and more transparently political. Demands have been made that the Alien Conspiracy Acts be repealed, thereby effectively squelching the Humanistos' source of power. The Minority, of course, would be delighted to limit Tien's power. We've hidden records, bribed, propagandized—and that's where you come in. The petitions for repeal are circulating now. If, during your trial, it can be demonstrated that you—a Branlow paranormal—constitute no threat to the sanity and souls of the people, then the petitions have sixty percent chance of success and Tien will be blocked. If the trial goes the other way, the Minority will have to either openly fight the Humanistos or join them and bore from within."

"If the Humanistos are so strong, why do they tolerate the Minority?"

"They're not strong enough to fight openly either. In fact, they had to agree to a public trial with a neutral judge."

"Neutral?"

"Yes. He belongs neither to the Minority nor to the Humanistos, as far as we can tell."

"Well, now I know where I stand," said Selena. "Right in a large pile of crap. You want me to help you spread it around." She paused, reflecting on what he had said. Her face settled into hard lines as she searched for the trap. "My conditions for helping you are freedom, money, and protection," she said finally.

"But I'm here to save your life," protested Molls.

"Bull. You're here to push the Minority. If I'm going to be used again, I'm going to be paid. Well paid. If you don't like my offer, I'll talk with the Humanistos and see what they'll do for me. They'd probably love to have a witness against the Minority in this little game, wouldn't they?" Selena smiled as Moll's mouth opened and shut soundlessly.

"Why, you conniving . . ." he finally sputtered.

"I was stupid once, as you so kindly pointed out," said Selena, her eyes brilliant with malice. "I won't make that mistake again."

Further recriminations stopped at a loud knock on the door. Selena walked over and opened it. An acolyte said, "There's a message for Mr. Molls. He's to call his superior as soon as possible."

"That's fine," said Selena. "I'm sure that they'll have a lot to talk about."

The next day Molls returned and wordlessly spread out a contract for Selena to read. His expression mirrored his distaste. Selena smiled coldly and skimmed the contract until she understood its three pertinent clauses: The government accepted her deal, would pay her very well, and guaranteed her freedom and protection. The only catch was that they requested the right to test and examine her every month for fifteen years.

"What if I refuse to be a guinea pig?"

"No deal," said Molls with relish.

Selena signed the contract without further question.

"Now," said Molls, gathering up the contract, "I want you to tell me everything you told Curien that bears on your paranormal powers, particularly anything to do with contacting the Rynlon." He switched on a recorder.

Selena closed her eyes and repeated the pertinent conversations verbatim.

"Is that everything?"

"That is all that you requested. My memory is flawless."

Her certainty made the lawyer pause and look at her golden eyes with something approaching disbelief.

"No, Mr. Molls, I don't know that my memory is part of the Branlow syndrome. I do know that I don't forget anything, ever."

"Ummm. That must be quite useful."

"It has its drawbacks," said Selena bitterly.

"Well, at any rate, not too much of what you said to Curien is really damaging. The dreams are bizarre, of course, but hardly dangerous. And you can't read minds, so all the Brotherhood really has on you is the fact that you're a Branlow mutant and Branlows are parans. Ah, that is, they have paranormal mental abilities."

"The word 'paran' is nothing but convenient slang, Mr. Molls. I don't attach obscene or derogatory meanings to it. If you want to insult me, you'll have to find another way," said Selena.

Molls ignored her final comment. "Fine. As you said, the shortened form is convenient. Now, being a paran is not per se illegal. What is illegal is to use your powers to make contact with the Rynlon. You have not done so?"

"No."

"You're sure?"

"Yes."

"Good. Now about the trial. I don't care whether you lie from one end of the proceeding to the other, so long as you continue to say that you've never contacted the Rynlon. You're a smart girl," he bowed sardonically, "and you should be able to handle the prosecution—now. If you can lie to good effect, do so. There's too much at stake to quibble about 'truth.' Your arrest was a matter of politics and the trial verdict will certainly reflect this. Understand?"

"Yeah. I'm a poor orphan who's had a lousy time of it and I don't know nothing about those wicked parans who want to cause trouble for the good kind Humanistos."

"Don't overdo it."

"Don't worry. I'll keep my part of the contract. You tell the Minority to do the same."

Molls eyed Selena's hard young face and decided that there was little he could add to her education.

Selena moved her back in a futile effort to get comfortable. Only the court could educate her now—in the time and means of her death. Soon. The last of the tapes were being played. She listened with curious aloofness to the clear, low voice and periodic bursts of laughter which tied past to present. A pleasant numbness permeated her mind, shutting out the hissing invective of her lawyer as he heard her recorded words close off chance of defeating the Humanistos.

High in the ancient building a window passed warm sunlight into the room. Selena watched its minute, silent progress across the defense table, across her fingertips, until finally the warmth enveloped her. With a tiny sigh she relaxed into the light, basking in its gentle heat while she listened to the marvelously spliced tape tell of alien lands, treason, and conspiracy with the Rynlon.

The judge's gavel woke Selena out of her reverie; the rectangle of warmth was gone, leaving her more alone than before. Without prompting she rose to hear her sentence.

"—death by vaporization. The right to appeal is suspended under Title VIII, paragraph 3 of the Alien Conspiracy Act. Sentence will be carried out by 24:00 this tenth day of—"

A corner of the wandering sunlight caught Selena's eye. It was just within reach. She stretched out her hand toward its golden warmth, heedless of the stir her movement caused in the packed courtroom.

With everyone else, Mark looked at her hand turn slowly until the sunlight seemed to nestle in her palm. For a moment his face was no longer a careful mask;

pain and hunger pulled deep lines around his mouth as her fingers stroked the sunlight.

The gavel rapped sharply, signaling the end of the trial.

Molls gathered up his meager notes and turned toward Selena.

"If those tapes were faked—as you claim—it was a job to confound both man and machine. It seems that you have outsmarted yourself by making a deal with both sides. But try not to worry," he smiled. "I understand that death by vaporization is painless. More than you deserve, in my opinion. Goodbye, Miss Christian."

Selena didn't reply; she was relieved to be rid of him. In a moment she was surrounded by green as Earther guards prepared to take her from the courtroom. One of them brushed against her wrist as he led her from the table. She didn't see the tiny needle taped to his finger, but she felt its sting. Before she could pull away, a spasm of pain shook her body. She gasped, then staggered as her legs refused to hold her. With a soundless cry she fell to the courtroom floor.

Immediately Mark began calling out orders in a voice of crisp authority. A cordon of Earthers pushed the rising crowd back and opened a path for him to reach Selena. He bent over her, long fingers searched for a pulse at neck and wrist. His hand slipped inside her black defendant's robe, but no heartbeat answered his touch. He shook his head and stood.

"She's dead," he said unbelievingly.

The crowd reluctantly shifted, then appeared to squeeze out a woman. She wore a green Earther jumpsuit. On her shoulder was sewn the insignia of the World Medical Corps. Without a word she taped various discs to Selena's head and arms, then checked the readout on her biomonitor.

"Very dead," she agreed. The discs came off with a soft sucking sound. "Take her to 12a. We'll want an autopsy."

None of the Earthers would touch her. With a gesture of impatience, Mark pulled Selena's body upright, then carried her as he would a sleeping child.

In the confusion that followed, no one noticed that both the doctor and one of Selena's guards had vanished.

Selena lay passively, listening to sounds drift in and out of the heavy darkness surrounding her. After a time the sounds resolved themselves into two distinct voices, arguing.

". . . still don't like it," said a woman's petulant voice. "She's the last paran we'll ever lift off Earth. The whole organization is blown. Mark should have known that—"

"He did," snapped a man's voice. "Who do you think gave the orders to disband? The colony has enough technicians and parans to survive. The only reason he didn't break us up years ago was his hope of finding a Branlow."

"Why a Branlow?"

"The mutation is prepotent. Branlow kids will be Branlows, and their kids will be Branlows and—"

The woman laughed harshly. "Some broodmare. She's a child."

The answering laugh was even less pleasant. "Green meanies again, Marion? Afraid that Mark was too interested in *this* Branlow? He really put our tails in traction for her; he wouldn't do that for you. He wouldn't even—"

"I'm not a Branlow."

"Amen. And you don't have any other claim on Mark, so for Chrissake, stop bitching and see how our prize is doing."

"She was breathing when we lifted, still breathing after the Fhlenn Distorter flipped us in and out."

"You're the nurse," he said coldly. "But she should have been awake hours ago and you know it."

"Just for you, sweetie, I'll check again."

Selena lay quietly while Marion gave her a cursory check.

"She's breathing just fine. Should come out of it soon."

"She'd better. If we lost her, Mark would—"

"I'll get some food."

Selena heard footsteps going away. The pent chaos of feelings and facts roiled across her mind until she forced herself to look at them one at a time. She was alive. Yes. And safe. Probably. Afraid. Yes, numb. Stupid. Of course. Afraid. Should be dead. Mutant, paran, FREAK.

Selena whimpered and thrashed against the webbing which held her on the bed.

"Miss Christian? Selena? Are you hurt?"

Selena turned her head toward the man's voice and tried to speak. With effort, her throat finally squeezed out the word no.

"Good. You've a long trip ahead of you, but not so long as the one you have behind you. My name's Al Martinez. I'm on Mark's 'recovery team.' And the woman bringing breakfast is Marion Baily."

Selena looked at the woman whose bitter voice still rang in her thoughts, and wondered why Marion was jealous of her. Marion was one of the most beautiful women Selena had ever seen. Heavy blonde hair and eyes as dark as a midnight sea. The mouth would have been more inviting, were it not flattened into a line of perpetual anger. Stiffness fought with grace in the rest of her body, too. She would have asked Marion why anyone so beautiful—and *normal*—would be jealous of a freak, but old habits of secrecy trimmed her response to silence.

"Look at those yellow eyes," said Marion. "Surprised you aren't panting, Al."

"Oh shut up, Marion," he said tiredly. "This ship is small enough without your help."

A bell code rang over the intercom. Martinez grabbed his food and hurried out of the sick bay.

"And what are you staring at, Missy?" rasped Marion.

Selena blinked and turned her head away; she hadn't meant to stare.

"Too good for us normals, huh? Not so much as a thank you."

Marion's antagonism penetrated the drug-haze which had dulled Selena's reactions. The thin string of her patience snapped.

"For what?" Selena said coldly.

"Mark Curien risked his ass and ours to get a Branlow off Earth alive. Got that, Missy? On Earth you'd be so much cold meat."

"Thanks to Mark Curien."

"You've got to be the dumbest Branlow in captivity—or a spy. Did you really believe the Minority would turn loose of you? You were a marker. If they won, you'd be given to the labs. If they lost, you'd have been given to the mob. Mark knew it. He tricked you into talking and then slip-snapped the tapes. And we both know why you talked. He's quite the man, isn't he?"

Selena's face paled until her eyes looked like pools of dark honey.

"It worked, didn't it, Missy? You fell for him just like a normal woman. And all he wanted was a Branlow—any Branlow—for the colony."

Selena felt her body tighten, and the denials she wanted to scream scalded her throat. Memories of Mark made a spiral of pain and humiliation which nauseated her. For a sliding moment she nearly gave way to confusion, despair, and the enervating drug which still gripped her body. Even Marion's spite faded, leaving only the truth of her words. She was a freak. On Earth she was loathed and feared. She had been saved because she was a freak. Whatever else she was interested no one, then or now.

Wearily, Selena closed her eyes. Maybe with more sleep she could gather the strength to fight. Maybe . . .

When Selena awoke again, she was alone and hungry. She tried to sit up, but a network of straps and webbing held her firmly. She stopped struggling and took the time to review all that had happened since the trial. The memories of Mark's humiliating pseudo-friendship and Marion's mockery burned, but she dismissed them. Emotions, no matter how painful, were luxuries a freak couldn't afford. Except one. Revenge? Not quite, but close. Vindication is a kind of revenge, and so is power. For either, she must again set up the poles of her life, restring the wire, and resume the act. The dumbest paran in captivity was going to learn. She was going to be the smartest Goddamned freak they ever caught. She'd never be loved, but they would learn to fear as she had feared.

"If you're awake, Selena, I'll bring you some food."

Selena's eyes snapped open, but there was no one in the room.

"I'm awake," she said aloud.

"Push the knob by the top of the bed. It releases the harness."

Selena waited for the intercom to click off, then released herself. The first few steps were shaky, but she set her jaw and walked the small room until her body felt normal.

"Glad to see you up, Selena," said Al as he set down what appeared to be a small, multicolored bagpipe. "That's breakfast. Just suck and squeeze."

The shape of breakfast convinced Selena as no half-remembered conversation could. "I'm on a spaceship, by the looks of that. Rynlon?"

"Only kind we have," said Al.

Selena stood quietly for a moment, then sat and

began to wrestle with her breakfast. Spaceship or no, a body needed food.

"While you eat, I'll tell you what has happened. I don't have much time, so save your questions until after the spiel."

She nodded, squeezed a patch of orange on the bag, and sucked on the matching orange straw.

"As you might have guessed after your, uh, talk with Marion, Mark Curien is not a Humanisto. He arranged the details of your escape—"

"After he arranged my capture, trial, and death sentence."

Martinez made an impatient gesture. "After the trial, I slipped up to you and gave you a paralytic drug. It's a lethal poison unless the antidote is given within six hours. Dangerous, but we had to make sure you got past the real Humanisto doctor. The 'doctor' who checked you first was Marion, incidentally. As we expected, her opinion and the drug convinced the real doctor that your heart had failed. After that, it was just a matter of juggling bodies and caskets until we got you on a private launch. The scout picked you up at sea, and here you are."

Selena sighed. "Where is here?"

"Can't tell you. We're on our way to a Recovery and Development colony. The exact location of the colony is secret. Earth has been building—or trying to build—spaceships ever since the Rynlon gave spec sheets to us. By now, World Government must have a few operational ships. And what WG has, Tien will eventually have. That's why Mark, and a few others, stayed behind to destroy references to the colony."

Al frowned. "I hope they got all of them, but I doubt it. Anyhow, the colony is as close to a secret as we can keep it. There is no direct communication between Paran—that's the name of the planet—and Earth. So if you're a spy, forget it and settle down to a new life."

"A spy?" Selena laughed coldly. "I'm a freak and Earth never let me forget that. The planet can take a short orbit into the sun for all of me."

"Good. It's a relief not to have a homesick refugee. I've nursed hundreds of them. Until they learn that home is a death sentence, they can't be useful members of the colony."

"Your homesick hundreds must not have been parans, or you wouldn't have had to teach them such a simple fact."

Al smiled grimly. "Not everyone is as . . . realistic as you, Selena."

"I'm learning. I expect to learn even more."

Al looked at her eyes, at their cold topaz brilliance, and shuddered inwardly. He'd seen a look like that once before: a dying lion that stalked its killer with a grim intensity he'd spent years trying to forget.

He cleared his throat and shook off the memory. "Paran is suitable for human life without supplementary life-support systems. It was a supply depot for the Rynlon. When the World Government realized that it was losing, the colony was started. The Rynlon paid for it; in return the colonists work for them.

"Present population is approximately 2500. Most are refugees like you. The rest are specialists who volunteered their skills to get Paran on its feet. The purpose of the colony is to develop any and all paranormal abilities. When you've completed the set courses, you'll have the choice of staying and developing other parans, returning to Earth to work against Tien, or going out to the stars with the Rynlon as contact agents.

"There is evidence that everyone is a paran to some degree. Your job is to find your level of ability. Ours is to help you. When you're not working on yourself, you'll do some ordinary work for the colony. Everyone works part-time in support of the colony. If you don't have a skill we need, you'll be trained. Any questions?"

"What about—"

The intercom drowned Selena's words.

"Martinez to control room. Immediately."

"Sorry," said Al. "Maybe we've got some old pamphlets around. You're our first lift-off in over a year, but we should have something left. I'll put Marion on it."

"Don't bother," said Selena, but he was already gone. Selena swore and turned back to her breakfast. Before she had wrung out the last drop, Marion entered.

"These pamphlets explain the physical layout of the colony, its history, facilities, and rules. You *can* read, can't you?" said Marion sweetly.

"Shove it," said Selena. It was time Marion learned that parans had teeth when they weren't drugged. Besides, something about Marion brought out the gutter years.

"Such manners. I wonder how Mark stood it."

"He didn't. He took it lying down."

After that, Marion left her alone.

II

The loudspeaker droned the final landing warning. Selena hurried to the bed and strapped herself in, wondering a bit apprehensively what the landing would be like. Her worry was useless; she didn't know the ship had touched down until the announcement of disembarkation instructions came.

Selena walked quickly to her designated area and fidgeted until the port opened. The air smelled incredibly rich and exotic. Neither city nor spaceship had prepared her for the undiluted scents of a wild planet. Eagerly she walked down the ramp until she noticed a man checking names off a list. "Damn," she sighed. She stood impatiently as he gave her a list of people to see and directions on how to get to them.

Holding a small map on which her route had been marked, Selena hurried off the landing apron toward the walkways, choosing the one with the cryptic message "Med."

As the belt walkway took over, she looked up, and shivered with pleasure at the beauty around her. To her left was a low-profile building of amber rock which the map told her was a power plant, but which looked more like a temple. Beyond the plant stretched mile upon mile of field crops, gold and mauve and lime green under the turquoise sky. Where the crops ended, orchards began their lithe, silent march toward the copper hills and tumbled mountains.

Soon trees limited her view of the distant mountains, bringing her eyes back to the immediate area of the walkway. Varicolored plants grew in casually ordered profusion along pathways leading to small houses hidden in scattered groves of sea-green trees.

The walkway sped quietly through the groves to an artificial clearing which surrounded the heart of the colony. To the right rose several apartment buildings made of native wood and the curious amber rock which had given the power plant such beauty. The apartments rose in sweeping tiers of crescents, freedom captured in an alien architect's mind.

The walkway slowed as it approached the curving medical center. When she walked toward the center more buildings seemed to slide unobtrusively out of the ground until an entire administrative-medical-laboratory complex was revealed in a series of fluid golden curves. It began to dawn on Selena that for all their flowing grace, the buildings were immense.

She decided that her medical examination could wait until she had explored further. She chose a meandering walkway marked "Park." The walkway slowly moved away from the medical center toward an artfully landscaped green area which the map showed separating the central complex from the living areas. Halfway through the park, the walkway crossed a small stream which fed an unseen lake. As she looked to her right, toward the dormitories and commissary, her pleasure faded. The dormitories were rows of grey plastic and cement boxes hunched against the squat bulk of the commissary. Even landscaping couldn't blur the ugly functionalism of the buildings. Selena sighed; obviously the colonists had been in a hurry to get their first buildings up, and now she would have to live in them amid the tantalizing beauty of the rest of the colony. She turned back toward the medical center.

The nurse at the medical center looked both relieved and angry when Selena gave her name. "Where were you? The doctor has been waiting for fifteen minutes."

"I wanted a few minutes outside."

"Well, young lady, you'd better learn right now that duties come before whims on Paran. Now follow me."

Selena swore under her breath as she followed the crisp yellow uniform down the corridor, but she offered no resistance when the nurse told her to strip and put on a flimsy paper gown.

The nurse looked at Selena's slender body critically. "Your records say that you're twenty-six."

"Yes," said Selena shortly.

At the nurse's doubtful look, Selena said, "I'm a Branlow mutant. I'm told we mature slowly. Most don't live long enough to test the theory. Anything else bothering you?" Selena turned her back on the nurse and slipped into the paper smock. When she was finished the nurse was gone.

After half an hour of staring at shiny instruments and aseptic tile, Selena began to regret her temper. At the end of another fifteen minutes she decided to get dressed and leave. But the nurse had taken her clothes. "Damn her," muttered Selena.

Fifteen minutes later and she'd had it. Semi-nude bodies couldn't be that novel in a medical building; she'd just go and find her clothes. She walked over to the door and yanked the handle. It was locked. Just as she was getting ready to break into the cabinets to find a lock-picking tool, the door swung open and Dr. Johnson walked in, accompanied by the elusive nurse.

Three hours later she was released, still in her smock, to the eager psychology department.

"Dr. Nelson, this is Selena Christian," said the nurse to the young man who was to examine her mind.

"Don't give her back her clothes until you're finished testing."

"Gladly," he smiled.

Color blazed on Selena's cheeks as she preceded him down the hallway to the testing room. When he closed the door, she hissed, "Let's get one thing straight. I'm not a prize animal or a piece of property. I've been poked, prodded, and pawed for four hours. I haven't eaten since last night so that their damn tests could be run. I want food and clothes now or you can forget your tests. And if you lock me in here I'll scream until the bloody walls shatter."

"They must have given you a rough time. Tell you what," he smiled engagingly, "if you'll promise not to disappear, I'll get your clothes and we'll have lunch together. There're too few pretty women around here; I don't want you mad at me before I've had a chance. And call me Hugh."

Selena hesitated. "It's a deal."

He returned in a few minutes, triumphantly carrying her dress. "Hugh Nelson to the rescue. Snatched them right out of the dragon's jaws." Selena had to laugh at the sight of him waving her dress like some exotic flag. "Now," she said, "go away while I dress."

"Five minutes," he said over his shoulder, then added with a leer, "After that, you take your chances."

Selena quickly put on her clothes. She was just tying her sandals when the door opened.

"That was a very short five minutes," said Selena.

"Can't blame a guy for trying. Ready for lunch?"

"Do you have a comb?"

"A comb. Let's see." He fished through his pockets. "Here you are."

"Thanks." Selena unbraided her hair and tried to comb it, but every time she raised her left arm she winced. The immunization series the doctor had given her had about paralyzed her arm. Hugh took the comb out of her hand.

"Let me. I used to do this all the time for my sister."

"I'm not your sister."

"Yeah. Isn't it great?" he said, carefully unsnarling her long hair. "Quit thrashing around or I'll strangle you with your own hair," he said when she turned to retrieve the comb. Selena's lips flattened into a line, but she stood still.

"That's better," he said.

As the last of the tangles came out, Hugh admired his handiwork. "Sure you want me to braid it up again? It's such a shame to hide all this lovely hair," he said, moving his hand lightly over the shining mass. Selena jumped as though she had been burned.

"Right," he said, "braids it is," and quickly finished the job. "Now let's get some lunch."

The food was standard, but Selena's stomach was in no mood to quibble. Hugh watched in awe as she dispatched three helpings with ravenous delicacy.

"You weren't kidding about being hungry. Feel better now?"

"I'm working on it," said Selena around a mouthful of cake.

"Ready for the tests?"

"After I ask some questions."

"You're stalling, but go ahead."

"What kind of tests?"

"Everything we could think of from cards to crystal balls, plus the usual assortment of psychological tests to determine IQ, stability, motivation, sociability, etc."

"Sounds like it'll take all afternoon."

"And part of tomorrow, too."

"I doubt it," she said. "What are all these tests supposed to prove?"

"Damned if we know. Oh, they have their uses, but what we really want to measure no one has devised a test for. That's where we hope you can help us."

"The gutter school wasn't very long on psychology."

"Don't let that bother you," said Hugh. "What we really want is to compare your test profiles with those of other parans in the colony, as well as with those of us apparently untalented normals. If we could just find some common area of response. It's so damn frustrating; we're sure that almost everyone has some psi potential, just as almost everyone can at least hum even though they're not musical geniuses. But getting at and training the normal psi talents has been impossible so far. Why, we've even . . ." Hugh's voice trailed off under the impact of Selena's ambiguous yellow gaze. "Anyway, I'm eager to see your test results."

Selena finished the last of the tests by early evening. There was just enough time for dinner before she had to report in to the computer for the first in a series of orientation classes.

While she ate, Selena glanced over the instructions that Hugh had given her. One sheet was headed "Required Classes for All New Colonists" and listed such topics as "Dangerous Flora and Fauna of Paran," "Edible Flora and Fauna of Paran," "Geography of Paran," and "Self-Defense." At least the last class showed some promise, she thought; she could use a few lessons in self-defense. At the bottom of the page was an inconspicuous warning. "Please note that satisfactory completion of the above courses is a requisite for continued use of your Ident Card. Standard time for completion of these courses is six weeks."

No courses, no food. She wondered what they would do if she told them to stick it in their omniscient computer. But she wouldn't.

Yet.

Promptly at seven o'clock Selena let herself into a small cubicle containing a standard computer console and desk. She put her card into the slot and settled back to learn about the "Dangerous Flora and Fauna of Paran."

After fifteen minutes of text, illustrations, and creeping boredom, Selena pressed a red button. Almost immediately the door opened and a middle-aged man stepped in.

"I'm Mr. Gomez. Are you having difficulties?"

"Not with the computer," said Selena. "But could you speed up the information output."

"The lesson was carefully planned so as to give maximum information in the minimum time," said Mr. Gomez. "However, if you can pass the test which is given," he glanced at the screen, "after the next illustration, I'll give you manual speed control. Then so long as you pass the tests, you'll be able to choose your own rate of learning."

"Wait while I take the test."

Mr. Gomez looked curiously at Selena. "You're very sure of yourself, aren't you?"

"Yes."

Mr. Gomez watched in growing amazement as Selena's fingers danced over test response buttons without an error. New questions appeared the moment the previous question was answered correctly. Selena finished the ten-minute test in less than two minutes.

Wordlessly, Mr. Gomez reached behind the console and flipped the manual override lever. "The dial to your right controls the speed. If you run out of lessons before your time is up, call me again. I'll set up the rest of the required lessons on another console."

Selena twisted the dial to maximum speed. Mr. Gomez shook his head in disbelief as pictures and text flashed across the screen at split-second intervals.

Three hours later, the computer finished its two-week program and quietly shut off. Selena stretched and rubbed the back of her neck wearily. What she needed now was sleep, but she was due back at the psych lab. She sighed as she fumbled for the button to call Mr. Gomez.

"Yes, Miss Christian?"

"Could I call the psych lab?"

"Of course. Come with me to my office."

When Selena stood up, the room swayed gently. She set her teeth and waited for balance to return before she followed Mr. Gomez.

Once in the office, Mr. Gomez watched with barely concealed curiosity as Hugh's face appeared on the screen.

"I'll come in tomorrow. Now I need sleep," said Selena.

"Mr. Gomez told me that you were tearing through those lessons. We're curious to see what physical effect—if any—such concentration has."

Selena looked at Mr. Gomez and said acidly, "How many extra credits do you get for spying?"

"Selena!" said Hugh.

"Forget it. And forget the appointment." Selena slowly reached out to break the connection.

". . . wait," Hugh was saying reasonably. "You're too tired to be rational. I'll . . ."

Selena never heard the rest; she had quietly folded up and was sound asleep on the floor.

When she woke up she wanted food, and the longer she thought about it, the more intolerable her hunger became. At last she located a buzzer by her pillow and pressed it. Immediately the door opened and a nurse entered.

"Is this the starvation ward?" said Selena.

The nurse whipped out a small packet and strapped it under Selena's arm before she answered. "Just lie quietly for a few minutes, Miss Christian," she said as she checked a small panel which read out Selena's temperature, pulse, blood pressure, and other things which Selena could not identify. The readings must have been satisfactory, for the nurse retrieved the packet and told Selena to sit up.

"Feel dizzy?" said the nurse as Selena swung her legs over the edge of the bed.

"Hungry."

"All right. Now take my arm and stand up," said the nurse.

Selena slid off the bed, refusing the nurse's arm.

"Still feel all right?" said the unruffled nurse.

"No. I'm still hungry."

"Now we'll just walk around the room and—"

Selena pulled away from the nurse. "I can walk alone."

She walked swiftly around the room several times. "Is that good enough, or would you like to see a few cart-wheels?"

"That won't be necessary," said Dr. Johnson from the doorway. "Nurse, give her back her clothes. She'll have dinner with Dr. Nelson and me in the cafeteria."

Selena realized that it must be very early morning when she reached the cafeteria; there was no one there except the two doctors.

Hugh waved her over and pointed to a steaming tray of food waiting for her. She eagerly attacked the food as Hugh and Dr. Johnson exchanged smiles.

"Ever see such an appetite?" said Hugh.

Dr. Johnson shook his head as he watched the food disappear.

Selena ignored them until the tray was empty. Then she settled back in her chair and said, "Okay, ask your questions."

Dr. Johnson nodded to Hugh.

"First," said Hugh, "you don't seem the least bit upset over what happened. Do you do this often?"

"Not since I was ten," said Selena. "I used to do it all the time when I really pushed myself mentally. But during and after the Revolution it was too dangerous. If an Ear was nearby, I'd be caught."

"An Ear?" said Dr. Johnson.

"Street slang for a Receiver," said Hugh. "A person whose talent is to sense other parans at work."

"Oh. Well, no need to fear that anymore. But your exhaustion. Do you think that will happen again?"

"Probably. At least until I'm used to using my mind again. It's been years since it was safe to really think and my brain is sluggish."

"Sluggish!" said Hugh. "You call that performance today sluggish?"

"That 'performance,' as you call it, was mediocre, an exercise," Selena shot back. "According to what little I've learned about Branlow mutants there's just one hell of a lot more than I should be able to do. But so long as my brain is flabby I'll get nowhere."

"Look, Selena," Hugh said gently, "your brain will do you no good in a burned-out body. Why don't you just take it easy until you know your limits?"

" 'Burned-out,' 'limits,' crap," Selena said. "For someone who was so eager to get a real live Branlow mutant to study, you're pretty backward. Tomorrow I'll be able to concentrate for three hours before I quit; the day after four, and so on until I've reached eight hours. That's as far as I got when I was ten. There's absolutely no physical damage to me that sleep and food can't handle. I simply fold up before that happens. There's no way you can stop me, so why don't you just put a bed and some food in the computer room and cut the shrill."

Hugh looked helplessly at Dr. Johnson.

"Relax, Hugh," Dr. Johnson said. "Selena's right about her physical condition; she wasn't the least bit hurt by her 'exercise.' In fact, I'm willing to bet that her reflexes have improved." He looked at Selena questioningly.

"Very good, Doctor," said Selena. "My reflexes do improve along with my mind—up to a certain point."

"I give up," Hugh said. "But would you at least agree to doing your 'exercises' in the psych lab? We could easily arrange for it and poor Mr. Gomez wouldn't have to spend half his time in shock. I'd feel a lot better, too."

" 'Poor Mr. Gomez' could spend the rest of his life in hell for all of me," said Selena. "But I'll work in the lab if you don't bother me or shut off the computer when you think I've had enough."

"Such trust," said Hugh, "is touching."

"I have damn little reason to trust anyone," Selena said tightly.

"This isn't Earth," said Hugh. "We—"

"The next thing we wanted to talk with you about," said Dr. Johnson quickly, "is the job you'll have in the colony. Unfortunately, our library is fully staffed right now, so we can't use your experience in that area. However, according to your file, you spent some years of your childhood on a small, ah, farm."

Selena nodded. "Dad was afraid to have me around too many people. And it wasn't really a farm; he bred dogs and horses. But so few people could keep a dog, much less a horse, that he busted."

"Did you enjoy the animals?"

"Yes." A small smile played across Selena's face as she remembered the clumsy eagerness of the colts and the puppies' moist friendship.

"Excellent," said Dr. Johnson. "We have many animals here, some from Earth, some from Rynlonne, and a few natives of Paran. As you pointed out, very few people these days are familiar with animals. You could be useful if you'd work in the animal compounds."

"Doing what?" Selena said.

"Don't worry," laughed Hugh. "There won't be any cages to clean. Most of the animals run loose within large areas which are as close to their natural surroundings as we could manage."

"Yes," said Dr. Johnson. "What we would like you to do is more or less be a companion to those animals— such as the horse and dog—which are amenable to such a relationship. There are many documented cases in which a singular rapport has developed between animals and people. Naturally, we hope that something similar will occur with you. We would like to study the phenomenon, as we believe it possible that a type of mental communication occurs as the basis of rapport. Of course," he added, "if nothing beyond a normal friendship develops, you'll still be useful in that your presence will help to inhibit these animals from reverting to a wild state."

"How about it, Selena?" asked Hugh.

As Selena looked at the intent faces of the doctors, she wondered why it should be so important that she accept this particular job. But the work itself was too tempting to resist.

"I'll try it," she hedged.

"Good," Hugh said. "Great. I can take you out there now if you want to look around."

"It's a little early," Dr. Johnson said. "Unless, of course . . ." He looked at Selena.

Selena shook her head.

"Hey," said Hugh, "we forgot about the bonus."

"Bonus?" Selena said.

"Yes. If you want it, that is."

"Get to the point," said Selena.

"As an animal tender, you're allowed a small house adjacent to the compounds. And, if you like, you can have as many pets around the place as there's room for."

"Can I move in now?"

"What'd I tell you, Doctor?" said Hugh.

Dr. Johnson smiled wryly and said to Selena, "Hugh took the liberty of moving your belongings while you slept."

Selena's annoyance at being so transparent was short-lived. To have a house of her own, and to be allowed to have dogs and maybe even horses around again . . .

"I'm glad I didn't upset your plans. Now, if you can stop being smug long enough to tell me how to get home, I'll be on my way."

"I'll take you there," said Hugh.

"No."

Hugh hesitated, then gave her directions. "You take walkway four—it says AnComp on the marker—until you reach the veterinary hospital and lab, then you take the walkway marked 'Eq.' At the end of the walkway you'll see a huge silvery tree. There's a small box on the tree trunk which has the lighting controls for the path. Push the white button and the path lights come on. The house is keyed to your card. Got all that?"

"Yes."

"Then we'll see you today at the lab at 11:00."

Selena found her way to the secluded house without difficulty. The living area opened upon a serene, uncluttered garden surrounding a still green pool. Concealed lights silhouetted graceful trees, and turned foliage into delicate silver. Selena took a long, deep breath as the peace of the setting drained away her tension.

When Selena reported to the psych labs later Hugh whistled wolfishly. "If that's what country living does, I'm moving today." His eyes appreciated her loosely flowing hair and lithe, relaxed body. "Got an extra room in that house?"

"No, but I could have the computer make me a kennel."

"That wasn't what I had in mind."

"I'll bet. Speaking of rooms, where's mine?"

"Right next door. Do you want to start the lessons now or would you rather look at your test profiles?"

Selena's face showed interest. "I thought that information would be for everyone but me."

"And we thought it might help you if you knew a little more about your potential."

"Then let's get it done."

Hugh walked over to a console and began pushing buttons.

"Here we are," he said as the printout began spitting sheets of plastic. "We'll start with the easy stuff. IQ: Subject exceeded scale."

"Meaning?"

"It means that it was a lousy test." Hugh grimaced in disgust. "You're the twelfth person so far that has ruined our nice, neat curve. Sociability," Hugh continued, "thirty out of a possible one hundred. In other words, you think you don't like people. You do, of course. In fact, you need companionship so much you are afraid of it."

Hugh looked at Selena intently, but she showed no reaction to his comment.

"Stability: reasonable."

"Meaning that I'm not insane."

"Right."

"What about all those absurd tests I took with cards, dice, crystal balls?"

"I'm just coming to that. Before I give you the results, I want to explain something. Do you know Probability Theory?"

"No. Should I?"

"You're going to. I'll make it fast and simple." He picked up a paper clip and put his hands behind his back. "Now, if I asked you to guess which hand has the paper clip, what would be your chances of picking the correct hand?"

"Fifty-fifty."

"Right. And if you guessed one hundred times—"

"—I should be right fifty times," finished Selena impatiently.

"Approximately, yes," said Hugh. "Of course, it rarely happens that way, and we have long formulas to cover our embarrassment, but the fact remains that the further you deviate from fifty percent accuracy in this test, the less probability there is that chance alone dictates your answers. In other words, you're using paranormal abilities to gather information. Okay so far?"

Selena said crisply, "I'm not an idiot, Doctor, if your IQ tests are to be believed."

Hugh carefully replaced the paper clip. "All right, Selena, I'll just say one more thing. A negative score—one less than is mathematically probable—means just as much as a positive score. The further a score deviates from the mathematically probable, the more interested we are." He picked up the next printout sheet. "A few results at random. In the card test, which was the first one, you had seventy-five percent accuracy. From our standpoint, that is the kind of score that makes psych dance around the lab. However, it isn't that unusual; we've at least five hundred such scores on file now. Some never did as well again, and some fall in the seventy-to-ninety-five range every time. We don't yet know whether your score is a fluke or a reliable index of paranormal ability. What makes this test really interesting is that when you took it late in the afternoon, you dropped to ten percent accuracy. That's an even larger deviation from probability than before." Hugh smiled dryly. "What you were telling us was that you were sick of our games and wouldn't play anymore, so you used your ability to guess wrong, instead of right. And motivated by spite, you made a truly fantastic score."

Selena looked thoughtful. "You mean there's no way to muffle paran talents?"

"Not until you're able to use them consciously, as you do your ability to concentrate."

Hugh rummaged through the plastic sheets in front of him until he found another profile. "Here's a similar case. You scored seventy-three percent. Again, we've had several hundred people who have done as well or better. The interesting thing is that only a relative handful of people score high on both card and image tests. Then, when we asked you to repeat the same test, using a crystal ball as a focus of concentration, your accuracy dropped to five percent! It's the highest score we've ever had on this test!"

"But—"

"But nothing. You were so mad when we made you use a crystal ball that you really wanted to hamstring us." He laughed out loud. "Looks like the knife cut you more than us. But we felt the edge, too. We don't know whether it was the crystal ball or the anger that upped your score. Maybe it doesn't really matter; concentration and motivation seem to be the key."

"It wasn't the crystal ball," Selena said indignantly.

"What's the shame in a crystal ball?" said Hugh. "We've got people who use balls, rings, navels, lights, drugs, anything that helps them to focus their attention. Eventually most of them outgrow their need for props, but even if they don't, it's the results we care about."

Selena poked through the scattered sheets on the console and held one up for Hugh's inspection, quoting. " 'Subject manifests symptoms of acute invasion phobia.' What does that mean?"

"Roughly it means that you refuse to give up any control of your actions to another person. And not only do you dislike people, you have such a phobia against trusting others that we couldn't hypnotize you. And when we can't hypnotize anything above IQ 40 it really burns out computer circuits. I didn't believe it when Mark said you probably couldn't be hypnotized, but he was right. It'll make our job a lot tougher. Most of our successful parans began their development under post-hypnotic suggestion. Later hypnotism isn't necessary, but it had been our most useful tool so far."

"I didn't try to resist hypnotism," said Selena flatly.

"Perhaps not consciously. At some level, though, you refused to allow it. And with your ability to concentrate, we're helpless to get around you. But don't look so worried. Your first classes will be in auto-hypnosis. You'll probably allow self-hypnosis where you'll have nothing to do with us. It's risky, though, so be careful and don't throw yourself into it the first time out."

Selena gestured negligently. "I'm not likely to lose control if what you say is true."

"I certainly hope so," Hugh said.

"Is that all of the test profiles I'm to see?"

"Those are the most interesting. I'll give you a non-technical summation of the overall results, and then if you have any specific questions now or later I'll try to answer them."

"Let's have it."

"The total series of tests indicate that you are of very high intelligence, that you are potentially one of the most gifted parans we've studied, and that you're damned stubborn. Normally, with someone of your paran potential, we'd put you in with other parans and await results. However, with your distrust of people, and your invasion phobia, putting you close to other parans could be a quick disaster."

"Why?"

"Three years ago we had another paran with invasion phobia. We thought that all he needed was to participate in mind-speech and he'd lose his fear."

"What happened?"

"He went insane," said Hugh bluntly.

"So that's why you gave me the house. It fairly oozes tranquility."

Hugh glanced sideways at her, then nodded. "Until you decide to trust us, we thought that everyone would be happier if you lived alone. Besides, your dossier indicated that you were an exceptionally able animal trainer, in spite of your youth. We'd like to know if that was accidental or the result of paran abilities."

When Selena remained silent, Hugh looked at her appraisingly. "You don't resent being alone, do you?"

"I don't like being ostracized, if that's what you mean," said Selena. "I never have. But then I don't like being forced into 'suitable friendships' either." She walked around the room, picking up and replacing various apparatus. "Does this job mean that I'm not to participate in the colony life beyond my assigned duties?"

"Oh no, Selena. You're entitled to the same social freedoms as anyone else. We just didn't think you wanted to participate at all," said Hugh.

"And you thought that the quickest way to make me interested in colony life was to appear to forbid it. Right?"

Hugh moved in his chair uncomfortably. "Dammit, Selena, that's not fair."

"Not fair or not true?"

Hugh slammed his open hand against the console, then turned to her. "Selena, we want to help you, but we can't unless you're willing."

"That doesn't answer my question."

"All right. All right! We do want you to make friendships with the other parans. And the normals. And we did hope that in your perversity you'd do just that if we appeared to forbid it."

"Sweet God," said Selena wearily, "is it any miracle I don't trust people? Why couldn't you just tell me what you wanted and then let me decide?"

"Because you're too goddamned stubborn," said Hugh.

"Amen," said Selena coldly.

Abruptly the anger left Hugh's face. "Selena, I'm sorry. Your willfulness is a virtue, as well as a vice. It's the thing that will give you the strength to push yourself to the limit of your potential." He smiled and put out his hand. "Truce?"

Disconcerted at Hugh's sudden reversal, Selena found herself taking his hand.

"Am I interrupting?" said a musical voice from the doorway.

Selena snatched her hand back and turned toward the voice. She saw a petite woman with short dark hair fluffed around a pretty oval face.

"Lea," said Hugh, "what—"

"I came to brief the new paran about the compounds," said Lea. She turned to Selena with a smile, "You're Selena Christian, aren't you?"

Selena nodded.

"I'm Lea Nibuku." Lea's smile widened and Selena caught herself relaxing in its warmth.

She looked at Lea sharply. "You're a paran."

Lea looked surprised, then laughed. "If I am, psych hasn't told me. What makes you think I am?"

Hugh waited for Selena to answer, but she said nothing.

"How does she remind you? What did she do?"

Selena turned away. "It's not important."

"Yes, it is. It's very—"

"Don't push her, Hugh," said Lea softly. "You'll only make her mad."

Selena faced Lea again. "You are a paran. You know how I feel, yet a minute ago, you weren't even sure who I was. You're an Empath."

Lea shook her head slowly. "I don't think so, Selena. Ask Hugh: he knows how I always blurt out the wrong thing at the wrong time." Lea chuckled at some memory, then added, "If I were an Empath, I wouldn't have called you a paran—you don't like the word and you showed it."

Selena shrugged. "I knew you didn't mean it as an insult."

Hugh said suddenly, "That's it."

Lea looked at him, her dark eyes questioning.

"You're not a paran, Lea. At least not in the sense we use the word here. You just, well, project warmth; people look at you and know you're not a threat to them." He smiled fondly at her. "That's why nobody's strangled you for your left-footed remarks—yet."

Lea laughed. "You know me—never an unspoken thought."

Hugh nodded ruefully. "I know."

Selena watched closely, but could discover no malice in their teasing, only a tacit understanding and mutual regard.

"Now that we have that settled," said Lea, "I'd better brief Selena so I can get back to my guinea pigs." She handed Selena a pamphlet and small disc. "This disc allows you to enter the animal compounds."

"What do I do with it?"

"I had mine put on a chain," said Lea, pulling a similar disc from beneath her blouse. "I kept forgetting it and those fences don't fool around."

At Selena's perplexed look, Lea added, "The fences are energy barriers; you can't see them until you run into them. If the intial shock doesn't stop you, your nervous system takes on a whopping overload. The animals avoid the fences completely, unless we're with them." She turned the disc over. "This dial controls the volume of space that is neutralized by the disc. Usually it's set on one, which means that only an opening large enough for a human body is neutralized. At number ten, you can neutralize fifteen yards in any direction from the disc."

"Handy little gadget. What am I supposed to do once I'm inside?"

"There's no program for you to follow. You just pick the animals you want to work with and do whatever you like." Lea sighed wistfully. "It should be a picnic."

"Guinea pigs don't go on picnics," said Selena.

III

As Selena walked toward the animal compounds, her face was a mask. Lea's natural warmth rang too many painful memories. She wondered at her own unthinking response: it was hard to go back to being alone.

Irritably Selena increased her pace. Lea was no threat to her. Nor was Hugh, really. The only hold anyone had over her was her meal ticket; she had been careful to stay within the colony rules. So nothing threatened her but her own craving for friendship. And now that could be taken care of as she had in childhood; animals made excellent companions—speechless, undemanding, uncomplicated, and affectionate.

Only a slight tingling sensation told Selena that she had passed through the barrier into the horse compound. She stopped and remembered what the pamphlet had said. Thirty-nine purebred Arabians, that breed having been chosen by the colony's founders for their intelligence, adaptability, and long, meticulously recorded bloodlines. Now used as a control group to detect genetic mutation in alien environment.

Selena spotted the first herd grazing quietly in a large meadow. The stallion must have been young, for there were only three mares and two colts in the herd. When Selena stepped out of the cover of the trees, the stallion pranced restlessly.

Selena moved slowly toward the horses, but they trotted further up the meadow and resumed grazing. Selena followed them quietly, yet the horses moved away each time she came within twenty yards. Even the aromatic grain she shook in her hands did not tempt them.

"Well," sighed Selena. "I guess I'll have to do it the hard way. Hope I haven't forgotten how."

She settled herself comfortably on the grass, holding her grain-filled hands in front of her. "Which one of you will it be?" she said softly as she scrutinized the six animals. A sorrel mare caught her eye; the mare didn't have a colt to distract her.

Selena closed her eyes and carefully visualized the mare in exact detail. Once satisfied with her mental picture, Selena thought of the mare moving cautiously toward her, nostrils flaring at the fragrance of the grain. Selena's mind lingered over the mare's hunger, the irresistible flavor of the grain, and the friendliness of the girl who held the gift.

Sweat slid down Selena's cheeks as she poured energy into her visualization of rapport between the mare and herself, of irksome itches scratched, of thirst slaked, and of the wild beauty of a thundering run through the forest.

A soft, snuffling sound penetrated Selena's concentration; the mare was calmly licking the last of the grain from Selena's outstretched hands. The other horses had fled.

"So, my little Ember," murmured Selena soothingly, "I haven't lost my touch." The mare's ears flicked at the sound of Selena's voice, but she did not shy away. Instead, the horse nuzzled Selena's hair and licked the salty sweat from her neck. Selena gently pushed Ember's nose away; the next thing she knew the mare would be eating the clothes off her back.

Undaunted by Selena's touch, Ember crowded closer to Selena, nearly knocking her over. Selena laughed as she reached up to rub the top of Ember's head. "Holding me to my promises, aren't you, girl?"

Concentrating once more, Selena envisioned Ember following her through the barrier where more grain was waiting. When she opened her eyes again, the mare nudged her impatiently.

"All right, greedy. You'll get your grain."

Selena slowly got to her feet, flexing quivering muscles and wishing for a hot bath. The meadow dipped crazily.

"Uh, oh, Ember, we'd better hustle. I won't be awake too much longer."

When Selena approached the barrier, Ember shied nervously. Selena groaned and once more fell into deep concentration. Time and again she visualized herself and Ember moving safely through the fence.

Selena opened her eyes and saw that the mare was standing calmly near her. She shook the sweat out of her eyes and with trembling hands pulled the disc out of her pocket. After several attempts she fixed the dial at four.

"Come on, Ember. I'm about finished."

Wrapping her fingers in the mare's mane, Selena led her through the barrier to a small mound of grain. As Ember began to eat, Selena sank gratefully onto the grass.

She awoke as the evening sun was falling slowly into the grove, sending tawny beams slanting through the soft air. Ember's gentle nudge startled her until she remembered her new friend. She reached up to stroke the mare's head.

"Well, you're finally awake."

"Hugh! What are you doing here?"

"Lea came over here to check on you and found you passed out. When that long-toothed watch dog," he indicated Ember, "wouldn't let her close to you, she called Dr. Johnson. And here I am. You hungry?"

"Starved."

"Introduce me to your friend and I'll bring over some food," he said, getting to his feet. Ember laid her ears warningly against her skull as he took a step toward Selena. "See what I mean?" Hugh said, hastily stepping backwards.

"I think she'll be all right once I'm on my feet," said Selena. "I must have brought out her mother instincts."

Hugh looked skeptical. "You'd hardly pass as a colt," he said, inching toward her. When Ember again threatened him, Selena laid her hand reassuringly along the mare's neck.

"It's okay, girl. He won't hurt us," Selena soothed.

Ember's eyes did not budge. Selena closed her eyes and urged reassurance through Ember's fear. The mare's ears twitched and she moved restlessly, but she no longer looked at Hugh with blood in her eyes.

"Okay, Hugh. Just don't get too close to her. And walk slowly."

"Don't worry. I won't get any closer to that beast than I have to. Why don't you send her back through the fence?"

"I'm going to keep her at the house for awhile. She has to get used to people sooner or later."

"How about later?" he asked hopefully.

"She won't hurt you now that I'm awake."

"Yeah, sure. She's tripping all over her sharp hooves in her eagerness to be friends."

"I didn't say she liked you. I just said she wouldn't attack. Now quit grousing and bring that food."

Grumbling, Hugh crossed the remaining distance and handed Selena the bag of food. "It won't taste like much, but it'll give you energy in a few minutes."

Selena made a face as she bit into one of the brown wafers. "They'd better," she mumbled through the crumbs. "They taste like they were scraped out of the lab cages." Flavor notwithstanding, Selena rapidly ate five more.

"Ugh, I need a drink. Let's go to the house," Selena said.

"If you don't mind, I'll go first," said Hugh, keeping a respectful distance between himself and Ember's hooves.

Selena smiled, but for once held her tongue.

Once at the house, Selena asked, "How am I supposed to keep an eye on Ember? I didn't see anything that could be used for a barn or even a corral. I don't want to put her under mental restraint."

"Set up an energy fence."

"How?"

"You haven't done your homework," chided Hugh. "Didn't you find a book explaining the functions of the house?"

Selena waited patiently.

"The house computer also takes care of the grounds. All you have to do is pick your spot, program the computer, and you'll have instant fence. And the fence will be keyed to a special disc, just to keep some poor soul from crossing one of your 'pets.' "

"I could learn to love this house," said Selena. She turned to Ember and concentrated.

Hugh said curiously, "That's the second time you've done that. What, exactly, are you doing?"

"I'll explain later. Let's get that fence up fast. I don't want to put too great a strain on Ember at this stage."

Hugh quickly programmed the computer, following Selena's instructions as to location. "This disc will be in the transport chute," he said, going over to a portal in the kitchen. Selena picked up the disc with a rueful grin. "Now I've got two of these to keep track of."

"Make them into rings," suggested Hugh.

Selena did not answer; she was already out of the house to check on Ember.

When she returned from the new compound, Hugh was sitting expectantly in the kitchen. Two full glasses bubbled crisply in front of him.

"You wouldn't be hungry, would you?" said Selena.

"Miss Christian," he said with great dignity, "I spent over three hours watching your angelic sleep. It was indeed a rare privilege, but it cost me my lunch. What's for dinner?"

Selena hesitated, then shrugged; she might as well answer questions here.

"I'll check," she said, activating the selection plaque. She punched out the desired meal. The words "ten minutes" appeared on the plaque. When she turned around, Hugh handed her a glass.

"What is it?"

"Just drink it and don't be so damned suspicious," he laughed.

Selena sipped cautiously. "Whew. It's good, but I'll bet too much would flatten me."

"Yup," said Hugh. "But it wouldn't give you a hangover. The antidote is right in the drink."

Selena took another sip, then put the glass down reluctantly.

"You'd better ask me your questions now. Much more of that and my tongue will go to sleep."

Hugh stretched out his legs comfortably. "To begin with, how did you get that beast—"

"Ember."

"—Ember to be your devoted pet? I know those horses are nearly wild; they certainly haven't been close to a human being for several years."

"It wasn't easy."

"I guessed that by your nap. How did you do it?"

"It's hard to explain," said Selena. "When I was a little girl, there was a certain pony that I wanted to make friends with. But the pony would have nothing to do with me. Dad told me to talk to the pony and tell it that I was its friend, that it didn't need to be afraid—you know. So I took a handful of grain out to the barn and stood there talking to the pony. The pony was quite patient about it all, but after the grain was gone he lost interest."

Selena broke off and looked at Hugh. "When you were a child, did you ever want something so desperately that you were afraid even to think about it?"

He nodded.

"That's how I felt about that pony. When I saw that I hadn't gotten through, I hung on to the edge of the stall and *willed* the pony to like me. When I woke up, he was mine." Pain flickered in Selena's voice. "It was a mistake; it broke his spirit. I hadn't given him a chance to come to me. I never again forced an animal to like me."

Hugh waited for Selena to continue. When the silence lengthened, he asked gently, "Then how did you get Ember so quickly?"

Selena sipped from her glass several times before answering. "I began by reconstructing Ember in my mind, in order to make her the sole focus of my concentration. Then I visualized her eating out of my hands while I 'explained' to her what good things would happen if she chose to be my friend. When I opened my eyes, there she was."

"Does this method always work?"

"No," said Selena sharply. "I told you that I never again forced an animal to like me. What I offered her she wanted. It's that simple. Sometimes an animal is just not interested and I send it on its way with no regrets."

Hugh hesitated before asking his next question. "Selena, could you communicate like this with human beings?"

"I've never tried. Verbal communication is much less tiring." She paused, then added, "Besides, I think that most people have an innate block or filter that would require a conscious effort on their part to overcome. At least I hope that they do; I'd hate to think someone could rape my mind."

While Selena unwrapped the food trays, Hugh asked,

"Would you try to communicate with me like you did with Ember?"

"No. It's too . . ." Selena floundered for the right words.

"Intimate?" suggested Hugh.

"That's part of it," said Selena. "You see, when I talk to Ember, I receive certain background information from her mind. Whether she's hungry, frightened, curious, things like that. Naturally, I don't know what she receives from me along with the desired message. Frankly, I'm afraid that more information might be exchanged than either of us want."

"I'll take that chance," he said.

"I won't," said Selena and began to eat dinner.

"Will 'talking' with Ember always be so tiring?"

"I thought you were hungry. You can't eat if you keep asking questions."

"I'll eat while you answer."

"God, but you're persistent," said Selena. She sighed. "Talking with Ember will become easy as soon as my mind toughens up."

"Does Ember give you a headache?"

"You mean like those image tests?"

"Yes."

Selena shook her head. "The only time I ever had that reaction was when I tried to guess the pictures you were seeing."

"We'll have to try that test again," Hugh said.

"Thanks. I really need another headache."

"But you'll try the test again, won't you?"

"Oh, all right. But not today. There's an autohypnosis class this evening that I want to go to."

"Sure it won't tire you too much?"

"We've been through this before, Hugh. Either I pace my own development or psych can forget it. Besides, there's no guarantee the class will help."

"I think it will. In fact, I think you use some type of self-hypnosis already."

"Perhaps. I'll know in a few hours either way."

"Mind if I tag along? I'd like to see how it turns out. And I promise not to interfere," he added before she could object.

"Suit yourself," she said, yawning indelicately.

Hugh stood up quickly. "I'll see you this evening. Try to get some sleep."

"Yes, mother. I'll do just that."

Halfway through the class, Selena became acutely bored. The films and lecture on the various methods of autohypnosis had proceeded at a snail's pace. Then each student had been assigned to a console to have his knowledge tested. The tests were to continue for another hour, but Selena had finished the program twenty minutes ago. Hugh watched her fidget for a few more minutes and then motioned her outside.

"Ready to try out your knowledge?" he said.

"I've been ready for quite a while," Selena answered impatiently. "I want to try the black dot method. Do I have to wait?"

"No. I told Dr. Han that this would probably happen and he agreed to have his assistant take over the class if you wanted to try autohypnosis tonight."

"You mean the class isn't going to do anything but research tonight?" said Selena.

"Not everyone learns as rapidly as you, Selena. They'll try their luck in a few more nights."

"Let's find Dr. Han."

"He's in the next room, monitoring the test results. If he agrees that you're ready, we'll start right now."

"He'd better agree," said Selena. "I'd like to have an experienced person around for the first few times, but it isn't necessary."

"What's the truth?" said Hugh reasonably.

Selena stopped and looked directly into Hugh's eyes.

When she spoke her voice was low, but there was neither warmth nor intimacy in it.

"As long as I can remember, I've been a freak. On Earth I was loathed. It was a crime for me to live, much less to develop my talents. On Paran, I'm still a freak. You won't kill me, true, but all anyone cares about is the extent of my freakishness. Don't bother to deny it," she said cuttingly. "You'd have walked through an energy fence without a disc to see the test results. And that's fine by me, Hugh. You're honest about what you want from me. After Curien, honesty is a distinct pleasure."

"Just what does that mean? Mark is—"

"It means I'm going to be the best goddamned freak you've ever tested. It means I'm through being shit scared and worm defenseless. I'm going to have power, Hugh, power that—But you don't want to hear about it, do you? You'd like me to stay nice and docile, a glorified guinea pig for the psych labs."

"That's hardly fair, Selena."

Selena shrugged impatiently. "Maybe, maybe not. But that's how it is. Now let's get Dr. Han."

Dr. Han rose to his feet as Selena and Hugh entered the room. "You must be Miss Christian," he said, bowing slightly. "Your test results indicate that you have a thorough understanding of the various mechanical aspects of autohypnosis, as well as what I might call an intuitive understanding of the discipline. Have you had any previous training?"

"Not that I'm aware of," said Selena. "Hugh thinks that I use some sort of autohypnosis at times. If he's right, I'd like to refine the technique. Beginning now."

"Such zeal is commendable, and gives great promise of success. Have you selected the method you wish to use?"

"Black dot," said Selena.

Dr. Han showed surprise. "That is a rather difficult

method, requiring unusual powers of concentration. But I forgot, you have just such an ability. The black dot, as you call it, is an excellent choice for you."

Dr. Han led them to a soundproof room. When Hugh started to enter the room, Dr. Han turned to Selena. "Do you wish Dr. Nelson to be present? Too many people often are distracting."

Selena was silent for a moment, then reached a decision.

"One of the dangers of autohypnosis is that I may go so deeply into a trance that it is both difficult and dangerous to recall me. Is that correct?"

"Precisely," said Dr. Han.

A smile that was halfway between amusement and bitterness briefly crossed Selena's face. "In that case, Hugh is the only one in the colony who has a chance of recalling me. He's the only one I know." She turned to Hugh. "I'll set a half-hour limit on myself. If I don't come out of it at the end of that time, I want you to say 'Ember needs you.' If that doesn't bring me up, nothing will. She's the only living thing that I feel responsible to."

Dr. Han nodded. "An intelligent precaution. I hope it will not be necessary. Shall we begin?"

Selena stretched out on the couch and concentrated on relaxing each individual muscle in her body, beginning with the toes. Once fully relaxed, she visualized a tiny black dot hanging in her mind. She made the black dot slowly grow, encompassing first her mind, then her body. It replaced the room, the building, the colony, the planet itself. Stars flickered and died at its edges; whole galaxies were subsumed by the gentle ubiquity of the dot. Blackness became the alpha and omega of universes in all times and planes, silently dilating into unknown and unknowable dimensions. Inexorable, unbearable blackness, sated by its being, rent itself at its source. A tiny circle of white appeared. Selena's reeling mind surged gratefully toward the light and tumbled ignorant into freedom.

Infinite light shaded into rainbows of sound bridging immense fluid shapes. Her mind slid downward, struggling for symmetry amid primal malleability. Just one color; all else is distraction. There, below, the consummation of asylum, the olive shade which dissolved into gentle laughter; Mark. But the danger . . . to her? No, the benign olive shade, sinking, struggling against the virulent ravenous green, green, GREEN. Hooded green enfolding, smothering. Mark! And now fire, fire everywhere, searching, aching, needing, burning itself out, guttering feeble defiance against the returning blackness. Breathe on it, hurry, the ember needs you, ember needs, needs. Ember needs you. Ember needs you.

Shivering violently, Selena returned to consciousness.

"Thank God," Hugh said, his voice trembling with exhaustion.

"Nurse, hot wraps, quickly!" snapped Dr. Han. "Selena, can you hear me?"

"Yes," she whispered.

"Who am I?"

"Dr. . . . Han."

"Where are you?"

"I'm back . . ."

"Where are you?" Dr. Han insisted.

"Colony. Ember needs me," murmured Selena.

"Ember is all right, now that you're back," soothed Dr. Han. "Just rest for a few minutes; sleep if you like."

"Mark," Selena said faintly.

"What's that?"

"Mark. Danger. Hooded green . . ."

"Selena . . ."

"Leave her alone, Dr. Nelson. She's asleep," Dr. Han said sharply.

"Will she be all right?" said Hugh.

Dr. Han turned his hands palm up. "I don't know. She appears to have retained her identity and some grasp of reality. I think she will recover. You know her better than anyone; did her last words seem rational to you?"

"She obviously felt that there was some danger to be marked, to be aware of." Hugh shook his head ruefully. "That's a rational statement if I ever heard one. But as for the 'hooded green'—I just don't know."

"At least she is sleeping normally. I suggest that we do the same," said Dr. Han.

"I'd like to stay with her."

"She will better benefit from your presence when she awakes. But, if you wish, I'll have the nurse prepare another bed in the clinic. That is where I am spending what is left of the night."

Hugh nodded.

"Nurse, we will be in the clinic. Call us if there is any change whatsoever in Miss Christian's condition," said Dr. Han.

"Yes, sir."

"Now, Dr. Nelson, I would suggest a sedative for you and then a good restoring sleep." Dr. Han led Hugh out of the room and quietly shut the door.

Selena awoke late the following morning to find herself the object of intense scrutiny by Dr. Han and Hugh.

"Hi, Hugh," she said weakly. "You always seem to be around when I wake up. Something scandalous about that."

"How do you feel, Selena?" asked Dr. Han.

"Drained," she said simply.

"Are you hungry?" asked Hugh.

Selena shook her head. "I don't have the energy to be hungry."

"Would you eat if we brought you something?" he said.

Dr. Han gestured to the nurse, who slipped quietly out of the room.

"I'll be hungry later, I suppose. How long was I gone?"

"You were in the trance state for something over six hours," said Dr. Han.

"That long? It seemed like bare seconds." Selena closed her eyes and shuddered. "I thought the white would never come. The black was . . . so complete it seemed not to need its opposite."

"Selena, did you feel a sense of personal danger during your experience?" asked Dr. Han.

"I was afraid that the blackness would never end, but when the white appeared I left the dark behind."

The nurse returned carrying a glass and some small wafers. Dr. Han gave the glass to Selena. "Drink this; it will restore your energy."

Selena sipped from the glass slowly at first, then greedily as the cool, tart liquid sharpened her thirst. When the glass was empty, Selena looked at Dr. Han hopefully. For the first time Dr. Han smiled.

"Would you like some more, Selena?"

"Yes. And even those awful wafers look edible."

"Now we're getting somewhere," said Hugh. "As long as you're hungry, I know you're all right."

She made a face at him, but didn't let his teasing prevent her from dispatching the wafers and another glass of whatever it was. Even as she settled back comfortably into the bed, Selena could feel energy returning to her body and revitalizing her brain.

"What is that stuff, Dr. Han?" she said, indicating the empty glass.

"It has a very long chemical name," he said, "but we refer to it as Bi-Res, a shortened form of Biological Restorative."

Selena, seeing that Hugh was stifling laughter, asked, "And what do you call it, Hugh?"

"Joyjuice," he said, breaking into laughter.

Dr. Han looked pained at the flippance. "Really, Dr. Nelson, Chemistry worked over twelve years to develop that formula; the least we could do is respect their effort."

Hugh winked at Selena as he smoothed the laughter from his face.

Dr. Han cleared his throat.

"Do you feel strong enough to answer questions, Selena, or would you prefer to rest for a few hours?" asked Dr. Han.

"I'd like to talk with you about what happened. I keep feeling that there is something important that I should remember. Perhaps your questions will bring it out." Selena turned restlessly onto her side. "I rarely forget anything and I don't like the feeling."

Hugh cut in before Dr. Han could frame his first question. "With your permission . . . ?"

At Dr. Han's nod, Hugh turned to Selena. "Just before you fell into a natural sleep, you said the words 'mark,' 'danger,' and 'hooded green.' Apparently you felt that there was—"

Selena's mind whirled and she was back among the viscous colors, searching, finding, and losing that precious olive green. She moaned in renewed pain, clawing the covers blindly, then screaming as pernicious Earther green engulfed her mind.

A sharp slap brought her back to the room, shaking and covered with sweat.

"Selena, what in God's name happened?" demanded Hugh.

His hands on her shoulders, the concern in his eyes and voice told her that Hugh cared about her, that he would be a friend if she let him. She abandoned caution, reached out to him in a desperate attempt to make him understand.

"It's Mark. He's in terrible danger. The Humanistos will kill him. We've got to help him. I'll go back to the colors and ask them; they'll know. Oh please, Hugh, help him, help him, help him!"

Hugh rocked Selena in his arms, murmuring reassurances. At a gesture from Dr. Han, the nurse picked up a hypodermic and approached Selena. Seeing the flash of metal, Selena cried out.

"No! Don't you understand? Mark will be killed if we don't do something!"

Hugh waved the nurse away. "It's all right, Selena, we'll—Mark! You mean Mark Curien?"

"Of course!"

Dr. Han paced the small room. "What exactly happened during your trance that makes you believe that Mark is in danger?"

"I don't know how much of this you'll be able to follow, but you must believe that what I discovered is real. After I broke into the white, I found myself floundering through endless sounds and colors. I was on the verge of losing my grip completely, when something told me to seek out just one color where I would be safe." Selena faltered as she realized how revealing her next words would be.

"And?" prompted Dr. Han.

"And that color was olive green."

Dr. Han and Hugh both looked puzzled and Selena knew that they weren't going to help her.

"Mark's eyes are olive green," she said tonelessly. "When I found that color I thought I was safe. But another green, that of the Earther uniforms, surrounded Mark, forming a net that was slowly strangling him. Before I could see any more, Hugh brought me back."

Selena tensed; she knew what was coming.

"I have a rather delicate question to ask," said Dr. Han. "Was there a special, ah, rapport, between yourself and Mr. Curien that could draw your mind when it is in a free state?"

"Yes and no." Selena examined the ceiling. "When I was first captured, I met Mark. I trusted him because I thought I was going to die. He used that trust to trick me into exile. Yet," her hands clenched, "even after betrayal, part of my mind refuses to end the rapport. I am quite literally of two minds on the subject of Mr. Curien."

"But, Selena," cut in Hugh. "How can you say that Mark 'betrayed' you? He saved your life; he's the only reason you're on Paran now."

"Answering that question won't help Mark. Beyond that, what I think is none of your damn business," she snapped, her eyes like chips of topaz.

"Selena," said Dr. Han, "can you be more specific as to the danger that he faces?"

"All I gathered was that the Humanistos were involved. He is more or less a spy for the World Government, isn't he?"

"Mr. Curien's loyalties lie with Paran. In that sense he is a 'spy' within the ranks of the Humanistos. His major function, however, is to suppress any information which may lead any government to confirm the existence of Paran. In addition, he has saved the lives of many exceptionally able parans such as yourself," said Dr. Han. "Of course, we would prefer that he leave Earth and help us with the colony."

"What Dr. Han is trying to say, Selena, is that Mark is very valuable to us, but is too stubborn to leave Earth. If we could prove to him that the Humanistos had discovered that he was a spy, he could no longer help the colony by remaining on Earth and would have to come to Paran. But we need some proof; he already knows his job is dangerous and that hasn't budged him yet."

"Dr. Han," said Selena, "is there any way I can go into a trance and pursue a specific goal? I was so terribly confused last time."

"There are a few, a very few, parans here who are able to consciously decide upon a destination for their mind and successfully reach that destination in the trance state. However, it requires both talent and control. You obviously have abundant talent; whether it can be controlled remains to be seen."

"I'll control it," she said. "I owe him."

IV

Selena's mind waited patiently for the blackness to sate itself. When the tiny opening appeared, she leaped eagerly toward it and sped heedlessly through color and sound and fluidity until she heard laughter. She followed the laughter, even though it led her to an emerald jungle which clutched at her mind. A green robe engulfed her, stifling, while the laughter faded through the enfolding cloth. She was caught! But the laughter was yet free. She must become as elusive as that sound; she must reach Mark. Her mind turned inside out, capturing the robe with laughter and smiling as the hooded green died.

No color; no sound; a void absolute. Selena's mind quailed as it tried to comprehend a complete neutrality.

Spread out, whispered a fearless part of her mind. *Fill the nothingness; envision that which you seek.*

Eyes.

Yes, olive green beneath dark lashes, reflecting strength and joy and love in a face corded by danger, darkened by futile deaths. And chestnut hair, thick and unruly in the shadow of the brooding cowl. A smile that denied the bitter lines of hatred and futility which pulled unwatched lips into thinness. Body, straight and powerful, seething inside the muffling robe, beckoning, calling, splintering neutrality into scintillating shards of passion which fled, slashing Selena's anguished mind.

Follow, whispered the undaunted part.
Reluctance.
Follow!
Numbed acquiescence pursued the glittering lights.
There, far ahead, it felt like Earth. Too far, too tired,
go back.
No. You must follow.
Searing pain blocked retreat, hurled Selena's reeling
mind into the cacophony of Earth's massed billions
where it huddled, shrieking for asylum, for Mark.
Mark made a startled exclamation and left the Humanistos' mess room with a bare minimum of cere-
mony. Selena's incoherent joy at finally touching his
mind made even the most routine actions impossibly
difficult. He lost his way twice because of her distracting presence, but at last he stumbled into his room.
Once safely locked inside, he lay on the bed and tried
to cope with Selena's undisciplined mind.
*Selena, you must control your mind. We can't
communicate unless you concentrate on just one thing.*
Chaos, slowly receding, then a barely coherent impression of shock as she realized the merest outlines of
his mind.
Paran!
*Of course. You're not the only paran in the uni-
verse,* he thought with gentle amusement.
His thought rang and shivered in her mind, and suddenly she felt an awful fear blooming, consuming, de-
vouring. Close, too close, being crushed, God oh
godhelpme.
Distant high mountains and an icy wind from a
glacial lake. In every direction unfettered space gleamed
under a warm sun. Selena gasped and shivered in the
wind. It had been hot, she remembered, hot and suffo-
cating, and she had been terribly afraid.
Gradually Mark let the image/experience fade as Selena regained control of herself. When she was calm he
delicately, tactfully, asked a question of her mind.

Is there something you want to tell me?

Assent, followed by a flood of incoherent images and words.

Slow down, Selena. Concentrate on projecting your thoughts verbally. One letter at a time to start. Visualize.

D

Good. Now more.

Daxprwv

Slower.

Danger.

What?

DANGER!

But the flood of associations that word had for Selena drowned specific meaning in a generalized flow of images out of her own past. For what seemed an endless time she struggled to transmit lucidly the words and only the words she saw in her own mind. Finally she summoned her new skill and attempted a question.

Easier way?

No. Even you have to learn this the hard way. Don't worry, you'll be talking me numb before long.

Impatience. *How long?*

That depends on your ability to concentrate.

Selena's mind strove to communicate her impression of danger, his danger, and her certainty that a trap waited to close around him. A kaleidoscope of Earther robes and locked rooms and fear surged through Mark's mind.

Selena, stop. I don't understand.

The images faded.

That's better.

Frustration.

Don't worry, Selena. You'll learn with time how to mind-speak.

Image of a clock disintegrating.

Mark's amusement warmed Selena's mind. *Of

course, we'll have enough time. It's a miracle that you've reached me at all.*

Mark began again, prodding Selena's mind, teasing words and sentences into clarity, praising, soothing, until she felt ready to try again.

Slowly, but coherently, Selena relayed her message of Mark's imminent danger. When she had finally finished, she could feel his skepticism.

But I know, she insisted.

And I guessed long ago that that was what you were trying to tell me. But I'm not in any worse danger now than I've always been.

If you knew, why—

I like having you around.

In Selena's mind Mark formed a picture of herself, as he had seen her on Earth. Her face was lifting toward him, lips curved in sensuous pleasure, eyes glowing like twin suns in the dawn of passion. But where he saw beauty, Selena saw mockery and humiliation.

Bastard! thought Selena, anger giving coherence to her mind as no lessons could. *I trusted you when all you wanted was to hang me with my own words and send me to Paran. And you gloat over it, you—*

Mark's surprise quickly turned to anger under the lash of Selena's mind. With swift power he demanded silence. His frigid command was obeyed.

What you want to believe about me is your problem. I have a different one. Every Ear in the country must be ringing with your blast. Now get the hell out of my mind.

Abruptly Selena found herself back on Paran.

"—can't go on this way much longer. Look at her; the last three weeks of sending her mind God knows where for hours and days—"

"I quite agree, Hugh," said Dr. Han. "But short of drugging her, we have no way of preventing her entrance into the trance state."

"Then drug her, dammit."

"No," said Selena. Exhaustion had reduced her voice to a ragged whisper. "I reached him."

Hugh's face showed disbelief. "But—"

Dr. Han motioned Hugh into silence. "Did Mark accept your warning?"

"No."

"Then it's all been for nothing," said Hugh.

"Yes . . . All of it. I . . ." Silent tears of exhaustion shone on her cheeks. "The Ears . . . damn Marion . . . damn . . . my stupidity." Her voice gained clarity. "I didn't know he was paran. *I did not know.* Part of me is blind and the other part is dumb and all is a fool and Earth is too far . . . not far enough . . ."

The voice disintegrated into silence, then she slept.

"Did you catch all of that?" said Hugh.

Dr. Han shook his head. "No, but it is obvious that she is at the edge of her resources. She must rest, preferably without drugs."

"You won't have to drug her. I understood enough to be sure of that. She won't willingly contact Mark again. Jesus, I didn't believe anyone could reach her."

When Selena awoke, she fumbled mechanically for the glass of joyjuice that she knew would be by her bed. Immediately a surge of energy overtook her. She got up and programmed a huge meal, ate it, and returned to bed. For three days she repeated the routine, the only interruption being when she curtly refused to see anyone.

Selena finally withdrew from the house, effectively cutting off even minimal human contact. The animals absorbed her completely. A visitor to the compound saw only a distant glimpse of her as Ember ran swiftly through the long meadow, her rider almost lost in a backlash of mane. Thunder rolled from Ember's hooves and behind her ran the dark shapes of huge Earth dogs.

"She hasn't spoken to anyone for two weeks," said Lea.

Hugh nodded. "Do you know how many animals she's reached since the day she contacted Mark?"

"No," said Lea. "But yesterday I saw her on five different horses."

"Those dogs—Jesus, they're huge. Saw her with ten of them a few days ago. Hope she knows what she's doing."

Lea listened; the thunder of hooves came redoubled. Suddenly she dug her fingers into Hugh's arm.

"Look!"

From the trees on the far side of the meadow burst Ember. The mare was running flat out, belly low, her tail a dark flag against the lime grass. Next to her, mere inches away from Selena's leg, ran a large grey horse. As they watched, Selena changed from her stride position to a kneeling crouch on Ember's back. With a fluid surge she moved from Ember to the grey. At once the grey's stride lengthened and quickened until Ember was left behind. With no slowing, the grey leaped a windfall at the meadow's edge and disappeared into thick forest.

Hugh swore, his voice shaking. "She'll kill herself. Maybe that's the whole idea."

"What happened that night?" said Lea as the last sounds of running hooves faded.

Hugh moved restlessly along the invisible fence. "I'm not sure. You know how defensive she is. I do know that she thinks Mark tricked her rather than saved her. I suspect she is—or at least was—in love with him. At any rate, he got close enough to hurt her."

"And Mark?"

Hugh shrugged. "I don't know Mark. I looked his records up, though. Very impressive. If anyone could fight Selena to a draw, he's the one."

"Selena doesn't need any more battles."

"Neither does he; if the Earthers find out what he is, he's dead."

"I wish I could help her. I keep waiting for her to cool down so we can talk."

"Luck," said Hugh. "I still have scars from the last time I mentioned Mark to her. Oh well, Dr. Han is happy; Selena has tamed damn near every animal on the planet in the last few weeks."

"She must be lonely."

"Not any more. She's got them." His arm swept in an arc across the animal compounds. "I'm afraid it was a mistake to put her to work here. Now she won't need us. And God knows we need her."

"She's a woman, Hugh. And you're a very attractive—"

"I'll tell you the same thing I told Dr. Han. No. You're all the woman I need or want. And if that's how Mark got next to her I hope the Earthers roast him over a slow fire."

Lea laughed. "You do care about her."

"Jealous?"

"Some. She's very beautiful."

"Do you really think so?"

"Yes."

"Funny. I never thought so until I watched her nearly kill herself to warn Mark."

"But what did you mean, that we need her?"

"Han wasn't too specific. All I know is that the last word from Earth was bad. Tien is the Majority Leader now and Han expects trouble."

"Then Mark really is in danger."

"Yes."

"Can't Selena help him?"

Hugh shook his head gloomily. "That's the balls of it. The 'Nistos have Ears—telepathic receivers— throughout their administrative and living quarters. Selena put him in real danger when she contacted him."

"Then why did she contact him?"

"There are two opinions going around: one, that she

just plain forgot the Ears in her haste to warn him; two, she's a spy."

"Which is the right one?"

"Why ask me? Just because I've spent a lifetime sorting through human psyches in general doesn't mean I understand one in particular. Selena once said she's of two minds about Curien. She's done nothing which would make me doubt her observation. But," he said hastily, as Lea showed outrage, "I don't think she's a spy. I'd bet my life on it. We may all bet our lives on it."

Lea looked at Hugh's troubled face, then stopped his futile pacing by wrapping her arms around him.

"Hey," she said softly, "remember me?"

The distracted look on Hugh's face faded. As he bent to kiss her smiling lips he whispered, "Remind me."

Neither one heard Selena approaching, though the grey hardly moved on tiptoe. The snort of the stallion as he caught their scent surprised them, but not as much as the near-wild pain on Selena's face.

"What's wrong?" said Lea.

Selena half-slid, half-fell from the horse's back and stumbled through the fence.

"Mark . . . caught . . . hate . . . hate."

Hugh grabbed Selena and shook her none too gently. "Get hold of yourself."

Selena gave him a glazed look, then visibly struggled for control.

"I must find Dr. Han," she said, forming each word as precisely as a machine punching metal parts.

"I saw him in Anlab 3 just before I came here," said Lea quickly.

Selena slipped from Hugh's grasp and sprinted toward the animal laboratory complex. Though the buildings were less than three hundred yards away, fear stretched the distance into miles. But in spite of fear, Selena controlled herself, slowing to a walk just outside the building. When Lea and Hugh caught up, she said between breaths, "Get Han without a fuss. Don't panic colony."

Hugh headed for the nearest intercom and calmly paged Dr. Han.

"Meet us in my office," called Lea.

Hugh nodded and waved them away. When he got to Lea's office, Selena was silently pounding her fist against Lea's desk. Hugh grabbed Selena's wrist, but one look from her blazing yellow eyes and he let go as though burned.

"You wanted me, Hugh?"

At the sound of Han's voice, Selena turned to face him so swiftly that even the unruffled Dr. Han couldn't control a start.

"*I* want you, Dr. Han."

Selena's voice was unnaturally low, yet so clear Hugh imagined he could see the words hanging in the air like a crystal bridge.

"Mark Curien is in a Humanistos jail. There will be no trial. His execution will take place at midnight, Earth time."

Dr. Han's face settled into folds of weariness. He didn't question the truth of her statement; a blind man could have seen what those words cost Selena.

"Did he say anything else?"

"You're to contact a Rynlon ship. Have them come in behind the moon and launch a scoutship. The men will be waiting in Old Park."

Selena paused, remembering. She had seen his mind flash through intricate calculations, searching for a possible escape, integrating probabilities, certainties, and unknowns with a speed which left her dizzy and finally awed as his mind outstripped her awareness in a complex resolution of data. She had felt strength drain from his body to feed his incredible mind and she ached to take the burden from him. And then he had coldly relayed a message to her. Permeating the message was the tacit assumption that while she would doubtless rather that he die, there were three other lives involved.

"Men?" repeated Dr. Han for the third time.

"Yes . . ." Her attention snapped back to the present. "Three others. The scout craft is to meet them north of the fallen arch. They can hold out one week, maximum."

"But," said Hugh, "a scout can't possibly hold more than two men and a pilot."

Dr. Han made an abrupt motion with his hand. "Mark knows that. His calculations must have indicated that no more than two would escape alive."

"No!"

Both sound and silence vibrated with Selena's intensity. Her eyes were as painful to look at as the sun, yet she forced them to look and each felt a cold tide rising.

"You are wrong," she said too quietly. "I relayed the message. Now no one will die."

Dr. Han removed his glasses and polished each lens slowly. "Mark rarely restates the obvious," he said carefully. "The relevant information is that a Rynlon ship must be dispatched to Earth immediately." He replaced his glasses. "I will attend to that now."

Selena spoke to his retreating back in words that would have vaporized steel.

"That's enough, Selena," said Hugh roughly. "It's not Han's fault that all he can do is call a ship. And the odds aren't too bad, considering."

"Considering what?" said Selena in tones that made him flinch. "Considering that a brilliant mind might die? Considering that my stupidity killed him? I think your odds have shit all over them!"

She turned away from him and started out of the room. In the hallway she paused long enough to say to Lea, "Tell Dr. Han that World Government had at least four operational spaceships before Tien took over.

And count your space communication units. Mark thinks there's one missing."

Selena disappeared down the hall before Lea could answer.

Selena rubbed her forehead wearily. It had been three days since Dr. Han had contacted the Rynlon ship; even with the Fhlenn Space Distorter, it would take another three days for the ship to reach the moon. She ached to contact Mark, to reassure herself that he was safe, but would not risk it. She had stupidly revealed him once to a waiting Ear; she'd not willingly do it again.

Her fist slammed against the house console. Moodily she sucked her burning knuckles. The house chimes called softly; Lea was outside. Selena hurried to the door.

"Any news from the Rynlon?" asked Selena.

"The Rynlon ship reached the moon undetected, and the scout will pick the men up at about two A.M., Paran time. We should hear from the ship again around six, if the scout has returned. Dr. Han thought you might want to be there when the call comes."

"Where?"

"The comroom above the library."

Lea watched the lines of tension bite more deeply into Selena's face. "Couldn't you sort of check up on them?"

Selena flexed her sore hand absently. "And give them away again?"

Selena stared with unfocused eyes at Lea. With an effort, she gathered her wandering thoughts. "Since you could have called and didn't, I guess you want to see the animals."

Lea smiled. "I hoped you'd ask."

As they walked slowly toward the compound, Lea covertly studied Selena's drawn face.

"Did anyone ever tell you how the Earth animals got here?" asked Lea, hoping to distract Selena from her obviously black thoughts.

"By spaceship," said Selena absently.

"I meant how these particular breeds were chosen."

"Someone had good taste."

"Don't let Han hear you say that."

Selena smothered a waspish reply; Lea was only trying to help. "Tell me about it," she said to Lea.

"According to Han," Lea paused to rearrange her face into aloof, straight lines and to lower her voice in an imitation of Dr. Han's measured tones, " 'The World Director at the time Paran was established had a special passion for wolves, Arabian horses, and assorted domestic and wildlife. One does not question the demands of the man to whom one owes everything. Fortunately, the Director was not an unreasonable man; once he became reconciled to the impossibility of transporting elephants and whales to Paran, he allowed us to fill the remaining cargo area with our own animal choices.' "

Selena laughed at Lea's imitation of the pompous Han. "Must have been the only joke that bastard ever hatched."

Lea made a face. "Oh, Han's not so bad. I caught him smiling once." Then, "Is that one of your horses?"

Selena followed Lea's pointing finger. A grey horse pranced along the invisible fence. "That's Smoke. He must be eager for a run."

"Is it all right if I come in and ride Ember?"

"Sure, Smoke won't bother you."

"It's not Smoke I'm worried about; it's them," said Lea, pointing to the two wolves who had not stopped watching her since she had first appeared.

"Oh, they're harmless, unless I'm threatened."

Lea cautiously stepped through the barrier and inched closer to Selena under the watchful eyes of the wolves.

"Stop sneaking," said Selena. "You'll make them nervous. That's better. Their names are Pacer and Shadow. Come over and get acquainted."

"Which is which?" said Lea.

"The bitch is Shadow. Don't be afraid. I wouldn't have let you come in if they were dangerous."

"But they weigh more than I do," said Lea reasonably.

Selena looked at the petite woman and then at the wolves. "You're probably right. But so does Ember, and you ride her like you were born there. Hugh weighs more than you, and you—"

"Truce," laughed Lea and approached the wolves.

After a few sniffs, they moved back to Selena.

"What did I do wrong?"

"Nothing. You've exchanged reassurances of good will, which is all they wanted."

"Oh." Lea turned away to look for Ember. Her shrill whistle brought Ember trotting out of the forest and across the meadow.

"I have to check the rest of the horses," said Selena as she mounted Smoke. "Come if you want."

"It's as good a way to kill time as any," said Lea.

Selena agreed, but said nothing.

As 2:00 A.M. approached, the people gathered in the comroom dropped the pretense of talk and stared openly at the web speaker, waiting. When the call came, Selena was frustrated to discover that she could not understand the ship's captain; she had not anticipated hearing an alien language. Everyone turned anxiously to Dr. Han.

"It was as Mark expected; only two escaped," he said quietly.

"Which two?" said Lea breathlessly, knowing Selena would never ask.

"Mark Curien and Pierre Beauvoir. They will arrive

here in approximately four days. We won't hear from them again until they are in orbit around Paran."

Selena began to breathe again. "Are they all right?"

Dr. Han spread out his hands. "They are physically exhausted. Mentally . . ." He paused. "They felt two friends die, slowly, and could do nothing. Mark is savage, it was his plan."

In a distant way, Selena regretted the two deaths, but her joy at Mark's safety left little room for intellectual sadness. He was coming to Paran! Thoughtlessly she bespoke Mark. His reply was swift and cruel.

Your Ear was good, paran. How much did Tien pay you? Or did you do it for free just to watch men die!

Selena sat unmoving, her face tight and pale, her joy gone. Hugh's features blurred in front of her.

"Are you feeling all right, Selena?" said Hugh. "Selena?"

Selena forced her mind to function.

"Yes. Fine."

"Are you sure?"

"Very," she said curtly as anger cleared her mind and whipped plans across her consciousness with a speed Mark would have appreciated. She must get out of the city and away from the incoming ship. She chose a plan quickly.

"Now that that's settled," she said, "I can get on with my work." She turned to Dr. Han. "I'm taking some of the animals into the mountains. The colony should know more about the immediate countryside. Satellite survey is fast, but lacks finesse. We don't even know which pass is best for human travel and which only looks good on the maps. Such information could be critical if the colony had to be evacuated for—"

Hugh cut in impatiently. "What happened? Why do you suddenly want to run off into the wild areas?"

Selena turned on him like a cat, but Dr. Han intervened.

"Hugh, I understand your concern, but it is

misplaced. The computer will judge the merits of Selena's request, not her motivation. If it deems her capable, she is free to go."

Selena's eyes glittered, but she kept her thoughts to herself as she walked over to the comroom's computer outlet. She sat down and opened up the channel to the main computer. It took scant time to outline her request. Hugh swore as he saw the computer's one word answer, "Yes," followed by a list of supplies and an aerial map of the country to be explored, with perforations indicating emergency pick-up points by the colony's one aircraft. The only restrictions were that Selena have a bio-monitor implanted in her arm and that she maintain radio contact with the computer once a day.

"I'll be damned," said Hugh. "It's as crazy as she is. Dr. Han—"

Dr. Han shook his head. "Selena is qualified, or the request would have been refused. The bio-monitor will warn of any untoward physical state, and she'll be picked up in a matter of hours."

"Hours," yelled Hugh. "That's damned poor comfort."

"The computer weighed probable danger against probable gain, and decided in favor of the latter," said Dr. Han. "I suggest you do the same."

Hugh muttered a suggestion as to what Dr. Han could do with the computer and left the room.

Dr. Han looked at Selena, who had calmly studied the map during Hugh's outburst.

"When are you going to leave?"

"Tomorrow morning," said Selena without glancing up from the printout sheets.

"The ship will arrive in a few days. Would you consider delaying your departure until then?"

"Why should I?"

"I had hoped that you would be interested in meeting the Rynlon," said Dr. Han.

"Some other time," Selena said as she gathered up the papers and left him standing alone in the room.

On the day the ship arrived, Selena was deep in the mountain ranges north of the colony. Pacer and Shadow roamed at either side, carefully avoiding the plants and animals which Selena had pointed out as dangerous.

When they topped a high ridge, Selena looked over her shoulder to check on the white mare who was carrying the supplies.

"Look alive, Lazy," she called, wishing the mare were not so eminently suited for her name.

Lazy flicked her ears, trotted obediently for a few steps, then fell again into her leisurely walk.

Selena shrugged. She had wanted a docile, unflappable pack animal, and that's what she'd gotten. The stallion she rode, on the other hand, was seething with curiosity and life. She rubbed Smoke's rippling shoulder appreciatively; even after hours of carrying her over ridges and through dense timber, his coat was barely marked by sweat.

Prolonged thunder shook the still afternoon as the Rynlon ship tunneled through Paran's atmosphere. Reflexively, Selena snapped on the distance glasses and scanned the sky. Minutes passed before she caught a metallic flicker against the deep turquoise sky.

She watched until the ship fell behind the range of mountains separating her from the colony. In her mind she visualized Mark leaving the ship, his lean body freed of the voracious robes, radiating life and strength and a unique grace. Desire for him twisted through her, firing memories of his hands touching her, his olive eyes alight with passion. She clung to Smoke, willing herself to forget, forget, forget.

Pacer whined anxiously and pressed his head against her leg.

"It's okay, boy," she said, rubbing away the dampness of her hand on his thick fur.

After a few minutes Selena urged Smoke down the ridge. The next camp was at least four hours distant and darkness came early to the deep canyons.

As Smoke picked his careful way across a talus slope, Selena felt an increasing foreboding. Automatically she signaled Lazy and Shadow to come closer and sent Pacer ahead to check the slope. Then she sorted through her memory of the last few minutes to discover what her subconscious might have noticed. Neither Pacer nor self-interrogation could pinpoint the source of her uneasiness.

Selena frowned; if not the country, what else could it be? Mark? She probed her painful emotions, but their sharpness was not at all like the vague malaise which permeated her mind. Gratefully, she abandoned that area of questioning and tried to analyze precisely what she did feel. Fear? No. Danger? She studied the possibility with care, as it seemed the most likely, but found nothing. Sickness? Homesickness? Yes, that was closer, but there was more. Delicately she picked over the feeling of homesickness. Ah, there it was . . . longing for your own kind, for . . . communication-companionship. That was it.

Although relieved at having defined the malaise, she was nonetheless puzzled. She honestly did not think that she missed the colony and the communication-companionship it offered.

As the miles slid beneath Smoke's agile hooves, Selena mulled and worried over the problem. When Pacer indicated that a campsite was just ahead, and the water was good, Selena sighed in exasperation and delegated the solution to her subconscious.

Halfway through dinner, her subconscious rewarded her with the information that the malaise had been increasing for the last four days. Four days, the ship, Mark, said her conscious mind, then rejected it. Selena stood up, impatiently muttering, "Lord deliver me from mine own speculations." She dumped the uneaten food in the fire and forced herself to drop the whole line of thought.

Selena unrolled a thermal bag, savoring the thought of hours of oblivious sleep.

But sleep was not oblivion. For the first time in months Selena dreamed of the cat-like beasts of the alien planet. The dream faded into olive green, dissolved into nothing encircled by longing, longing by the great beast whose crystal eyes knew her on Paran, not alien but Paran. Only one? Where are the other diamond eyes that shone upon that alien world of her dreams? Gone, so far, lost; alone faded two crystals, one mind, all longing.

Selena awoke shivering in spite of the mild night. Her eyes opened upon strange stars scattered above the desolate ridges, emptiness longing for empathy.

She rolled over, blotting out the stars, burying her face in Pacer's warm fur.

Dawn found her on the trail again, restive and depressed. She drove the animals through the rock-strewn morning until shame overtook her in a high mountain valley. She released Smoke and Lazy to enjoy fresh forage, and sat in the tawny sunlight. No sooner had she dozed off than the radio call signal shrilled through the still valley. Swearing, Selena scrambled up to silence the machine.

"Selena here."

"This is Hugh."

"Congratulations."

"What's the matter?"

"You woke me up."

"Oh. Sorry. Didn't you sleep well last night?"

"You must have had a reason to call. What is it?"

"Now I know this sounds absurd," began Hugh, "but part of the reason I called is to find out how you slept."

"Hugh—"

"Just answer my questions, then I'll explain."

"You better. I had a miserable night."

"How about yesterday?"

"Last night was the culmination of four days of malaise. Any other questions?"

"Four days? The other parans only felt it for the last day or so. Except for Mark, of course."

"Hugh, what's this all about?" she demanded.

"You said you dreamed. What about?"

Selena sighed. "A great big lonesome cat-beast."

"Describe it," said Hugh, his excitement registering even through the com device.

Selena's lips thinned in exasperation. Hugh, waiting eagerly back at the colony, heard only static.

"Please, Selena. It's important or I wouldn't bother you."

"Oh, all right. The animal gave the impression of bigness—how big I can't say. Just big, powerful, and built for speed. Four legs, very long prehensile tail, color ranging from neutral to silver. The head was large, even considering the beast's body. Its face was flattened—almost like a human's—and it had huge crystalline eyes. It was sentient, telepathic, and miserable. Except for its unhappiness, it was like the beasts I dreamed of years ago."

"Mark was right," shouted Hugh. "He said it resembled the dreams you told him about. When can you come back to the colony?"

"Why should I?"

"Don't you see? The Rynlon brought this animal back with them. It's here at the colony right now and driving everyone crazy. Even the normals are feeling edgy and the more sensitive ones are impossible to live with."

"Then why did the Rynlon bring it? Couldn't they feel its misery?"

"They had no choice. They had it knocked out for examination when Dr. Han's emergency call came. They couldn't just dump it out an airlock to die. But they're only going to stay at the colony as long as it takes to resupply the ship. Then they'll return the beast to its planet. They might be leaving within a week; that's why we want you to come back now."

"But it will take me at least four days to get back," said Selena.

"We'll send a cargo shuttle. If you can get your menagerie aboard and quiet, you'll be back tonight."

In Selena's mind arose two huge eyes, haunted by loneliness even greater than her own.

"I'm in a large, high valley between the second and third ranges of mountains approximately fifteen degrees northwest of the colony. I'll send up a homing signal."

"Good girl. See you in a few hours, if we're lucky. Out."

Selena began packing up and preparing the animals—particularly Smoke—for the coming ride. When she was sure they understood that the shuttle would not harm them, she sent them off to enjoy a last romp.

A few minutes later, the shuttle landed at the far end of the valley. Selena mounted Smoke and led Lazy toward the shuttle. The wolves offered no problem; anywhere Selena went had an irresistible attraction for them. Smoke, however, had different ideas; a hundred feet from the shuttle he balked, refusing to come any closer to that noisome lump of metal with the uninviting hole in its side. Selena jumped off and walked with Lazy to the shuttle. Lazy's nostrils flared at the unsavory smell of hot metal, but Selena's firm promise of rest and grain pushed her aboard.

After she secured Lazy, Selena called in the wolves,

leaving a near-frantic Smoke by himself in the empty meadow. Selena stood at the top of the ramp and sent out to him a picture of Lazy, nose deep in grain. Smoke edged closer. Selena visualized Ember nickering a welcome when Smoke returned. Fifty feet to go.

Selena bore down on the horrid loneliness of the valley, then offered Smoke the companionship of the cargo shuttle.

Smoke was aboard—tense, edgy, explosive—but aboard. Quickly Selena secured him, encouraging him to eat the lightly drugged grain.

She turned to go to the control room and nearly ran over a man who was standing quietly, watching her.

"We're ready," she said. They were the first words she had spoken for fifteen minutes.

"Incredible. I didn't believe him. No wonder Curien wanted you at the colony."

Selena looked through him.

"Excuse me. I'm Stan Morgan."

Selena nodded. "You're the pilot?"

"No. Rhanett's the pilot. I'm the translator."

"Translator?"

"Sure. The only craft big enough for this trip was the spaceship's atmosphere shuttle. Nobody but a Rynlon can make it move."

"I'd like to meet Rhanett. Or would that be tactless?" she added as Stan hesitated.

"Of course not. It's just that Dr. Han said you didn't want to meet any Rynlon."

"I didn't. Then."

"Oh." Stan struggled to smother a smile. "Come on up front then."

As Selena entered the control room she drew in her breath sharply. She had not known what to expect, but Rhanett was not it.

"He's beautiful," breathed Selena, as Rhanett walked gracefully toward her. Her eyes moved over Rhanett's steel-grey skin and curly russet hair. When he was but a foot from her he stopped, put his hands behind his back, and bent his long neck toward her.

Selena looked at Stan.

"Hands behind your back and touch your forehead to his neck," said Stan. As she complied he explained, "It's a gesture of friendship, like shaking hands."

Rhanett straightened, extending his hands. Before Selena could protest, she found her hands being placed around Rhanett's neck.

"Now what," said Selena. But when she looked into Rhanett's flame-colored eyes she knew the answer. She removed her hands and placed his around her neck.

"I don't understand," said Stan. When Rhanett dropped his hands, Stan addressed him in an alien tongue. Without looking away from Selena, Rhanett answered.

Stan shook his head. "That was the Rynlon version of the kowtow, a display of highest respect. He said he 'tasted' your mind as you worked with the animals. He is 'humble' before your talent."

"You mean he sensed my thoughts?"

"He must have. Some of the Rynlon who crew the reconnaissance ships are selected for telepathic sensitivity."

"I didn't know the Rynlon were telepathic."

"Neither did they. They hadn't even considered the possibility until Earth telepaths aided in the initial contact. Rhanett and others like him are the result of an exhaustive examination of the entire Rynlon population. The Rynlon are nothing if not thorough."

"Then why do they need us?"

Stan laughed. "Didn't you hear me? After culling an entire planet, only a few hundred Rynlon were found who had any psi ability, however small. There are far more parans at the colony than on all of Rynlon."

Selena looked speculatively at Rhanett, then shook

her head regretfully. "No time to experiment now—especially with that being pervading my mind."

"What being? Oh, you mean the Rynlons' animal."

"Tell Rhanett I'm honored by his respect," said Selena, "and would he please get this shuttle back to the colony quickly."

As Rhanett turned away, Selena again admired him. His eyes especially intrigued her; no whites, just a clear orange from corner to tapered corner. He was graceful yet undoubtedly masculine.

"Are all Rynlon that beautiful?" said Selena.

"Beautiful?" Stan shrugged. "I'd hardly call Rhanett beautiful, but then I'm not a woman. Rhanett looks pretty much like all the Rynlon I've seen."

Stan watched as Rhanett's twelve slender fingers flicked over the controls. "Now that you mention it, though, he does seem more, well, coordinated, than most."

Rhanett's hands paused as he spoke to Stan.

"We lift in two minutes," Stan said to Selena. "Are the animals secure?"

"Yes."

"Sit here and strap in," he said, pointing to an empty seat next to him.

Selena promptly obeyed, then released her mind for a final check of the animals. Both Smoke and Lazy had sagged against their restraining straps, blissfully relaxed after the drugged grain. Pacer and Shadow were nervous, but quiet, in their padded cabinets. Selena soothed them with a promise of freedom as soon as they were airborne.

When she opened her eyes, Stan was looking at her curiously.

"You haven't heard a word I've said."

"I was checking the animals."

"You were—" His eyes widened and he unconsciously drew away from her.

Selena flared at his rejection. "Don't worry, Stan; I

won't peep into your mind. It wouldn't be worth the trouble."

He flushed. "Sorry. I'm not really used to parans. I'm normal and . . ."

Selena let him flounder. When they were airborne, she unstrapped herself and left the control room, returning a few minutes later.

"Ask Rhanett if he would mind having the wolves up here."

At Stan's question Rhanett looked over his shoulder toward Selena, then beyond to the two waiting wolves. He locked the shuttle on the colony beam and gestured Selena over as he spoke to Stan.

"He says it's okay, as long as they're quiet. He's never seen a wolf."

"They'll be quiet," said Selena, signaling the wolves to sit on the floor next to her.

Rhanett approached them slowly, his manner a compound of caution and curiosity. The wolves watched him but showed no hostility. Selena pantomimed the proper way to greet the wolves. Slowly Rhanett extended his hand. Shadow sniffed it carefully; her sweeping tail gave a suggestion of a wag.

In a few minutes the four of them were sitting in silent companionship on the deck, leaving Stan to stare out the portal as Paran sped beneath the shuttle.

V

When the shuttle reached the colony port, Hugh was the only person in sight. Selena felt her depression return more strongly than ever after the interlude in the shuttle.

"Need any help?" called Hugh as Selena led the still woozy horses down the ramp.

"No. Just keep clear. Smoke doesn't like strangers."

Hugh hastily stepped back from the ramp. "I'll meet you at the house."

Selena waved acknowledgment and led the horses away under the watchful eyes of Rhanett.

When Selena entered the house she found Hugh pacing around the living room.

"I thought you'd want what background we have on the beast," he said. "The planet of origin is approximately Earth-type, of course, as those are the only kind of planets the Rynlon explore. The climate, however, is extreme. Literally freeze or fry. It's a tough, rocky, dry world. As there was no sign of technical civilization, we have to assume that any sentient animal life which evolved is highly adaptable, competitive and predatory." Hugh looked at Selena to see if she had accepted his oblique warning.

"Perhaps," said Selena. "But so is man. Besides, when I dreamed of these 'animals,' nothing occurred that made me believe they were dangerous."

Hugh looked skeptical. "When the Rynlon examined the beast they discovered, among other things, seven ways it could inject a nerve poison into its victim: two hollow fangs, a hollow claw on each foot, and a dart at the tip of its fifteen-foot tail. Not to mention sheer size and power, all controlled by a mind which is apparently of a high order of intelligence. Hardly my idea of a pet."

Selena shrugged. "If the animal's all that formidable, how did the Rynlon capture it?"

Hugh frowned. "They asked the same question. After the examination, they began to wonder who captured whom, so they kept the beast under mild sedation all the way to Earth and back. When we saw it we programmed a mile-square compound with an eighteen-foot-high energy barrier." An uneasy look moved over Hugh's face. "And I'll bet that beast knows the dimensions of its prison to a fraction of an inch. It walked the perimeter once, never getting close enough to be shocked, like it could somehow sense the barrier." Hugh got out of his chair and resumed walking. "I hope to God eighteen feet is high enough."

"Relax. If it wanted out, it would have escaped by now."

"I suppose so, but—"

"But nothing. You've done all you can. Is there anything else I should know?"

Hugh sat down again. "We don't know much else. The parans are sure that it's a 'sender,' but we don't know if it can receive. We think it's intelligent, but we have no proof."

"How about the fact that it was smart enough not to get killed when the Rynlon 'captured' it," said Selena drily.

"That could have been luck."

"Where's the compound? I want to see the luckiest animal in the universe."

Hugh hesitated. "I was hoping that you'd work with the beast from here."

"If I'd wanted to do a long-distance job on it I'd still be in the mountains. That so-called animal is lonesome. Mental contact is fine, but it has its limitations. A combination of body and mind touch is best."

"You can't be serious. That beast could kill you in a second."

"For God's sake, Hugh, I'm not stupid. I don't plan to rush through the barrier and give it a great big kiss. But physical proximity is essential to any relationship, be it between man and woman or man and animal."

"But you'll be very careful?"

Selena's eyes narrowed, sending splinters of yellow light flashing through dark lashes. "Yes, mother, I'll be careful. Now, where in hell's the compound?"

Hugh sighed and stood up again. "Take the park walkway to its end. On the right you'll see a new trail. It's marked by a red post that'll give you a mild warning shock when you pass it. The compound begins about a quarter mile up the trail." Reluctantly he handed Selena a disc. "The dial is on zero, to prevent accidental entry."

Wordlessly, Selena took the disc and left the house.

She fidgeted at the slow pace of the walkway; obviously it was meant for pleasure rather than business. She passed several intertwined couples enjoying the beautiful park after their own inclinations. The walkway glided past the ugly dorms, then moved faster as it entered the stretch of semi-wild woods that bordered the lake. When the shore was only fifty feet away, the walk hummed to a stop. Selena stepped off quietly, glancing around for the marker. A tight smile crossed her face as she saw another oblivious couple relaxing amid the remains of a picnic. The girl was leaning over her companion, kneading her fingers across his chest. He lifted his head to smile. Pain knotted through Selena as she recognized Mark. Her unguarded mind radiated pain, then rage, then nothing as she regained control and moved quickly into the forest. She didn't feel the shock as she stumbled past the trail marker. Her feet moved blindly down the new trail until a mental warning stopped her. The glowing disc showed the barrier was inches away.

A hundred feet away, the huge beast watched her with unblinking eyes. Suddenly it was running toward her, massive muscles rippling and bunching as the animal gathered itself, leaped the barrier with incredible surging power, and landed lightly next to her.

Mark's fear for her screamed through Selena's mind. Slowly she turned her head and looked into the eyes of her dream.

The beast was lying motionless inches from her, its head resting on massive paws. Into Selena's mind poured comfort, soothing her unbridled loneliness, promising friendship, shutting out Mark's fear. Dazed, wondering, she stretched out her hand to touch the great head and lose herself in the infinite crystal eyes.

At Selena's touch the beast's long tail wrapped gently around her shaking body, easing her closer until she nestled against the animal's neck.

For the first time since childhood, Selena felt sheltered, cherished, safe. With a long, long sigh she thanked the alien by laying her cheek against its velvet skin.

As Mark's mind caught the animal's loving thoughts, he turned to the hysterical girl beside him.

"Shut up, Marion," he said, shaking her until she stopped screaming, then releasing her abruptly. He resumed watching Selena, opening his mind to the flow of grief and tenderness between Selena and the alien. Some time passed before his concentration was broken by another scream. He turned toward Marion savagely and saw a panting group of armed men running up the trail. Hugh reached him first, only to stop in bewilderment as he saw Mark's relaxed face.

"What in hell's going on? You gave half the parans a headache yelling about Selena's danger."

Mark stepped aside, allowing Hugh to see Selena curled next to the huge animal. Hugh's hand tightened on the gun.

"Is she—"

"Obviously you didn't wait to hear the rest of the message," said Mark. "Now disarm that damn nerve gun before you paralyze what little brain you have."

Hugh flushed with anger, but he reset the gun to zero. Mark ignored him and turned to the restless group of colonists. "The rest of you heroes get out of here, and take her with you," he said, jerking his thumb toward the trembling Marion. As Hugh turned to leave, Mark's hand clamped over his wrist. "Not you."

Hugh began to protest, but stopped when he saw the look on Mark's face. After a few minutes of strained silence Hugh ventured a question.

"Curien, what's going on?"

"Can't you feel it?" grated Mark. "Are normals really so insensitive?"

Hugh flinched at the brutal reminder of his limitations.

"Sorry," said Mark curtly. "I've no right to attack you, especially on the score of sensitivity—I just learned how thick-headed I am." Mark's eyes darkened as he remembered Selena's loneliness. "Dr. Han made quite a point about you being Selena's 'friend'; that's why I made you stay. As her 'friend,' it's important that you understand that," he said, gesturing toward Selena and the alien.

Mark's tone made Hugh uneasy. "I'm her friend, period. I'm in love with another girl," he said bluntly. "But don't let that stop you from explaining. My psychology books didn't include aliens."

Mark looked at Hugh silently for a moment, then nodded. "Dr. Han's a meddling son of a bitch. I'll have a talk with him."

"You'll have to stand in line; I can think of at least three people ahead of you. And Selena burned him but good a few days ago."

Mark smiled briefly, but the mention of Selena drew his eyes back to her. He brooded over the strange pair at the end of the trail. Just when Hugh had given up hope of an explanation, Mark began talking quietly.

"I don't know how much Selena told you about her stay with the Humanistos. At the time her mind was undeveloped, her powers stifled because she feared discovery. She feared mindspeech, and was powerful enough to shut me out. In the time we were together I had to rely entirely on verbal communication. It failed. She felt I'd betrayed her. I didn't understand and we ended up slashing each other."

Mark paused and a bitter smile crossed his face. "Parans are not noted for their even tempers and general tranquility. She gave me a blast that made me furious. And then I was caught. Two men died; good men. On the way to Paran, she contacted me and—I gave her a blast neither one of us is likely to forget. I thought she had caused my capture, which she hadn't. And I thought she hated me." He shrugged. "If she didn't hate me before, she had every reason to after. So I started to look for someone to lick my wounds."

Mark flexed his hands absently, trying to drain off the tension of past mistakes. "Selena came across Marion and me in the woods awhile ago. Nothing spectacular, except to Selena. She . . . I knew that I had been wrong. I ran after her, saw her stop at that alien's command, saw that beast sail over the barrier. That must have been when I curdled the parans with my warning." Mark's laugh was like ice breaking. "I should have saved my energy. That alien is pure mush inside; Selena's unhappiness drew it to her. And now look at them. Sweet Christ! If Selena would be half open with me as she is with every goddamned stray animal—"

"What now?" said Hugh after it was apparent that Mark would say no more.

"We wait until Selena controls her mind and can tell us all about her lovely new friend."

"I should go tell everyone that Selena is all right."

"Don't bother. At the rate that alien is sending out affection every paran on the planet will be brimming with brotherly love. That damn beast is even getting to me. Now sit down and let me concentrate."

Hugh sat patiently as Mark once again immersed his mind in the interplay of emotions. Selena was noticeably calmer, which encouraged Mark to send her a questing thought. When Selena felt his mind, she recoiled with remembered hurt. Mark persisted, until sharp pain burned in his mind, destroying his concentration. Startled, he opened his eyes to find the animal watching him. He got the message and swore.

"What's wrong?"

"That obscenc beast told me to leave her alone."

"But why?"

"Because I hurt Selena," snapped Mark. "Oh hell, I can't blame it. I've balled things up enough as it is."

Mark fell silent, eyes unfocused in gloomy contemplation.

At length Selena stirred. With an unsteady hand she smoothed her tangled hair away from her eyes and looked around. Beyond the protective bulk of the animal's head she saw the motionless figures of Hugh and Mark. She looked quickly away, too vulnerable to face Mark and too tired to speak to Hugh.

Slumping against the animal, she began to collect her mind and regroup her defenses. Almost immediately she felt strength seep into her body and mind; somehow the alien was giving her energy as it had given her comfort. Selena relaxed and allowed the alien force to renew her sapped vigor. Dreamily she watched the sunlight shimmering off the animal's skin.

"Shimm. That's what I shall call you," said Selena softly. "For your mind and body shimmer with life." The name somehow comforted her.

Within a few minutes Selena's mind was once again under control. She tried to convey to Shimm her gratitude and affection. A strangely familiar throbbing sound came from Shimm. Startled, Selena could not at first remember where she had heard it before. Then the memory of a past dream arose, bringing with it a picture of many animals such as Shimm joined in a throbbing chorus of joy. Her reverie broke as she heard Hugh calling. Selena looked down the trail. Hugh was standing up, but Mark remained a motionless seated Buddha.

"Selena," called Hugh again.

"I hear you. What do you want?"

"What do I—Selena, don't you think it's time that we got back to the colony? You've turned that place inside out today. The least you can do is go back and let them see you're all right."

"Shimm's coming with me. She's not a beast to be caged and studied."

"She?"

"Yes. She. Didn't the Rynlon even discover her sex when they poked and harried her?"

"They didn't say. But I don't think you should bring that . . . her, into the colony."

Mark cut in before Selena could say anything.

"Shimm's harmless to us; she's too intelligent to take on the whole colony, which is more than I can say for some human beings."

In one fluid motion, Mark rose to his feet and left the three of them staring at his retreating back.

Hugh shook his head. "Let's go, then. I hope you and Mark know what you're getting all of us into," he added as Shimm stood up and he measured her size. "My

God, she must be at least six feet at the shoulder and twelve feet long."

"You forgot the tail," Selena laughed as Shimm curled it playfully around her waist.

Hugh looked anxiously at the tip of Shimm's tail but could see no dart.

"It's retractable, like her claws," came Selena's amused explanation.

Shimm in her turn studied Hugh closely, until he asked Selena nervously if anything was wrong.

"She's just puzzled. I think it's because she gets no response from your mind, yet senses that we are communicating easily. But I'm not sure; my exchanges with her are barely more complicated than with Smoke or the wolves."

"But Mark said she was intelligent."

"She is. It's my mind that's at fault, not hers."

They started toward the colony while Hugh chewed over Selena's last remark. When they were almost there, Hugh broke the silence.

"Are you sure?"

"Of what? Shimm's intelligence?"

Hugh nodded.

"Yes. I can sense that I'm only getting a fraction of what she sends. I hope that I'll improve as I get more familiar with her mind. A week won't be long enough."

"That's okay. We can keep her here."

"No. She has mates or friends, perhaps even children, that need her. There are enough exiles on Paran. When the Rynlon are ready, she goes back home."

"Suit yourself. But it seems a shame to pass up an opportunity to study an alien telepathic life form."

"Shimm is not an 'opportunity.' She's a sentient, sensitive being who has as much right to consideration as a human. How would you like to be yanked off Paran and studied by aliens on an alien world?"

"It was just a suggestion."

"Yeah. You and Dr. Han make a real team."

"Well, you and Mark aren't so great either," Hugh retorted.

"What's Mark got to do with this?"

"If you two parans can't do any better together than oil and water, I'm thankful that Lea and I are mere normals."

"I don't know what you mean," said Selena, her face tight.

Hugh laughed shortly. "That's exactly what I mean."

The rest of the trip to the lab was completed in silence.

In the days that followed, Selena spent all her time with Shimm. On the sixth day, Selena appeared in Dr. Han's office.

"Well, Selena, I thought we were going to have to hunt you down. The Rynlon are leaving tomorrow. Hugh said that you wished Shimm to return to her native world."

"That's why I'm here. I'm going with her."

"Do you think that is wise?"

"You yourself said that no one here could further my development."

"That was previous to Mr. Curien's arrival. If you would consent to work with him—"

"Shimm told me that my mind is that of a cub. The Lucents could train me, as they train all the young."

Dr. Han polished his glasses carefully. "Are you quite sure that you understood Shimm? I had thought that communication between you and Shimm was too rudimentary to convey such complex ideas."

"It took Shimm six days to get it into my head that her kind could help me. I want that help and I'm going to have it."

"You realize that you would have to go by yourself, as I doubt that anyone from the colony desires to accompany you."

"It's mutual," snapped Selena.

"Your supplies have been loaded aboard ship."

As Dr. Han noticed her surprised look, he said, "Really, Selena. Did you think that we would be startled by your request? It was quite obvious that you would rationalize a course of action which would remove you from the colony. I only hope that Shimm does help you; as matters now stand she is merely your escape from sometimes painful human intercourse. Beware of exchanging the infinite uncertainties of life for the cramped certainties of the womb."

"Are you quite finished?" said Selena.

"Be at the port no later than six this evening. The ship lifts at eight. You will find complete instructions in your quarters. That is all, Selena. If you will excuse me, I have work to attend to."

Shimm's appearance at the port halted all activity until Selena convinced everyone that Shimm was perfectly civilized and would harm no one without ample cause. Only Rhanett seemed undisturbed. His eyes glowed approval as he motioned Selena to bring Shimm to the cargo lock. They followed him to Shimm's hastily contrived quarters in the hold. He seemed apologetic that Shimm should have to travel with the cargo, but it was that or the laboratory cage. Shimm, however, had no objections, and promptly stretched out upon the resilient pad which served as her bed. Rhanett carefully secured the net which would immobilize Shimm during lift-off.

Selena turned to Rhanett, focusing her mind to convey gratitude for his kindness. As she watched his orange eyes, she felt sure he had received her thought. She opened her mind to his reply, but caught only the most tenuous suggestion of response. Disappointed, she followed him to her quarters.

Selena groaned when she saw a sheaf of papers conspicuously placed in the center of the bed. Muttering under her breath she strapped herself into the bed and began to read.

The first few sheets were an equipment inventory. Selena skimmed over the list, pausing only when she ran across unfamiliar items. One such item particularly intrigued her: a Molecular Analysis Unit. Selena's admiration for Rynlon technology increased as she read the explanatory note which followed: "MAU-2 analyzes any substance with reference to its suitability for human consumption and/or nourishment. Modified for Earth human chemistry from MAU-1 used by Rynlon." The remainder of the paragraph explained how to operate the unit and decode the results.

Selena continued through the list. When she reached the section dealing with supplies she was surprised at its brevity. Other than a large quantity of sustain wafers and dehydrated joyjuice, there was barely enough food to last two weeks.

In her anger she almost missed the explanation for the short supplies: "If, after one week, subject is unable to utilize sufficient native flora and fauna to sustain life independent of off-planet supplies, experiment will be considered a failure and subject will be returned to more suitable habitat."

Selena grudgingly admitted to herself that the computer was only being logical; she could hardly expect a Rynlon ship to suspend exploration merely to keep her in food. That MAU-2 was going to get a real workout.

A slight vibration told Selena that the ship was lifting. Hastily she flipped through the last of the inventory, forcing her mind to peak concentration. By the time that Paran had diminished to a small, silver disc, Selena had finished the last sheet of instructions and was on her way to release Shimm.

The trip was three days of frustration for Selena. She could not communicate adequately with Shimm, and there was no translator aboard for the Rynlon. She saw Rhanett only once. A day after lift-off he came to her cabin and indicated that she should lie on her bunk. No sooner had she complied, than she reeled under the two distinct attacks of vertigo. Rhanett touched her reassuringly, then left. When her mind settled down again, she realized what had happened. The Fhlenn distortion field had shifted the ship out of normal space, then back in at a far distant point.

Selena drew in a ragged breath and thanked Dr. Johnson for knocking her out on that trip from Earth.

The warning bell awoke Selena roughly. They were entering atmosphere. She sent her mind to check on Shimm, but Rhanett had already secured her. Satisfied, Selena quickly strapped herself into the landing net. At last the obnoxious clanging ceased; they had landed. Selena stripped off the net and ran to release Shimm before the last echo died.

In a few minutes, Rhanett joined them. Silently the massive cargo lock opened, extruding a metallic tongue to the planet beneath. Rhanett gestured them down the ramp. As Selena looked out she saw the remains of the hastily abandoned Rynlon camp. Beyond the camp three huge animals stood motionless, their great crystal eyes fixed upon the ship. With a joyous ululation Shimm flowed past Selena to join her mates. The three responded with a throbbing song which stirred the hair along Selena's arms. Shimm was soon the center of a tangled knot of caressing tails and affectionate pawing which would have incapacitated a lesser being.

Slowly Selena descended the ramp, ignoring the bustle as the Rynlon unloaded her supplies. She moved away from the ship and stood alone to watch Shimm's ecstatic homecoming. Abruptly she returned to the ship to help with the unloading.

In a short time, her supplies were stowed inside the tent which was to be her home. Rhanett showed her how to operate the tent's entrance, and various equipment. When he was satisfied that she understood, he inclined his head and departed for the ship. Selena stood at the entrance to the tent and watched as the ship lifted in eerie silence into the ochre sky. When even her imagination could no longer see the ship, she reluctantly went back inside the tent. She clamped down on her emotions; no hint of despair must leak out to the sensitive Shimm.

Mechanically Selena sorted the contents of the tent and put them out of the way. At length she came upon a large box marked MAU-2. For a moment she closed her eyes; from her mind poured every bit of information given to her in the instructions. As she remembered she manipulated the dials. She winced as a needle flicked out to match a sample of her blood against the information contained within the unit. Apparently her body chemistry matched the unit's program satisfactorily for the control locked into place and a hand-sized field unit popped into the receiving tray.

"Well, at least I won't have to lug this crate around," muttered Selena as she picked up the smaller machine.

Selena rapidly stowed the remaining supplies, leaving out only those things which she would use immediately. In a few minutes she had changed into thermal clothing which the Rynlon had provided. She placed the MAU, nerve gun, med kit, and emergency food in assorted pockets and sat down to study the Rynlon survey map.

She shook her head as the map detailed the rugged terrain. None of the rivers ran more than thirty miles before disappearing into jumbled heaps of rock or gaping holes. Life was concentrated along the rivers and around the frequent tiny lakes. Beyond these rose the broken, barren rock plateaus, jagged walls enclosing the random pockets of life.

Selena's map study was interrupted by the appearance of Shimm's head in the entranceway.

"Well, old girl. You finally remembered me, did you?"

She rose and approached Shimm. In Selena's mind grew a picture of herself riding Shimm away from camp.

Selena surveyed Shimm's sleek back and fluid muscles
doubtfully. There wasn't even a mane to hang on to.
When Shimm persisted Selena gave in.

"All right, Shimm. But it's a long way to fall."

Sensing acceptance, Shimm lay quietly on the ground
while Selena scrambled on. As soon as Selena was
seated, Shimm's long tail wrapped around her waist,
then around Shimm's barrel.

After the first few minutes Selena began to enjoy herself. It would take time to accustom herself to Shimm's
rippling gait, but while she learned, Shimm's tail prevented a broken neck. Selena watched the oasis glide by
and realized that Shimm's seemingly easy pace was
nearly as fast as a horse's gallop. Soon they had reached
the edge of the life belt and were headed into a heap of
jet-colored rocks. Without breaking stride, Shimm
glided over and around huge boulders. Deep cracks in
the earth flew beneath Shimm's supple body as she
flowed over terrain which Selena would have found im-
passable.

A distinct feeling of pleasure came into Selena's mind;
Shimm was enjoying herself. What was an impossibly
rugged trail to Selena was an enjoyable romp to Shimm.

"So you like this, girl," murmured Selena. "Why
didn't you jump the compound sooner? You must have
been wild for a good run."

If Shimm answered Selena could not discern it.

The rocks terminated abruptly when Shimm entered
another oasis. Selena reviewed the map in her mind;
Shimm had brought them almost twelve miles—most
of it over rock beds and crevasses—in a very short time.
And they were no longer alone; three of Shimm's kind
were silently pacing them. Beyond a clump of stubby
silver-blue brush waited many more.

Selena began to feel uneasy as she counted fifteen
waiting animals. Immediately, reassurances flowed
from Shimm. Selena resigned herself; this was no time

to abandon trust. She was rewarded by a surge of affection from Shimm.

When Shimm stopped, six of the animals moved toward her. Their scarred, mottled skin told Selena that they were the old ones, even as her mind quivered before their combined greeting. Sudden searing pain made Selena gasp as the Lucents explored her mind. Instantly the pain ceased, leaving Selena clinging to Shimm with sweat-slippery hands, enraged at the preemptory rape of her mind.

We are shamed, Selena-entity, whispered the Lucents in her mind. *One you call Shimm said you desired our teaching. We are shamed.*

Selena struggled with her whirling mind, but between anger and wonder at the Lucents' ease of communication, it was several seconds before she could bespeak clearly.

Why can I understand you, but not Shimm?

Our minds are ripe, and we are six. Still it is difficult.

But you speak words, not pictures.

The mature mind knows the energy which links sentience to sentience. The mind generalizes, the brain particularizes.

Selena withdrew into herself for a moment.

Does your teaching require entry into my mind?

Only if you desire. We thought your presence on Change indicated such desire. Your rejection showed us we misunderstood. Please believe we would never have presumed even such superficial contact had we known.

Superficial, muttered Selena, her head still throbbing.

Only mates and Lucents enjoy fusion. If you wish, we will limit your instruction to an understanding of the basics of our life on Change. Then, if you decide to continue, there will be no misunderstanding as to what is required of you in the Season of Becoming.

Selena sensed an undertone of danger behind the Lu-

cents' thought. Apparently knowledge was not without
its risks. Well, what was?

When can we begin? thought Selena.

Soon. The searfruit ripens, came their enigmatic
reply.

VI

In the days that followed, Shimm came for Selena at sunrise and carried her back to camp at dusk. Selena's hours with the Lucents were spent reviewing the life forms of Change. She discovered that the silver growth which thickly covered some of the rocks was the Changelings' main source of nourishment. When she tested the growth, the MAU told her that it was not poisonous to her and that it had a nutrition-energy index of 11.4 on a scale of 13.

Selena whistled; joyjuice's index was only 8.4 and the sustain wafers barely topped 7. Such a perfect food combined with the Changelings' efficient metabolism made the oasis positively underpopulated. If the stuff grew in sufficient quantity, that is.

Lucents, Selena thought, *what is this growth called?*

That-which-sustains-life.

Selena frowned; that was a definition, not a name.

Food? she asked.

That-which-sustains-life, came the firm reply.

Manna? persisted Selena.

There was a pause. Selena wondered into what symbols their brains had translated the concept.

Almost-manna, they finally answered.

Is manna plant or animal?

It has minimal awareness.

Selena mulled over the Lucents' answer. Apparently the Changelings did not classify life by physical structure, but by degree of awareness.

Is manna abundant?

When we wish it to be.

I don't understand. Either it grows a lot or it doesn't.

Manna is obedient.

Selena decided to try some other topic. Her own food problem was solved, even though manna did have a taste reminiscent of powdered kelp.

What is the Season of Becoming?

To answer that, we must first tell you about our life on Change, our racial history. Ours is a planet of extremes. The cycle encompasses the Time of Fire, the Times of Reprieve, and the Time of Ice.

A kaleidoscope of sensations rushed through Selena's mind: burning heat, brittle cold, warmth, chill; the oasis scorched, ice-filled, desolate, surging with life, always in flux.

These are the conditions of our evolution and our life. In the far past, we were a smaller people, prey of the torlen, hunters of unaware life forms.

In Selena's mind grew a vision of a leathery winged creature about the size of a human. The creature became a flock, swooping down on a young Changeling as the adults clicked and keened in rage, their combined cries sounding in Selena's brain as Torlen! Torlen! Selena shuddered as the torlen shredded flesh from the cub's body, sending freshets of bronze blood over its silver skin.

*The torlen and our ancestors hunted each other, but the torlen had the advantage of wings. To survive, we left the dark corridors beneath the earth, leaving the torlen to hunt skitters in the labyrinths. Only when we return to the caverns can torlen hunt our kind with success.

*During the time of transition, our ancestors, not yet

adapted to life beneath the sun, were indifferent hunters. Hunger finally drove the remnants of our race to eat the life forms of lowest awareness, whether they be found above or below ground. The discovery of manna saved our race; that of searfruit nearly destroyed us.

*It is not known who first tasted the searfruit. Many must have eaten it out of season, for many died. All but a few of those who lived became insane. Within one Great Cycle, our race was reduced to a few scattered groups of Changelings.

*Those who had eaten of searfruit and survived in body and mind found their awareness greatly increased; thus telepathy came to the Changelings. The survivors never again ate the searfruit, but still it destroyed. Their progeny increased in size, necessitating yet more food. Many of them were born deformed in mind or body. Those born normal were driven by some compulsion to eat the searfruit. If they were prevented, they died. And so began our history of death, deformity, insanity, and for the few, awareness.

Over thousands of Great Cycles, the race survived, each generation slightly less vulnerable to the deadly effects of searfruit, until today only one in five of our young are born deformed, and only one in eight fall prey to the Season of Becoming.

The flow of words and visions ceased. Selena blinked her eyes, surprised to find herself in the present as the past drama of Change echoed through her mind.

We will rest now, said the Lucents. *Though cooperative, a mind of such untrained power as yours is fatiguing to reach.* Silently they withdrew, leaving Selena to muse over their history.

Absently Selena lifted her hand to flick away an annoying insect. Insect? There were no insects on Change. Selena jumped to her feet, hand automatically yanking the gun from her belt before she realized that it was only Shimm's playful tail that had disturbed her.

"Shimm, you almost got your tail shot off," Selena

said as she replaced the gun. Amused apology filtered into Selena's mind, along with an invitation to ride.

"All right, you clown," Selena said as she rubbed Shimm's chin. "It's the least you can do for scaring me."

Shimm promptly lay down, allowing Selena to slip a light harness over her legs and around her neck. Selena scrambled up, grasped the harness, and told Shimm she was ready. Immediately Shimm bounded into the rocks.

As Selena clung to the harness, she realized anew that her first trip on Shimm had been the Changeling equivalent of a crawl. Now, with Shimm's tail free to perform its natural balancing function, Shimm fairly skimmed over the rocks, her mind radiating the joy of a mad, perfectly coordinated dash across the treacherous ground.

Within minutes they dropped into another oasis where three Changelings awaited them. As Shimm's thoughts finally penetrated into Selena's mind, Selena knew that she had been right; these were Shimm's mates. Selena concentrated on opening her mind to the others, and discovered to her surprise that one of the three was a female. She shot a question at Shimm, but at first felt no contact. Then she sensed that the Changelings were in the process of fusing. When Selena's question was answered, the communication had more clarity than Shimm alone, but not nearly so much as the Lucents.

Life unit, they thought, sending a picture of cubs romping around Shimm and the other Changelings.

Selena increased her concentration; this was going to be more difficult than her initial bespeaking with Mark. She visualized a man, a woman, and a child. Then she visualized Shimm with one male, and cubs, asking if this was a life unit.

The Changelings answered in the negative. Slowly they created one scene after another, until Selena finally grasped the idea that it took two males to impregnate one female, and that four Changelings—two male, two female—made up a life unit. Selena asked why four were necessary and received the vague impression that three alone could not care for the offspring.

As time passed Selena and the Changelings grappled with their limited ability to communicate until all five were tired. The fusion dissolved, leaving her frustrated; she would have to ask the Lucents about Changelings society at their next meeting.

After they had eaten and rested, Shimm indicated that Selena should once again mount her. With Selena firmly settled, Shimm led the Changelings across the small life zone to the edge of the rocks where a large patch of the silvery manna grew. There Shimm and her mates fell to tearing thick matted strips of manna from the rocks until they had harvested a large pile of the growth. Then each wrapped a tail around some manna, scooped up a large mouthful, and headed across the oasis.

Selena could not understand what the Changelings were doing, but she refrained from distracting Shimm with questions. As they reached the edge of the oasis, Selena noticed a dark opening in the earth. Without hesitating, Shimm and her mates dropped into it, landing lightly about ten feet beneath the surface. The tube wound steeply down into total darkness. Selena became completely disoriented as the blackness muffled her senses, playing tricks even with her ears until it seemed as though the swishing sounds of the Changelings' passage emanated from all directions.

And still Shimm padded swiftly through the darkness. Selena began to shiver in the chill dampness and cursed herself for not wearing the thermal jumpsuit. She lost all sense of time or movement; only her numbed hands clamped around the harness kept her from falling into the fathomless black.

After what seemed an endless time, Selena's straining eyes detected a faint lessening of the darkness. The Changelings increased their pace with the additional light until the passageway widened into a bell-shaped chamber festooned with lambent strings of vegetation. A silent stream wound through the center of the room, sending up tendrils of steam from its surface. Selena realized that she was no longer cold; the chamber enjoyed a natural heating system.

As her discomfort lessened, Selena began to appreciate the Changelings' winter-summer retreat. The vegetation was repugnant, but it provided adequate light. The water answered the demands of both thirst and warmth. All that was lacking was food; apparently the bulbs hanging from the stringy growth were good only for illumination, for the Changelings had stored a large quantity of manna in a corner of the chamber. After Shimm had deposited her load of manna on the growing pile, they all left the chamber and plunged into darkness again.

The return trip did not seem quite so interminable to Selena, yet the sight of a jagged circle of bronze light was a relief. She tightened her grip as Shimm's muscles bunched for the leap to the surface.

In sunlight once again, Selena relaxed and flexed her cramped fingers while Shimm crossed the life zone to the patch of manna. Without resting Shimm and her mates once again stripped the growth from the rocks. When it became apparent to Selena that they were going to return to the steamy chamber, she let Shimm know that she wanted off.

Selena watched as the four Changelings moved swiftly across the oasis. When she could no longer see them, she stretched out on the resilient woolly vegetation which carpeted the life zone.

She woke to Shimm's delicate but persistent nudges. When Selena glanced toward the patch of manna, she was surprised to find that nearly all of it had been harvested. Only random shreds of growth still clung to the black-veined rock. Selena clipped on the distances lenses and searched the rocky edges of the life zone for other silvery patches of manna, but found none.

She bespoke Shimm but there was no answer. Selena removed the lenses and turned back to the denuded rocks. The Changelings were in fusion, their opalescent eyes fixed upon the remaining manna. She sensed a flow of energy from Changelings to manna and was reminded of the strength which Shimm had once given to her.

The shreds of manna became larger. Selena's astonishment broke her concentration, but even without it she could feel the affection and power which the fusion radiated. As Selena watched the swelling manna in disbelief, the words of the Lucents echoed in her mind: *Manna is obedient.*

When the silvery growth reached a quarter of its previous size, the fusion dissolved. Shimm and the others ate from a small pile of food which they had set aside and then ambled over to a small pond to drink. Shimm's mates then lay down together, tails caressing each other until they knotted companionably. Shimm indicated to Selena that it was time for her to go back to camp; dusk was already spreading over the life zone.

After Shimm had dropped her at the tent Selena contacted Paran.

"Hi, Selena. How's it going?"

"Hugh. Since when are you the com-man?"

"Since yesterday. After all, I've got to keep track of my project, don't I?" he laughed.

"Your 'project' is doing just fine," said Selena tartly. "In fact, I've already found a native food source that makes your sustain wafer look as nutritious as plastic. I'll be able to stay on Change until winter comes."

"Change?"

"That's what Shimm's people call their planet."

Hugh grunted. "Fitting name, from what we know of it. The, ah, Lucents keeping you busy?"

"Only for short periods. Apparently communicating with me is quite a strain for them, even in fusion."

"Fusion?"

"A state in which their minds join and amplify each other," explained Selena. "I don't know yet whether fusion increases their power arithmetically or geometrically. If it's the latter, it would be a very useful tool."

"More than you know," muttered Hugh.

"What's that?"

"Nothing. Just babbling as usual. Say, you wouldn't happen to have time to snoop around Earth a bit?" said Hugh casually.

"I might. Why?"

"Oh, we've got a small problem. Most honorable Dominic Tien is feeling frisky."

"So what. Earth is past history."

"Not quite. The World Government had a complete file on 'Project Paran.' It's just a matter of time until Tien gives us a call."

"Again—so what?"

"So we can't take any chances. Particularly as some colonists are spies."

"You mean the Earthers are on Paran?" Selena said.

"Yeah. We've got a tag on all of them, of course."

"Hugh, this is ridiculous. What can spies do to Paran? They can't even communicate with Earth. Tien must think they're dead. Or for that matter, why would he even bother? We're certainly no threat to him."

"We know that. Hell, we couldn't threaten a butterfly. But Tien's a nut. He may ignore us, or he may declare a holy war. Mark thinks he'll probably use us to scare the world into unity. You know the routine—quit-your-bitching-we've-got-an-enemy-to-fight. Anyway, we don't know enough to decide whether fight, flight, or surrender is our best chance. We need any information you can get."

"All right, I'll do it. But I can't snoop just anywhere I please. I have to have been there before."

"Yeah. Mark explained it to me. He's willing to, uh, 'show' you some key places."

Selena trembled—to be that close to Mark again. Her thoughts scattered into glittering fragments of memory. Again his lips and hands caressed her and passion unfolded like a scorching flower. And again the pain.

"Selena. Selena?"

The memory exploded, leaving Selena shaken and dismayed. She could not trust herself to enter Mark's mind.

"Tell Mark I'll try it on my own," she said finally.

"But—"

"On my own or not at all."

Selena overrode Hugh's profanity. "I'll call you tomorrow at the same time to tell you if I've discovered anything. Out."

But of course she found nothing. Without Mark as a magnet, Earth was beyond her reach.

In the morning Shimm took Selena to the Lucents to continue her education.

Greetings, Selena-entity. If you desire we will tell you of the searfruit and the Season of Becoming.

I'm ready, she thought.

Twice each Great Cycle, they began, *occurs the Season of Becoming. In this time the fruit of the labyrinth reaches maturity; its chill luminescence signals ripeness. The cubs, who have been restrained by their life unit, are released to seek out the searfruit. The life units and we Lucents follow the cubs into the labyrinth, for their obsession renders them vulnerable to the ravenous torlen.

The life units guard the cubs' bodies after their minds have succumbed to the searfruit; we guide their sundered minds through the chaos of waxing awareness. When the cubs are able to integrate their minds and bodies at a new level of awareness they become Changelings.

An ineffable feeling of sadness which permeated the Lucents' thought prompted Selena to interrupt.

Do all cubs become Changelings?

The Lucents' sorrow became palapable. *No. Often our guidance is insufficient; mind and body sometimes remain sundered until the unnourished body dies.*

How long—

The body is given every chance to exert its affinity for the mind. Unless, the Lucents' sorrow became agony, *the uncontrolled mind threatens the well-being of Changelings. Then the body is slain, sending the nascent awareness into final change.*

Selena restrained her questions until the Lucents' feeling of sorrow diminished.

When will the searfruit be ready to eat?

Two days, at most. The cubs grow uncontrollable.

How long will the searfruit be ripe?

Six days. Then it bursts and new searfruit springs from the drops.

Will the cubs have recovered within six days?

Those that are able, yes.

Selena withdrew her mind for a few moments while she came to a decision.

If I should eat the searfruit after the cubs have become Changelings, would you help me?

The tone of the Lucents' thought became grave. *You, Selena-entity, are neither cub nor Changeling. Your mind has a staggering power; if it should elude our guidance . . .* Although the Lucents said no more, Selena knew a death sentence when she heard it.

But you will at least try? pressed Selena.

We will try. If you survive Change, perhaps you will consider aiding us.

Of course. How?

After—

A piercing mental cry broke the fusion. The Lucents sprang to their feet and turned as one toward a Changeling who was streaking across the life zone away from them. At a signal Selena did not catch, they moved swiftly to follow.

Shimm appeared beside Selena. Her tail snaked out and unceremoniously yanked Selena upwards. Selena's hands automatically locked upon the harness as Shimm ran with incredible speed after the Lucents. The land blurred and the wind tore tears from Selena's eyes. Into Selena's mind came suffering and despair and comfort, but Shimm was not their source. Dazed by the conflicting emotions, Selena clung to Shimm and waited for the ride to end.

Shimm's pace finally slowed at the edge of a small valley. When Selena's vision cleared she saw many Changelings fanned out in two crescents. Inside the inner curve of bodies a single Changeling lay against the glittering rocks. When Shimm took her place with her mates, Selena began to understand. The Changeling had been horribly injured; his silver skin was almost hidden by the outpouring bronze blood.

Selena looked away from the mangled, barely living body to the nine Changelings who formed the inner crescent. She recognized the six Lucents and surmised that the remaining three were mates of the fallen Changeling. The intense opalescence of their eyes told Selena that the nine were in fusion. The outer crescent contained twenty Changelings. Each life unit was in separate fusion; from these flowed comfort and that mysterious healing strength which Selena had sensed twice before.

Healing . . .

Selena's eyes returned to the injured Changeling. He had stopped bleeding and some of the jagged wounds were closing. But the healing was not without price.

Two of the Lucents were lying down, their strength depleted. As Selena watched, another Lucent slumped quietly to the ground.

Selena looked back to the Changeling, burnt orange beneath the mantle of drying blood. His pain laced through her mind as the fourth Lucent sank to the ground. An undertone of despair emanated from his mates; they knew the healing fusion could not endure much longer.

Selena closed her eyes to the scene, pulled between desire to help and fear of disrupting the healers. As the Changeling's pain stabbed again through her she slipped down from Shimm to lie on the ground. Her freed mind joined the remaining Lucents.

Agony twisted through Selena as her mind followed the Lucents into the maimed Changeling's awareness. Deep, deeper, they probed his mind-brain, forcing it to heal the body, channeling the massed Changelings' strength into him. Probing, stimulating, demanding, strengthening. And yet more, there is more. Pain lessening, still excruciating. Search; there. Strength, more strength, more, now *heal!*

Selena awoke to the gentle pressure of Shimm's tail on her shoulder. Her hand reached for a container of joyjuice before she remembered where she was. She fumbled at her belt, finally extracting a few sustain wafers. But when Selena tried to put them in her mouth, her exhausted body refused to obey. Shimm's tail delicately wrapped around Selena's wrist and guided the wafers toward her mouth. After more wafers and rest, enough strength returned so that Selena could feed herself. Shimm watched patiently, quick to help if needed.

Selena propped herself up on one elbow and searched for the injured Changeling. He was gone, as were all Changelings except Shimm and her mates. Selena longed to question Shimm, but her brain felt like it was held together by hot wires of pain. She lay back again and within seconds was asleep.

The second time she awoke she was inside her tent. Through the open flap she could see Shimm, crystal eyes unwinking as she guarded the entrance. From the angle of the sun, Selena judged that it was early morning. The question was, which morning? Her stomach tried to tell her it had been days, but she doubted it.

Cautiously Selena pulled herself upright, clinging to a crate as the tent danced in giddy circles around her aching head. When the tent resumed a more or less stationary position, she forced her reluctant body to crawl over to the supply shelf. After much fumbling and swearing she managed to make herself some joyjuice. As the restorative surged through her body, Selena began to think that eating just might be worth the effort. A few minutes later, she was wholeheartedly rummaging through the supplies, eating food at random until she sagged against the shelf, too full to eat more and too tired to move.

The day slid by in a dreamy river of bronze sunlight and patient Changeling eyes, the hours marked only by the intermittent call of the com unit—an irritant which Selena's mind ignored as long as possible. Finally the unit transmitted an unwavering, strident buzz which pulled Selena out of her daze.

"All right, all right. Get off the damn key," Selena muttered as she forced her stiff muscles into action. The obnoxious noise stopped when she activated the unit.

"Selena here."

"Thank God," came Hugh's worried voice. "We thought we'd lost you. Are you all right?"

"Sure. Fine."

"Where have you been?"

"Sleeping."

"Sleeping! You're supposed to call every flaming night whether you're sleepy or not. Dammit, Selena—"

"Shut up."

Silence gave Selena a chance to order her confused thoughts.

"Can you record?"

"The computer automatically monitors and records all communications," Hugh said curtly.

"Yesterday—I think it was yesterday—I, the Lucents . . ." Selena stopped and fiercely clung to her concentration, then began again. "My morning session with the Lucents was cut short. They streaked out of the valley. Shimm and I followed. We found them and twenty-three other Changelings in a small valley. One of the Changelings was a mess; he must have fallen from the rocks. He was barely alive. The Lucents fused with the mangled Changeling's mates. The rest formed separate fusions according to life units. These five units poured strength or power or energy into the main fusion. And the Changeling began to heal."

"What!?"

"The bleeding stopped and the wounds began to close. But it took so much energy. The Lucents began to pass out until the main fusion was down to five—two Lucents and three mates. With that few Lucents there wasn't enough power to sustain the healing."

Selena paused, remembering the subtle despair of the three mates and her own impetuous decision to help.

"What happened?" said Hugh.

"I . . . I fused with the Lucents. It was like being dumped unsuspecting into hell. To heal, you have to find the part of the brain which controls the injured areas. The pain—" Selena's throat constricted at the memory. "You feel the pain," she whispered, "as though it were your own. You hear each cell scream as it dies. The agony is a river you follow to its source, and then you dry up that source. And on to the next river, and the next, until the agony is gone." Selena's whisper dissolved into silence.

Hugh waited for her to continue. When she remained silent, he asked hesitantly, "Did the Changeling live?"

"I don't know; I passed out. When I came to, I was too weak to question Shimm. I slept again and woke up in the tent. God knows how Shimm brought me here. Today has been a dream; I didn't even care enough to answer your call . . ." Selena's voice sank into silence once more.

"Are you all right, Selena?"

"Oh, I guess so. It's hard to concentrate. I need more sleep."

"Look, I can get a ship to pick you up in a few days. Stay in the tent and rest until it arrives."

"No. Must eat searfruit. More awareness," Selena mumbled.

"Searfruit?" Hugh's voice became persuasive, soothing. "Now you just rest, Selena. The ship will be there soon and everything will be all right."

"No ship. Just sleep." Selena switched off the unit and dropped again into sleep.

The amber light of morning found Selena quietly sleeping. Shimm's tail moved gently over Selena's face, bringing her slowly into wakefulness. Selena stretched her cramped body.

"Morning, Shimm. That com unit makes a lousy pillow."

Shimm's throat vibrated reassurance as she pushed a small pile of manna over to Selena.

"Think I should eat, do you? Well, you're right, but I'll need some joyjuice to choke that stuff down."

Selena sat up cautiously, but the dizziness of yesterday was gone. Soon she was drinking and eating as though nothing had happened.

As Selena felt strength return she got up and walked slowly around the tent, testing her motor control.

"Everything still seems to be connected," she said to Shimm. "Now let's see if my mind is unscrambled." Selena focused her attention to send thanks to Shimm for her care. The ease and clarity of focus startled her, as did Shimm's immediate response.

"Well, Shimm, old girl. There's nothing like a good workout to toughen up the mind."

Shimm's throbbing approval rippled through the tent.

Selena laughed aloud, pleased with the world for no particular reason. Her glance fell on the com unit and laughter died. Hugh was going to send a ship; she would be forced to return to Paran. Forced to see Mark and Marion and—

"Not if I can help it," she said aloud, her hand opening the channel to Paran. Almost immediately she heard Hugh's voice.

"Selena, are you all right?"

"Yes. As a matter of fact, I called to tell you that I've never felt better. You just caught me in the recovery stage yesterday. This morning I'm fairly bouncing off the walls of the tent, I have so much energy. And my mind has never been sharper or stronger. Now will you cancel that ship?"

"I thought you'd get around to that."

"Well?"

"Dammit, Selena. You say you're fine, but I know you'd lie seven ways from hell to stay with Shimm."

"Let me put it this way, Hugh. You can send the ship if you like, but Change is a big planet."

"You wouldn't. Yes, you would."

"That is the first intelligent thing you've said in quite a while. No ship?"

"No ship, if you convince me that your mind is really okay. For instance, what in hell is 'searfruit'?"

"I'll tell you, but you're not going to like it. Just remember, there's not one thing you can do to stop me."

An expletive was his only answer.

"Searfruit is the fruit of a plant which grows in the deep caverns of Change. If eaten at the wrong time, it's lethal. Eaten at the right time, it's only lethal for some."

"Selena—"

"Shimm is going to bring me a ripe searfruit, which I'll test with the MAU. If it won't kill me, I'll eat the fruit."

"But why?"

"I'm getting to that. The cubs that eat the searfruit—and live—become Changelings. In other words, they move from animal awareness to a much higher awareness. How much higher, I don't know. Naturally, I hope that the searfruit will force my mind closer to its potential, what ever that may be."

"What are your chances?"

"Of success?"

"Of surviving."

"If I were a cub, about eighty percent. But I'm not, so I can't say. Look, Hugh, I know it's risky, but the prize is worth the hazard."

"Is it?"

"Of course," Selena said. "What's bothering you? I won't eat the fruit if it's poisonous so you don't have to worry. I'll be perfectly safe."

"Stop licking me," he said crudely. "Anything which can make a beast into a genius has got to be dangerous."

"That's my problem."

"It's Paran's problem. Except for Mark, you're our most valuable paran. And we need you now," he said harshly.

At the mention of Mark, Selena became angry.

"That's too goddamned bad. I'll do what I please when I please and you or anyone else can't stop me."

"Mark could stop you. All he'd have to do is—"

Selena slammed the switch down and sat trembling in the quiet tent. Slowly her anger drained away, to be replaced by a cold certainty: when the searfruit ripened, she would eat.

VII

At midday Shimm came to take Selena to the Lucents. With Shimm nearby, the sadness which had crept over Selena increased until it could no longer be ignored. Gently Selena bespoke Shimm.

What is wrong, my friend?

Shimm's answer came with difficulty. In Selena's mind grew a picture of the Lucents as they were at the healing. The injured Changeling was on his feet, walking toward the one Lucent who was still conscious. The Changeling's mates surrounded him; together they appeared to thank the Lucent.

The picture narrowed to the fallen Lucents. Selena had the feeling of time passing as one by one the Lucents recovered and ate the manna which an unknown Changeling brought. Finally only one Lucent remained down. Shimm's grief colored her vision. The Lucent would never rise.

Selena opened her eyes, surprised to find tears blurring her sight. Quickly she wiped them away and moved close to comfort Shimm. Shimm keened softly for a few moments, then asked Selena to mount. Selena sent Shimm a questioning thought and received a picture of a steaming cavern bright beneath the blue light of the searfruit.

"It's ripe," Selena breathed through trembling lips. Shimm again asked her to mount.

Wait, thought Selena. She set the com unit on record and spoke briefly. Then she reset it on repeat broadcast to Paran, and quickly threw supplies into a pack. After she had gathered enough for a week, she turned to Shimm and thought, *Ready.*

When they arrived at the valley of the Lucents, Selena stared in wonderment. The valley seethed with Changelings and their cubs. It took only a moment to tell which life units had cubs; the parent Changelings were very thin, their bodies drawn with fatigue from controlling the obsessed minds of their cubs.

The five Lucents bespoke Selena before she could dismount.

At another time we will render appreciation for your healing. The discovery of a natural healer is a great event. But now we have only moments before the cubs must be released. Shimm will take you into the labyrinth where you may view the Season of Becoming. Your questions will be answered after the last cub has recovered. Beware the wakening torlen. The fusion dissolved, leaving Selena confused and apprehensive.

At the Lucents' mention of the torlen, Selena's hand automatically moved to the belt of her thermal suit, checking that the gun was secure. She felt Shimm tense beneath her and grabbed for the harness. The valley appeared to explode as the cubs were released to seek the searfruit.

Shimm leaped forward, flattening herself into a sweeping run as she followed the cubs toward the mouth of a cave. Swiftly she overtook the howling cubs. Selena risked a glance over her shoulder and saw that Shimm's mates, along with the rest of the life units, were only yards behind.

The entrance to the cave was upon Selena before she thought to reach for the night lenses which hung around her neck. She fumbled the band into position on her head, praying that Shimm wouldn't suddenly change direction.

Once inside the dark passageway, even the lenses gave Selena little visibility. The sounds of hurried feet and heavy breathing bounced and reverberated off the cold stone walls until Selena felt as though she were being shaken inside a box. As Shimm continued ever deeper into the earth, the sounds of pursuit subsided. At first Selena thought that Shimm had outdistanced the other life units, but then she realized that the Changelings were stationing themselves along the passageway to see that the cubs came to no harm. Soon only Shimm's running feet echoed through the darkness, and the sound of her rhythmic breathing expanded in the emptiness.

The blackness began to dissolve into glacial blue as Shimm ran toward an unknown destination. Soon Selena was able to see the jagged edges of the tunnel, the wet brown rocks like decayed teeth in a waiting mouth. Without warning Shimm catapulted into a huge cavern which pulsed beneath the ghastly blue light of the mature searfruit. She leaped a steaming pond, not slackening her pace until she reached a dark alcove away from the shimmering bulbous growths.

Selena sat quietly as Shimm's sides rose and fell beneath her legs. Loud, broken howling issued from the tunnel as the cubs neared consummation of their obsession; a surging, cacophonous wave of flesh broke over the silent cavern.

The cries of the cubs ended as they filled their mouths with phosphorescent bulbs. The silence was short-lived; the Lucents entered the cavern, bringing with them sharp warning of the torlen.

Shimm trembled with a horrible eagerness; her blood lust washed over Selena, leaving her weak and nauseated. Hastily she slid down.

Dark, winged shapes flew into the cavern, pursued by the Changelings who had been guarding the cubs. Oblivious, the cubs continued to feed until convulsions overcame them as the searfruit began its work.

The torlen, called from their skitter hunting by the piercing cries of the cubs, swarmed ravenously over a convulsed cub. Instantly the Changelings defended the cub, tails lashing like whips as they sought to pierce the leathery skin of the torlen with poison darts. The coughing, wailing battle cry of the Changelings echoed and reechoed in the steamy cavern; their killing lust filled Selena's mind until she sank retching to the rocky floor.

Selena fought to control herself as the sight of the transformed Changelings overcame her again. She closed her eyes, but the vision of Shimm, cobalt eyes glittering as she slashed and whirled in an ecstasy of slaughter, burned unquenchably in Selena's mind.

The cries of the Changelings rose to a shriek. Selena looked up. The torlen had reached two cubs and were swiftly stripping the defenseless flesh from their bodies. The cubs' blood flowed purple in the gelid light. Selena shouted futilely as she freed her gun and shot into a swirling mass of torlen. Strange joy shook her as four torlen dropped flailing to the cavern floor. Selena's voice climbed to a scream as the flock dove again at the bleeding cubs. She turned the power to full and jammed the firing stud down. Torlen fell like black rain, their shrill whistles mingling eerily with Selena's echoing scream.

In time, silence returned to the cavern, broken only by an occasional whine from the cubs. Selena lay across Shimm's paws, exhausted by the emotions which had raged through her unprepared mind. Several life units were in fusion as they healed the minor lacerations of their mates. Four of the Lucents were also in fusion as they guided the cubs into awareness; the fifth Lucent slept until it was time to relieve one of his peers. The two injured cubs were watched anxiously by their parents— no healing could be done while Lucents were totally occupied with the cubs' minds. Several Changelings moved slowly across the cavern, gathering dead torlen. Selena watched listlessly as the mangled carcasses were placed in searfruit grottoes to provide nourishment for next season's fruit.

Selena struggled through a nacreous blue nightmare into wakefulness. Shimm's tail stroked soothingly over her arm, but Selena's eyes told her the nightmare had not ended; the cubs still lay scattered over the cavern and the water vapors were heavy with the smell of death.

Reluctantly Selena got to her feet and rummaged through her pack until she found the MAU. It was still intact. Satisfied, Selena worked her way across the cavern, detouring around the viscous puddles which marked the death of a torlen, until she reached a searfruit grotto. Most of the ripe searfruit had burst, leaving fading phosphorescent blotches on the dark rock. Selena picked the few ripe fruit that were left and moved on to the next grotto. No fruit remained. Selena examined the growth more closely; there was fruit, but it gave off little light. She picked one of the immature bulbs and placed it with the others in her pack.

After harvesting along one side of the cavern, she returned to Shimm and began to test the fruit. Each ripe searfruit registered identically on the scale: consuming more than .005 percent of her body weight in searfruit would be lethal. Selena eyed the small fruit and decided that, conservatively, she could eat one or two, perhaps even three, without killing herself. She tested the immature searfruit. The MAU responded with a short, blunt reading: Lethal. Carefully Selena tucked the deadly bulb into a separate pouch.

A mournful ululation rose from the parents guarding one of the injured cubs. Selena shoved the ripe searfruit into her pack and hurried over to the Changelings. Their cub lay in the complete stillness of death. Selena glanced at the other cub and was relieved to see his flanks moving slowly. When she turned back to the dead cub, she saw him being dragged across the cavern toward a large grotto. Her stomach lurched as she realized that the Changelings fed even their own to the searfruit.

Disgust rose in her as she watched the cub's parents push him into the luminescent grotto. The Changelings' tails lashed the grotto walls, limning the lifeless form in a chill blue blaze of shattered searfruit.

As the phosphorescence died, the Changelings' voiceless sorrow left Selena shuddering and ashamed of her former disgust. The silent chant faded from her mind, only to be replaced by the audible mourning of the parents. Their keening climbed beyond endurance, yet Selena's mind resonated with grief and death. Abruptly the threnody ceased. Selena pressed her hands to her head, mind reeling under the impact of silence.

She turned and stumbled back to Shimm.

The hours and days passed slowly in the blue light of the cavern. One by one the cubs recovered and left the labyrinth with their parents, until only the injured cub lay upon the damp rocky floor. Selena could see that he was very weak, his breathing ragged. At a signal from the Lucents his parents entered into fusion. Once again Selena felt the pulsing strength flow from the fusion, but there were no visible signs of healing. At last the cub's breathing became more regular. Selena unclenched her hands. The Lucents were controlling the cub's respiration; he would have more time to integrate his mind and body.

But the fusion could not continue without pause. Selena knew that the Changelings would have to rest and the cub's life would once more be endangered. She went to her pack and lifted out the canteen. Quickly she filled the tough, flexible bag from the steaming lake. She emptied several packets of joyjuice powder into the canteen. If manna was good for her, Bi-Res should be good for the cub. In any case, the cub was too weak to eat and would soon die without nourishment.

The neck of the canteen was narrow and elongated, ending in a small, round tube. Selena slid the tube into the cub's mouth.

She watched in increasing frustration as the liquid trickled out the corner of the cub's mouth. If only he could be made to swallow. Fiercely Selena demanded the Lucents' attention. When she felt their minds, she explained what she wanted them to do. With their assent Selena knelt by the cub and grasped the canteen. At a signal from the Lucents she squeezed the bag firmly and watched anxiously as the fluid gushed into the cub's throat. The cub swallowed convulsively. Selena squeezed again. Again the cub swallowed.

When the bag was empty Selena sat and awaited results. The Changelings rested and watched curiously. The cub's breathing seemed a little more even, but Selena could not be sure. At least the restorative had done no obvious harm. She watched the cub for a few more minutes before deciding to risk another dose of joyjuice.

When the canteen was ready, Selena asked the Lucents for help. Once again they controlled the cub, forcing his muscles to respond to their directions. The second bag of restorative flowed smoothly down the cub's throat. The Lucents released their control and watched with Selena for some response from the cub's body.

After a few minutes Selena smiled in triumph: the cub's flank rose and fell with increasing regularity. The joyjuice had helped to give him strength, but was it enough? The Lucents went into fusion while the other Changelings rested. Selena settled herself more comfortably and opened her mind, trying to discover just what the Lucents did to help the cub into awareness. But her tired mind could not follow the rising spiral of the Lucents' fusion.

Selena returned to the corner of the cavern that had been home for the last few days and lay on the rock floor, her head resting on the pack.

A feeling of excitement woke Selena. The Changelings were gathered around the injured cub; a healing had begun. Within a short time the barrier of Changelings parted, allowing Selena to see the risen cub. He was still weak, but he would live.

Hurriedly Selena filled her pack. With the last cub transformed into a Changeling it was time to leave the cavern to the steam and searfruit. Selena looked for the last time at the dark walls of the chamber. The searfruit vines, stripped of fruit, were once again lambent strings clinging to the damp rock. An occasional cobalt glow marked the place of late-ripening searfruit.

Shimm nudged Selena; it was time to go. Selena fastened Shimm's harness in place and mounted for the long ride into light.

Once on the surface the Lucents told Selena that they were willing to begin her education at once.

The fruit will last for a few days yet, Lucents. After we have all rested, I will eat.

As you wish, Selena-entity. We will come to your dwelling with tomorrow's sun.

Shimm swiftly returned Selena to her camp. Even before she entered the tent, Selena could hear the wailing of the com unit. With a sigh she left Shimm to her mates and went to face Hugh's wrath.

"Selena here."

"It's about time."

"I explained everything in the message. You've no complaints coming."

Hugh was silent for a moment. Then, "It was very kind of you to leave a message, Selena. You've no idea how it eased our minds. We're also happy that you've dropped the idiotic idea of taking the searfruit yourself."

"Who said I wasn't going to take the searfruit?"

"You mean that's what you've been doing for the last four days?"

"Of course not," Selena snapped. "I've been watching the cubs. They took it and became Changelings."

"All of them?"

"No."

"And how many did the searfruit kill?"

"Just one. And it wasn't really the searfruit. The torlen injured him too badly; his body lacked the strength to hold his mind."

"Selena, won't you . . . couldn't you be reasonable and wait until the labs have had a chance to work on the searfruit? Then you could take whatever chemical is responsible for the change without the risk of death or insanity."

"No, for two reasons. First, the searfruit is only ripe twice each Great Cycle. I don't know how long I'd have to wait for the next season, but it could be years. Second, I've a feeling that the chemical which induces awareness—even if you managed to isolate it before I lost patience—would still cause death or insanity."

"Let me get it straight. You mean that the only time it is even moderately safe to eat this fruit is during a certain time of the year, so you can't wait even a few weeks?"

Selena thought of the cavern and the tardy searfruit. It would probably not all ripen for a few weeks. She could wait and—"No, I can't wait. It has to be done now."

Hugh finally abandoned patience and began swearing in a clear, cool monotone. Selena was reaching for the cut-off switch when she heard Mark's voice telling Hugh to leave. She wanted to shut off the machine, but her hand betrayed her.

"Selena, this is Mark."

Selena could only stare at the unit, her mouth too dry

to speak, afraid that her voice would betray her as had her hand.

"I know you don't want to talk to me, Selena. Just listen and say 'yes' when I'm finished. I'm not going to give you a long list of reasons why you shouldn't eat the searfruit. You know the reasons better than I, and you haven't told Hugh more than a part of the truth. For another, I—" Belatedly, Selena's hand followed her command. Quiet came to the tent, but not to Selena's mind. As though her hand had never moved Mark's voice continued in her mind.

But you can't reach me. You've never been to Change.

Mark's reply was gentle and tinged with laughter. *Selena, darling Golden Eyes. Many possibilities exist that you've never dreamed of. You don't have to risk death to extend your knowledge. Come to me; we have so much to learn and share and enjoy.*

Selena wanted to cry Yes, but it was strangled by old fear and recent hurt. She tried to shut out Mark, to hurl him from her mind, but he was by far the stronger. When she realized his strength, she fought like a cornered animal, tearing, rending, destroying even herself in a frenzied attempt to escape. Suddenly she was alone with only the ghost of Mark's last words to disturb her: *Again I've been stupid, Selena. I thought it was rejection you feared, but it's love.* Rich with anger and sorrow, his words echoed through the frightened pathways of her mind.

Selena awoke an hour before dawn. She busied herself mixing the joyjuice she would need, laying out sustain wafers, and calming her mind. In her last task, she was not entirely successful; she ached to contact Mark, but feared it even more.

Dawn brought the Lucents to Selena's tent.

Selena-entity, we feel your unease. Their quiet statement waited patiently at the fringes of Selena's embattled mind.

Selena left the tent and entered the circle of blazing eyes. On the ground were four ripe searfruit.

May we assume that you have decided to eat the searfruit?

Yes.

Shimm and her mates appeared at the mouth of the valley, closely followed by another life unit. All were carrying manna.

*The life units have arrived; it begins. Selena-entity, we suggest that you eat the fruit slowly. After you have consumed an amount sufficient to cause convulsions, you will feel great physical pain. The pain will be of short duration; the agony of the mind soon overshadows all else. Do not struggle; seek to be the agony rather than feel it, for in becoming agony you shall no longer be its subject. Seek not to retain your mind, your identity, for that shall only ensure insanity. When your mind has attained freedom we doubt that we will be able to guide you as we did the cubs. Your voyage will be made alone, in a solitude that we are unable either to alleviate or comprehend. In this lies both your danger and your greatness.

Do you still desire the searfruit?

Yes.

Selena placed the container of joyjuice to one side and told the Lucents she would require it upon awakening. She tested the searfruit. It registered as before: barely safe.

Selena sat down and lifted a searfruit to her lips. Carefully she bit off the tapered top of the fruit. A sweet yet bitter taste covered her tongue as she chewed the resilient outer skin. The remaining skin was a cup from which she drank the viscous pale liquid inside. When the liquid was gone, she ate the shell and waited for pain.

More.

Selena consumed a second searfruit, then slumped to the ground as a huge tiredness turned her muscles to sand. Shimm's life unit surrounded her, rolling her body until it was firmly held by their rope-like tails. Gently the Lucents filtered into her mind.

Pain was suddenly an enraged animal inside her, clawing out strangely distant screams. She must release it, she must turn— But pain was only the mewling infant of an agony which seared her mind like sheet lightning, burning fresh passageways, severing former certainties, a flaming chaos in which only agony had identity, only agony itself could survive.

Selena's scream for Mark rose until it too became agony and in agony was unity and in unity release.

"She's gone."

Mark's words lingered in the quiet room until Hugh's harsh question scattered them into the night. "What do you mean, 'gone'? If you've let her die, I'll—"

"That is enough, Hugh," said Dr. Han. He turned to Mark. "What, exactly, has happened to Selena?"

Mark's eyes closed as he recalled the scene on Change. "There were thirteen Changelings present when Selena ate the fruit. Four of them restrained her through the convulsions, so I don't think her body suffered extensive damage."

Lea drew her breath in sharply, but Mark continued his description in an emotionless voice.

"The convulsions lasted only a few minutes, although it must have seemed longer to her. Yet the convulsions were a caress compared to what the fruit did to her mind." Mark stopped, his face reflecting vicarious agony.

"Go on," prompted Dr. Han.

Mark rested his head against the top of the chair and stared with unfocused eyes at the ceiling.

"The searfruit catapulted Selena's unprepared mind into at least sixth level awareness."

"What does that mean?" said Lea.

"Very little, Lea, except to someone who's been there," said Mark quietly. "But I'll try to explain it to you. We postulate many possible levels of awareness, ranging from that of a stone to that of the most developed mind we can extrapolate. Roughly the scale is: inanimate matter, zero level; plants, first level; animals, second level; normal man, third level; paran, fourth level."

"What about the others?"

"At the fifth level, a person has simultaneous awareness of all sentient life in the universe." Mark forestalled Hugh's protest. "No, not an encyclopedic knowledge of all sentient life, merely an awareness, a feeling, a rapport, a . . ." Mark shrugged. "You'll just have to accept my words. It is a qualitative, not a quantitative, experience. Each person who has experienced the fifth level describes it somewhat differently, but the essence remains unchanged."

"The sixth level—what about it?" said Hugh.

"At that level your awareness includes nonsentient and nonliving matter. The rapport extends to the most minute particle of matter or energy, as well as to all lower levels of awareness. Again, the experience is qualitative. Yet enough remains that you are . . . changed."

Dr. Han interrupted. "It is Mark's attainment of the sixth level that permits him to project his awareness to places he has never visited physically if a compatible mind receives him."

"And the seventh level?" whispered Lea.

The lines around Mark's mouth deepened and he spoke slowly. "At the seventh level you are no longer merely aware of each component of the universe, you are the components. You are the nutrino and the galaxy, the dead and the living, the dark and the light. For one timeless instant you Are.

"And if you are very lucky, you return still sane. The eighth?" Mark shrugged. "Perhaps two sevens in rapport could tell you. I can't."

"You're crazy," said Hugh quietly. "Dr. Han, tell him he's crazy."

Dr. Han polished his glasses in silence. With a deep sigh he replaced them and turned to Hugh.

"You are an excellent psychologist, Hugh but neither your science nor your emotions are equipped to understand Mark. What he has told you tonight is the truth insofar as he and a few other parans have experienced it."

"But why weren't we told?"

A suggestion of a smile appeared around Dr. Han's lips, then vanished.

"You have been told, Hugh," he said softly.

"But—"

"Exactly," said Dr. Han. "Your first reaction was that Mark was insane. And right now, you are thinking that if he is not insane, he is either to be worshipped as a god, or to be destroyed as a devil. Being civilized, a man of science, you will of course suppress your reactions as unworthy. And in the future you will endeavor to avoid Mark, because he represents a possibility which you can neither comprehend nor attain."

Hugh's patent discomfort was all the answer Dr. Han required.

"Now, perhaps you are able to understand why the abilities of parans such as Mark—while not kept secret—are not the topic of luncheon conversation among the rest of us."

Hugh brought his eyes up from the floor and turned to face Mark. "I'm sorry, Mark. I—"

"I'm sorry, too."

Mark sank deeper into the chair and suddenly Hugh realized that Mark was very human, and very alone.

"But that's unimportant now," said Mark. "It's Selena who is in trouble—and the colony. We have many parans, but few who are both highly talented and stable."

Mark raised his eyebrows and looked at Dr. Han, who nodded.

"This is your night to learn unpleasant truths," said Mark with a sardonic smile. "In any case you would have been told at tomorrow's meeting. Paran is under attack."

"Under attack?" said Lea. "But who, I mean how, I mean—"

"Who, is Dominic Tien," said Hugh, looking toward Mark for confirmation.

Mark nodded. "As for how—Tien has suspected Paran's existence for years. I stayed on Earth to make sure that suspicion didn't become certainty. Obviously I failed."

"Nonsense, Mark. A secret the extent of Project Paran cannot be concealed indefinitely," said Dr. Han. "By your own calculations Paran's existence would have been discovered five years ago if someone did not deliberately misdirect the search. I, for one, am grateful for the five years which your stay on Earth secured for Paran."

"The point is that Paran is no longer a secret," said Mark bluntly. "For the past six years, Tien has been sentencing his own agents to death as parans. Naturally, we did not know who was legitimate and who was not. We just rescued people and hoped for the best."

"But if Tien didn't know for sure—" began Lea.

"He didn't care," said Mark. "He's not one to quibble over the possible death of loyal agents. If they escaped to a mysterious colony, fine. If not," Mark shrugged, "better luck next life."

There was a pause while Mark dragged the last of his mind away from Selena. Then, "Before I left Earth, I compiled a list of probable agents. We're watching them closely. But the list covered only the last three years. Besides, Tien is a master of political intrigue. There is a probability that he either has several secret files, or that he never puts the most important plans and names into any sort of permanent record—however secret." Mark rubbed his forehead. "In other words, only Dominic Tien knows for sure what's in the file, and he's not telling."

Without looking up, Mark said, "All right, Hugh. Ask your question."

"I . . . ah," Hugh cleared his throat and tried again. "Couldn't you just sort of read his mind?"

Mark smiled crookedly. "Parans are just like anyone else, Hugh; we have our limitations—and ethics. I'm no philosopher, so I'm unable to debate the virtue of raping a man's mind on the off chance it might prove valuable to the colony. Frankly, if I thought I could; I would. But 'reading' a mind isn't like reading a book. The book is passive, has no defenses, and is generally designed to be read. Man's mind is not passive, has many defenses, and is a hodgepodge of the trivial and the essential. Even if Tien were passive—drugged—he would still have some defenses against mindsearch. And if I breached those defenses without irreparably damaging the mind I hope to make use of, there would still be the problem of rummaging around, hoping to find useful information. And I do mean hoping; without his cooperation I'd be damned lucky to discover one useful fact. Or, instead of purposeful search, I could simply become 'aware' of Tien's mind, and then spend a considerable time as a dual personality until my knowledge integrated. And there's always the chance that the two minds can't be integrated."

"Have you ever become 'aware' of another mind?" said Hugh.

"Partially. It was part of my training."

"Then you could do it."

"The mind I used was both cooperative and compatible. Tien is neither." Mark looked searchingly at Hugh. "I'm not a miracle man, or a mobile bag of tricks. If the colony is to survive, it will have to fight for life like any other living organism. And in such a fight,

Selena—and the Changelings—would be very welcome."

"Is that why you didn't stop her," said Lea, with an anger that cut deeply because it was so unusual for her, "so you could use her all over again? The least you can do is help her now. She needs you."

Mark's eyes glittered as coldly as green stones under moonlight, but his reply was controlled. "I could have stopped her—by bending her mind until it broke. I wouldn't do that to Tien, much less to a woman I— Help her now? You don't understand, Lea. Selena is gone; alone; unreachable. Only her genes and endurance can help her. But if she does want to come back, she will."

"Why wouldn't she want to come back?" said Hugh. "I heard part of what you told her. She knows that you—"

"She's afraid of me," said Mark savagely.

Silence.

"Perhaps," said Dr. Han finally, "we had better concentrate on those parts of our present problem which are amenable to control. Hugh, I want your opinion as to how the people of the colony would react if one, the colony engaged in full scale war with Earth, or two, Tien launched guerrilla-psychological warfare against the colony, or three, the Rynlon fight against Earth forces, or four, any combination of the foregoing. Bring your answers—however tentative—to the meeting tomorrow."

"Tomorrow?"

"Yes. And keep quiet about what you've learned tonight."

Hugh nodded. "Come on, Lea. As of now you're my assistant."

Dr. Han turned to Mark, who was again staring at the ceiling.

"I believe you spent the day calculating the probabilities for the colony's survival under the conditions I outlined to Hugh. What conclusions did you reach?"

"Lots of them. None good. I wish to hell we knew more." Mark straightened in the chair. "On the basis of the information we have, the colony is dead. If Tien conducts a conventional war, we can't last a week. But conventional war has less than ten percent probability. Tien has enough trouble consolidating his position on Earth without lifting royal soldiers to Paran except as a last resort. Besides, his mind runs to subtlety; G.P. warfare is more his game."

"And our chances?"

"I'll know more after Hugh gives his opinion, but I'm afraid he'll just confirm what we both know: this colony will shatter into factions at the least pressure. You saw Hugh tonight; most normals just can't accept parans without a lot of work on both sides. It could be Earth all over again. All Tien would have to do is promise a free ride home in exchange for turncoats and we'd be killed in the stampede to the spaceport. And who blames them? They were shanghaied here. Sure it saved their lives, but that's not worth shit against a ticket to Earth."

"How long could we endure?"

"Anywhere from six days to forever. Depends on what you mean by endure. The original Project called for the colony to be a safe place for paranormals to develop until such time as the government ousted Tien and his filthy prejudices. Then we were all supposed to be reabsorbed into Earth's culture. It never occurred to those fatheads that Tien might win. So we're screwed. To beat Tien we need people loyal to Paran. But if we somehow manage to transfer the colony's loyalty to Paran, the Project is dead: Earth would still be closed, paranormal talents still stifled. We'd save our skins, but only by deepening the chasm between parans and normals. We'd become in fact, as well as in Tien's propaganda, aliens. Heads we lose, tails he wins."

"We must hold the colony," said Dr. Han. "When

that is accomplished, we shall debate the problem of Earth. Under what conditions is it most probable that we will survive?"

"As a colony, we're lucky to be alive now. As groups in hiding, living off the land, we could last indefinitely. Tien doesn't have the material to incinerate the planet."

"There is one source of help that you have not mentioned."

"Yes," said Mark. "The Rynlon. They're our last resort. If necessary, they can lift us off Paran and dump us on another planet. Then we could wait for someone to steal another space-com unit, report to Earth, and begin the whole cycle again. Goddammit, Han. There just aren't enough good parans here. We've got to return to Earth and teach, or what we've learned about the mind will die with us. When I think of the latent psi talents of most so-called normals, I could almost enjoy breaking Tien's mind."

Dr. Han adjusted his glasses beneath Mark's glare, then said softly, "Tien's death would accomplish very little. His power stems from the supine, superstitious masses of Earth."

"Exactly," said Mark wearily. "And how can we teach the ignorant and afraid if we are quarantined on Paran? Even on Earth, the job would be almost impossible. Mind training requires time and cooperation."

There was a long silence while Mark brooded over the talented children of Earth. Finally Dr. Han cleared his throat. "Mark, I feel you should know that I've dispatched a ship to Change. It will arrive in approximately ten days."

The lines of Mark's face hardened until it seemed he wore a mask of wood.

"If Selena wishes," continued Dr. Han, "we will return her to Paran. If not, we will collect samples of the searfruit for analysis."

"Don't give me that 'if she wishes' crap. We both know that in ten days she'll probably be dead or totally insane. You don't give a damn about her, you just want to get your meddling hands on the searfruit."

"As you pointed out, mind training is a lengthy process. It is possible that searfruit would shorten that time considerably. That possibility must be explored."

Mark made no reply, thinking only of the clear golden eyes which might be lost irretrievably in the seventh level of awareness.

VIII

At first the blackness was familiar, an old friend whose depths had been fathomed, whose boundaries had been ascertained. But the ebony intensified until even memory of light receded and the former dark seemed as grey. And yet deeper it became and blacker and Selena's mind twisted upward. Where was light? No. What was light? Ah, yes. What was . . .

The spiral collapsed, leaving Selena's mind without support, but with awareness increased. Fear not blackness when it is but oneself. A different self, seething with infinite yet discrete sentience, compilation of awarenesses, but not plural because self is singular obsidian and obsidian is all.

But not all, no, never all. All must have its opposite or it becomes nothing-at-all and being nothing cannot be all. And what of all-darkness whispered awareness, haunted by remembrance (s) of not-darkness long before. Where is the not-darkness that makes all-darkness exist? Awareness pondered, spread itself, searched itself for its other self. And one singular note of awareness screamed for identity, for otherness unwashed by the irresistible tide of massed sentience.

"Mark, it's been two days. Is Selena . . . have you . . ." Lea waited, her black eyes pleading for help.

"Her body lives. Her awareness, if not her identity, probably also lives." The green of his eyes was heightened by the black marks of fatigue surrounding them. "Is that why you woke me up?"

"Yes. No. I'm sorry. Dr. Han sent me—there's a meeting now in his office."

"Another? What happened while I slept?"

"I don't know. Maybe a ship has been spotted, or more propaganda, or murder, or—"

"Lea, you should get some sleep," Mark said gently.

"Hugh needs me. He—"

"He'd tell you to see Dr. Johnson."

A look of rare stubbornness hardened the gentle lines of Lea's face.

"In my new capacity as Controller," said Mark, "I order you to go to Dr. Johnson immediately."

Lea's stubbornness flickered, then dissolved in streams of tears. He held her until her sobs became far apart, then ceased.

Mark tilted her chin upward until he could see her dark eyes and smiled gently. "Feel like you can sleep now?"

Lea nodded. "You won't tell Hugh?"

"Won't tell him what?" teased Mark. "That I held his woman?"

A smile hovered over Lea's lips, then settled into its natural place.

"That's better," said Mark, smiling in return.

"I don't think I'll need Dr. Johnson," she said. "By the time he gets out of the meeting, I'll be asleep."

Mark looked at her closely; the shadow of hysteria had passed from her eyes. She would sleep without drugs.

When Mark reached Dr. Han's office his ears were assaulted by loud arguments. He looked at Dr. Han quizzically. Dr. Han shook his head slightly and motioned for Mark to sit down. Mark found an empty chair and glanced around the room, cataloging the occupants and their opinions.

First, though by no means the loudest, was Al Martinez, copilot of the Earth rescue ships and a man dedicated to the exploration of space. Mark listened to his penetrating, yet pleasant voice.

". . . damn it all, it'd be murder not to evacuate some of these people, especially the children. So we might end up transporting some agents to another planet. Hell's fire! If we don't evacuate, the colony will be wiped out and Earthmen will never ride out to the stars. Look, Stan talked with Rhanett and some of the other Rynlon, and they agreed that evacuation is the only sensible plan. Here's how we'll do it. . . ."

Mark knew most of the plan, and could guess the rest. His attention shifted to Shandara Jorgenson, who had just returned from an exploration with the Rynlon. She was one of the few parans who could lay claim to the title Sensitive: she could sense the existence of any sentient life, and often could give an accurate assessment of its emotional state. For a moment Mark toyed with the idea of lining up the colonists one by one and having Shandara ferret out Tien's agents. Then he laughed at his pleasant daydream: Shandara was indeed talented, but even she could not say whether a person was hostile because he was an agent, or because he resented even a mild form of mindsearch.

Still laughing silently, Mark listened to her words.

". . . must choose between what are presently conflicting goals: contact-communication with intelligent alien life forms, and training and development of paranormal talents on Earth. As the latter is impossible under Tien's rule, we should concentrate on the former."

"But Dara," said her husband, "there aren't enough of us to do any real work. We need the talents of Earth to explore and understand the life forms we meet."

Dara turned to him, her dusky face flushed with excitement. "Sven, there's always the chance of discovering other talented life forms. It's at least as good a chance as working successfully with Earth under Tien's rule."

"And if we do find a talented, cooperative life form, what of Earth?"

"Earth will obtain her just karma—stagnation."

"You can't mean that," said Sven. "What we are and will be we owe to Earth. It would be monstrous to leave her children in darkness. Surely Tien could be persuaded—"

Mark shook his head and exhaled his breath slowly, letting the arguments whirl soundlessly around his head. The colony had three choices: run, fight, or give up. And the choice had better be made soon. He stood and walked to the center of the room, leaving silence in his wake.

"Unfortunately, Tien won't wait until we talk ourselves to death. When I left Earth, the World Government had four ships ready for test runs. The ships were to have been used—secretly—by Earth in exploring our sector of space. We must assume that Tien now has the ships and will use them against the colony."

Hugh looked at him strangely. "Did Lea tell you why this meeting was called?"

"No."

"One of Tien's ships will be here in two days, if we can believe his broadcast."

"And then?"

"Supposedly, Tien will transport all defecting colonists back to Earth. Anyone not waiting at the spaceport will be killed."

"Pure bull. One ship couldn't carry all the agents, much less defectors. And Tien couldn't kill the rest unless we were stupid enough to stay at the colony. But he could certainly raze the spaceport."

Hugh laughed humorlessly. "Yeah, but try telling that to a bunch of stupid, homesick—"

"We have to try."

"We are," said Dr. Han. "But human beings will believe that which is most appealing to their needs. I fear that our point of view is unheeded by many colonists."

"How many?" said Mark.

Dr. Han looked toward Hugh, who shrugged. "Maybe four hundred, maybe five, maybe more."

"What would happen if we closed off the spaceport?" said Mark.

"We'd have at least five hundred enemies."

"Just what we need," Mark said.

"You mean you're going to let them line up at the spaceport like sheep?" said Martinez. "You can be goddamned sure that Tien isn't going to land his precious ship here."

"We know that, Al," said Mark softly. "The point is, what are we going to do with five hundred actively hostile colonists?"

"Evacuate them with the rest of us."

"It will take at least two months for the Rynlon to take every last person off Paran. That's what your plan calls for, isn't it?"

Martinez nodded.

"There are three Rynlon ships in orbit around Paran now," said Mark. "If we started loading in an hour, and broke every safety rule, three hundred colonists could lift off for Rynlonne within thirty hours. That leaves approximately twenty-two hundred people on Paran, a good part of them eager to slit our throats."

Martinez was silent; he could subtract as well as anyone in the room.

"But," said Mark, "we'll evacuate as many colonists as possible. The ships will land tonight. Dr. Johnson, I want you to go through your medical files. The old, the ill, and the very young have the first claim. If there are less than three hundred who fit that description, or if there are less than three hundred who are willing to go, contact me immediately. If there are more, I'm afraid you'll have to play God."

Dr. Johnson nodded and prepared to leave.

"Don't go yet. You'd better hear the rest of the plan," said Mark. "By the time we leave this room, the computer will be jamming all communication frequencies. They will remain jammed until the colony is empty."

"But how will we organize the people?" said Martinez.

"That's your problem. As of now you are in charge of evacuation for the colony." Mark smiled. "It's not that bad, Al. The computer was programmed to set up a shell of interference, with the colony at center. Within the shell, com devices will operate. All the shell does is make it impossible for any agents to alert Tien's ship to what is going on in the colony."

"What's to prevent someone from slipping outside the colony?"

"The shell is lethal," said Dr. Han. "Without a disc— and none will be made—nothing living can pass through it. When the colonists are ready to leave, the barrier will be dropped. After we have left, it will go into force again."

"You mean we're all going out of the colony?" said Sven.

"What about the people who want to go to Earth?"

"Of course we're going to abandon the colony," said Martinez. "It's every bit as good a target as the spaceport."

"One fusion bomb would do the job nicely—or Tien might want the buildings intact for his own purposes. After all," Mark laughed, "he wouldn't be the first politician to need an escape hatch. But so long as the computer exists, the physical plant of the colony will remain intact and unapproachable."

"What if we want to get back in?" said Dara. "Surely some provision—"

"None. We want no one to run back to the colony. And as for the people who want to return to Earth, Hugh and I will cope with them. Any questions?"

No one admitted to any.

"Al, I want you and Hugh to stay with me and hash out the evacuation. The rest of you keep in touch with Dr. Han. When we have a plan, we'll need you."

Mark waited until everyone else had left the room before turning to the two men.

"You first, Al. For the last month the Chemical Complex has been turning out only emergency items: all-weather camouflage clothing, knives, sleeping bags, medkits, canteens, emergency rations, etc. By tomorrow afternoon each colonist will get his gear through the supply tubes. Your job is to divide the colonists into groups of twelve, and choose leaders and points of exit from the colony. You'll brief the leaders, give them each a nerve rod and map, and a special com device to be worn at all times."

Mark walked over to Dr. Han's desk, opened a drawer, and picked up something which looked like a wrist compass.

"This is the com device. The groups should be scattered all over the continent by the end of the month and the Rynlon would have a hell of a time finding them. That's what the com units are for. A Rynlon cargo shuttle will fly over a segment of the continent and drop caller units about every twenty miles. If the leader of a group is within ten miles of the caller, his wrist device will show two points of light—blue for the group location and red for the caller. Using the lights, the group should be able to find the caller. After the group reaches the caller, the leader reverses the unit's signal and it calls the shuttle."

"Sounds all right, but—" began Al.

"There are holes," said Mark. "I know, but it's the best we could do. If you and the people you choose as leaders can close some of the holes, do it. But any plan you finally use has to be based on the capabilities of the caller and the wrist device. They're all we have."

Martinez nodded glumly. "And what about the

groups? What if some of the people I've assigned to a group want to go to the spaceport instead?"

"Let them. The computer figured that six to twelve people would comprise an optimum number for group survival. If more than six leave, scatter the remainder into other groups which have lost people."

When Martinez left, Mark turned to Hugh. "You're the psychologist—what are we going to do with the people who believe Tien's propaganda?"

"I'd like to escort them to the spaceport, wave good-bye, and run like hell."

Mark smiled. "I'd thought of the same thing. But some of them are just trying to get back to people they love."

"Yeah, I know. About the only thing we can do is trick them into believing that they'll be allowed to go to the spaceport. They'll be mad as hell when they find out, but at least they'll be alive." Hugh hesitated, then continued. "Are we sure that Tien's men will kill who-ever goes to the spaceport?"

"We're not sure of anything."

"What about the colonists we are sure are working for Tien?"

"They're locked in their rooms. Why?"

"The colonists who want to go to Earth won't listen to us. But if we were to tell the spies that they were going to be sent to the spaceport—deported, we'll say—and the spies refused, that might shake up the rest."

"And if it doesn't?"

"Then," Hugh said, "the spies will go to the spaceport while the rest watch from a safe place."

Mark stood silently as he considered the plan. "We can always hope that the offer was real, that the ships will take them to Earth."

"You don't believe that," said Hugh.

"No, but those spies will be at the spaceport just the same."

Hugh nodded, started to ask a question, then glanced

quickly away. He walked to the desk and fiddled with the wrist unit. He cleared his throat, but no words followed. Mark waited for a moment, then said, "Selena is still alive."

Hugh nodded, then left the room without looking back.

Awareness reached, flexed, threw off countless shards of light, then reshaped itself until discrete awarenesses coalesced as bright drops on a spiral of sentience stretching through time and space. At the center of the spiral a minute sphere of darkness enwrapped a waiting mote. Bright drops dissolved in moving toward the hollow sphere, merged with other drops as the shimmering spiral began an ancient lay of galaxies and mesons and the hearts of neutron stars. And yet more drops dissolved, bringing to the shadowed mote quicksilver knowledge of life, all life, and the death of nescience in an iridescent implosion of knowledge.

Drained of song and sentience, the spiral waited, beckoned. The mote expanded along the curving spiral, straining, pulsing, heaving, until in a final rhythmic expansion cognizance became omniscience.

I AM.

Silver galaxies spun in the silent void.

I AM.

Planets brought forth their children.

I AM.

Life birthed sentience and

I AM.

Death.

The barrier dropped and anxious groups hurried away into the darkness. In the port control center, sunk into concrete and resting on massive springs deep beneath ground level, Mark and several men waited in coiled silence for the ship from Earth. Waited, and watched the viewscreen which showed fifty unwilling guinea pigs imprisoned in an immaterial cage of energy.

"Are you sure you can get the rest of us out of the hills in time to load?" asked the man who represented the colonists who wished to return to Earth.

"We've been over that before, Carl," said Mark. "We've got two cargo shuttles waiting. When I give the signal, they'll bring the colonists to the spaceport before Tien's agents are even aboard."

"I still don't like the idea."

"Tough—"

Mark shut off his reply as an approaching craft tripped the warning circuit.

"Here it comes." Mark released the barrier around the spies. The viewscreen seethed with their frantic attempts to find cover.

"Still wish you were out there?"

Carl shifted uncomfortably. "Tien said he would transport—"

"Bullshit," Mark pointed to the tracking screen. "That's a two-man scoutcraft."

Ten figures still remained on the viewscreen when the scoutcraft became visible to the unaided eye. Mark's knuckles whitened on the console as he saw the ten remain motionless, apparently watching the approaching craft. He opened the line to the surface speakers and yelled, "Run, you stupid bastards!"

The agents jumped at the unexpected voice and began to run from the exposed concrete apron.

But the scout was faster. Light bloomed from the craft's belly and chemical bombs skated crazily across the smooth concrete surface, scattering white flames and death as they fragmented.

Within minutes the blazing chemicals sputtered to a sullen phosphorescence, then died into darkness.

Except where the chemicals had combined with organic substances—then a curious low-flamed fire burned whitely.

Mark counted eight patches of fire. "Still believe Tien?" he asked softly.

"You tricked us," shouted Carl. "If we'd been out there we'd be on our way home. Tien's right. You parans can't be trusted. You—"

A nerve rod slid from its wrist sheath into Mark's hand. "We've got ten minutes before the barrier goes up for good."

He pointed toward the emergency tunnel with the rod, and the surly colonists moved out of the control room. A slidestrip carried them swiftly to the elevator shaft. When they reached the surface they had five minutes left. Mark scanned the area, but felt no other people. At his signal the men moved beyond the barrier marker, their reluctant steps speeded by Mark's waiting weapon.

She awoke into a chaos of uncontrollable perception. Sound of her own and the others' breathing, of pumping blood, and the harsh grating of her clothes against the earth came as an avalanche upon her unprepared senses. Her rising scream masked but could not overpower the numberless sounds of life which surrounded her.

And then sound ceased.

She opened her eyes reflexively, trying to determine what had happened to the sound. Colors and shapes fought for her attention in a silent frenetic dance. She knew she was screaming, but could hear nothing, when sight, too, was taken from her. Comfort seeped into her mind.

Entity, do you wish to receive instructions in the control of your awareness?

I am . . . Selena. I wish to be taught.

And so began the endless days in which the Lucents taught Selena to hear, but only as well as she wished to hear, to see, but only that which was desired, to perceive completely, yet selectively. She had no difficulty with mindspeech, as that talent was unfettered by past habits, but physical responses had to be divorced from old habits of perception. After three days she could feed herself. After six days she could walk. On the eighth day she felt a Rynlon ship approach.

Shimm, a Rynlon ship will land here soon.

Yes. We feel their minds.

Does my speech hurt you?

Selena sensed Shimm's rueful amusement before her reply came. *Not any more. The first days were awful; most of the Changelings entered fusion just to block you out.*

I thought so. How did the Lucents ever manage?

They just knotted their tails and took it. It was either that or kill you.

For that Selena had no answer.

Are you going back to your own kind? asked Shimm.

I don't know. I have so much to learn that the Lucents could teach me.

Not any longer, thought Shimm.

What do you mean? I don't have nearly the precise control of mind that they do. There's a lot they can—

You're only eight days old.

Selena laughed. *How old do I have to be to win an argument with you?*

You'll never know, unless we can go back with you.

Selena caught the periphery eagerness of Shimm's thought.

We? You mean your life unit?

Yes, thought Shimm, no longer trying to conceal her desire. *I have a request to make, in the name of my race. That you may understand, will you fuse with me and my mates?*

Selena hesitated fractionally, then agreed.

The life unit wrapped gently around her mind and Selena suddenly understood that the Changelings' four minds were truly complete in each other in a way that surpassed even the Lucents. She relaxed and reveled in an unparalleled feeling of wholeness.

Selena, came Shimm's soft thought, *my name is Light-That-Dances-on-Water. I accept your friendship-call of Shimm. Would you accept my mates?*

Yes. What must I do? asked Selena.

Selena heard no answer. The feeling of friendship wavered, and Selena felt loneliness creeping in to take its place. Without hesitating she called out, seeking the full friendship that she had felt a moment before.

And the Changelings returned joyously, their pleasure telling Selena that they, too, had felt a wholeness in her presence.

Shimm, she asked, *why did you leave?*

It was the only way to be sure that we would miss you, and you, us. It is the way we seek mates, and know them. All Changelings speak to each other's minds, but all Changelings are not mates.

Then what am I?

You are Selena—neither mate, nor Changeling, nor alien.

You have told me what I am not. Selena withdrew into loneliness until a gentle thought asked for her attention.

My name is Light-That-Shines-Through-Falling-Water. Would you give me a friendship call?

Selena felt the compassion of Shimm's male counterpart, and was ashamed of her reaction to Shimm's honesty. For Shimm was right—she wasn't a Changeling and could never be a mate. But she could share their minds and affections. She waited, but the male Changeling sent no further thought. She visualized one of Earth's magnificent waterfalls, lingering over the light-shot mist which encircled the fall like a wreath of diamonds. The response was a sigh of wonder in her mind, for Change had few waterfalls and none of great height.

And what do you call the silent children of the thundering water?

Mist.

Selena felt their approval of the name.

My name is Light-That-Ends-Darkness.

The thought came from the second female. *On Earth, the end of darkness is called dawn.* Selena visualized the spreading, many-colored splendor of an Earth dawn for the Changelings, and felt their acceptance. Only the second male remained to make the exchange complete.

A questing thought swept her mind, surprising in its suggestion of suppressed power. *I was conceived out of season in the black corridors of Change. But I survived to be called Light-That-Explodes-In-Darkness.*

Nova, flashed across Selena's mind, and with it a vision of the awesome fury of stellar destruction.

Selena, came the amused thought, *I've never seen the stars which your mind describes, but I'm pleased to be thought so powerful.*

Now, Changelings, you have felt my mind and my affection. What would you ask me in the name of all your kind?

It was Dawn who answered, yet her words were permeated by images from the others.

*Changelings are a dying race. Our own birthplace destroys us. To survive at all we must live much of our lives in the caverns of Change. There we are protected from the savage climate of the surface. There we enter sleep and dreamwalk our lives until the Times of Reprieve. And there we die as the corridors of Change shift and crumple upon us.

*Within the memory of our race, since the Awakening, the rumbling death has increased. We know little of the forces which move Change; our time is consumed by mere survival. To conceive, raise, and control two cubs takes the total effort of four Changelings. The cubs themselves do not become fertile until four Great Cycles after their Awakening. They cannot grow manna until they enter fusion; they cannot fuse until mated; they cannot mate until fertile.

Yet they must eat. In the short Reprieves between ice and flame, life units must grow enough manna to feed all through the dreamwalking. Manna will not grow in caverns, no matter how we Changelings encourage it. Thus, though we are fertile, no life unit has more than two cubs every eight cycles. The eight-cycle span of time is called the Great Cycle and is the basic rhythm of our life. Yet every Great Cycle the earth shifts, killing and crippling more adults than there are cubs to replace them. The coming winter ends a Great Cycle. More will die. As a race, we will not survive thirty more Great Cycles.

Dawn's thoughts stopped. Even the flow of images ceased while Selena integrated what she had been told. If more food were available, more cubs could be raised, but would they survive the treacherous movements of Change? Selena summoned from her memory all that the Rynlon had discovered about the planet. Change not only had a large axial tilt—the cause of its savage seasons—but it also had five satellites. Three of them were half the size of Earth's own moon. All of them had a higher specific gravity than Earth's own moon. All of them had a higher specific gravity than Earth's moon. Their ever-shifting orbital waltz put severe strains on the planet, pulling appreciable tides across Change's crust. Should all moons ever line up to add their pull to that of the planet's sun, the very core of Change would be shaken.

Change was a deathtrap waiting to be sprung.

You must leave the planet.

*We, too, have decided that. For many Great Cycles our Lucents have searched and called to the unknown for a means to leave Change. They touched many minds, more dreams.

Yes, Selena, even yours. You and others like you dreamed of us, but in only one sentient people did our dreams strike fire.

The Rynlon! thought Selena.

We called them the Seekers until we knew their name. Yet, after they found us, they did not know it was our race they sought. All those thousand Cycles of Changeling dreamwalking and Seeker effort, all for nothing. The Lucents could not even reach an individual mind to explain. Those you call Rynlon still do not know why their race roams the emptiness.

But, thought Selena slowly, *the Lucents did well enough. The Rynlon who came here did not fear you, or Shimm would have died.*

So little. So very little for the dream-striving of two sentient races.

Little! Changelings, your Lucents touched an alien people and sent them out into the void on an endless, barely understood quest. The Rynlon aren't even parans. I wonder . . .

Yes?

I wonder if even Earthmen didn't hear your call. Many of my race have yearned toward the stars. But many more have feared, she finished bitterly.

Do not hate them, Selena. They are like cubs before the Season of Becoming, minds ruled rather than balanced by body needs.

Not all are as unaware as you think.

Then they are to be pitied.

You pity them; I'd rather beat some awareness into their tiny minds.

Selena distinctly felt Nova's sympathetic response, then all felt the thunder of an approaching spaceship.

It will probably land at the camp, thought Selena.

She scrambled up on Shimm. *The Rynlon will take you four with me now if I have to pull every curly hair off the pilot's head.*

What about your people? Will they allow us to live with them?

Paran is a big, fertile planet. We'll find a way to grow manna for you, and searfruit. Then we'll bring other Changelings to Paran. I won't tell the Rynlon that it was your race that urged them to the stars. At least not until I know how—or if—they rationalized their drive. But I'll make flaming certain that the Rynlon don't stop until every last Changeling is safe on Paran.

We appreciate your feeling, Selena. But the planet is not yours to give. Nor can you ensure that we could live peacefully with your race. During your Becoming, your memories told us of your life on Earth. If differences of mind cause war among your people, how could they accept us? But if . . . if they do, we will ask that a few other life units be transported, that our race may not die.

For the first time the life unit felt the full force of Selena's will.

If not Paran, then another planet will be found. Now let's go meet that ship.

The fusion dissolved. With Selena clinging breathlessly, Shimm and her mates ran their fastest, savoring what could be their final dash across the harsh landscape of Change.

All too soon the slim shape of the Rynlon shuttle rose above the jagged rocks.

Within a few minutes the ramp slid silently to the ground and the Rynlon appeared. One of them walked toward the Changelings. It was Rhanett.

He stood in front of Shimm and looked up at Selena. She dismounted to stand before him. Something was wrong.

Dawn, what do you sense about this man?

Sadness follows him like a flock of torlen. His mind is closed to me beyond that, as was yours before the Season of Becoming.

Rhanett gestured toward Selena, then toward the ship. Clearly he expected her to leave Change. But why would that trouble him? And why had the ship come for her in the first place?

Selena decided to attempt mindspeech. She reached out to him carefully, afraid of hurting him through lack of skill.

Rhanett, do you understand me?

Rhanett's eyes widened, making their orange depths even more startling.

Selena waited, but his response was too weak to catch. She allowed herself more power and tried again.

Rhanett, if my mindspeech hurts you, raise your hands and I will stop.

Rhanett's hands stayed at his side.

Good. Now try mindspeech with me.

Selena waited again. This time his response was clearer, but still difficult to understand. She followed the Lucents' training and systematically blanked out all sensory intake to concentrate on the Rynlon. The results were immediate.

. . . must leave quickly, as soon as the searfruit is gathered. Paran is at war and the colony has been abandoned.

Abandoned? When?

Rhanett raised his hands and Selena quickly cut the intensity of her mindspeech.

Sorry, Rhanett. Your news surprised me.

It's all right. It's worth a headpain to be able to communicate with you. The few interpreters we had are on their way to Rynlonne with some colonists. I was sent because you knew me, and might cooperate better.

Selena felt the humor underlying his statement, and knew that Stan had told Rhanett about her favorable opinion of him. She wondered what Rynlon customs were like, and if she had insulted him by her frank admiration. Well, he didn't seem hostile.

We don't have much time, Selena. Dr. Han wants us to gather searfruit and take it to Rynlonne for analysis. He also told us to pick you up, if you were in a condition to be helpful.

He would use those words exactly. What happened at the colony?

Can you take the information from my mind? It would be quicker.

I—all right. With all the care she could summon, Selena crept into Rhanett's mind. Pictures of the colony permeated with voices and plans and fear. When the last of the story was hers, she prepared to withdraw. As she was leaving, she stumbled over a thought which Rhanett had placed before her: *I, too, find you beautiful.* Selena's pleasure swept over Rhanett, for she could no more conceal her feelings from him than he could lie to her while their minds were joined.

When was your last contact with the colony? she thought.

One of the other ships contacted me a few days ago. They were going to Rynlonne with all the parans.

What about the others?

I believe they scattered into the wilds.

But then how do we know where to land?

Stan will contact me as soon as his group finds a fairly safe place for the ship. If that's impossible, I'll take you down in a shuttle, and take colonists back the same way.

Who does Stan have with him? asked Selena, hoping he did not catch the importance of the question.

The top administrators, Dr. Johnson, and several others, thought Rhanett. *Dr. Han took all but one or two parans with him. Now we'd better get the samples Dr. Han requested. Would they help?* He indicated the Changelings.

They might. For a price.

Selena felt Rhanett's puzzlement.

Well, it is their planet, said Selena. *The least we could do is pay them.*

How?

Oh. . . . How about offering them a ride to Paran? They're very curious about us. And they want to go.

Rhanett laughed, then became serious. *They could be killed. Paran's not very peaceful these days.*

I'll tell them what they're getting into. If they still want to go, will you take them?

Yes. But only the Great Spiral knows what they'll eat.

Selena outlined the situation to the Changelings. As she expected, they still wanted to go.

Rhanett, do you have a place in the ship where they could grow manna?

What does manna require to grow?

Light, air, rock, and Changelings—I hope. If not, Paran will see some real predators in action.

Rhanett looked at the huge Changelings and hoped that manna would survive the transplant.

By sunset the last of the manna and searfruit vines were safely stowed. The Changelings had taken leave of their kind and were returning to the camp. As Selena watched from inside the ship, the Changelings hesitated, then flowed as one into the waiting ship.

IX

Selena waited impatiently while Rhanett set the shuttle computer to take them down to Paran. At last his nimble fingers were still.

Where are we landing? she demanded.

In the mountains north of the colony site.

What about Tien's men?

We're supposed to watch for snipers. And you're to send the Changelings into the forest—the meadow grass could never conceal them.

The approach alarm shrilled, sending Selena hurriedly to her couch. As the shuttle penetrated further into the atmosphere the high pitch slid into a deep hum which resonated throughout the shuttle until she felt as much as heard it.

All secure, Shimm? she asked.

Yes. But the humming makes our tails ache. Why the special alarm?

I don't know, but I think it's because they're unsure of the landing field—and the reception. You're all supposed to go to the forest immediately.

Trouble?

Just being cautious.

The humming died to a whisper, then stopped. Selena released the landing harness and hurried to the cargo hold. The Changelings were already up and waiting by the port. Selena fidgeted, wondering why the port remained closed.

Selena, the ship's heat sensor showed no radiating bodies other than those in the camp across the valley, but be careful anyway, thought Rhanett.

Right. Are you going to stay with the shuttle?

No. I must speak with Stan.

The door mechanism clicked to life and within seconds the sweet air of Paran had filled the hold. Quickly, Selena and the Changelings ran down the ramp. She flattened herself into the tall grass as the Changelings sped to the forest. She felt Rhanett drop beside her.

Rhanett, why are all the top people of the Project in one camp? Isn't that dangerous?

Maybe. But if they were scattered one to a group, it would be too great a temptation to the others.

Temptation?

Selena felt Rhanett tense beside her.

Some might decide to trade an administrator for safety. Rhanett's thought faded into sadness as he added, *Or kill him out of sheer malice.*

The old fear surged up in Selena, and with it a choking bitterness. People were unutterably stupid.

Shouldn't we go to the camp? said Selena when Rhanett made no move to get up.

When he did not answer she turned to him questioningly. His body was rigid, hands clenched in anger or fear.

Rhanett, what's wrong?

Slowly Rhanett's fingers uncurled. *We must go to the camp.*

Wait, she said as he began to stand. *I just thought of something.* She blanked her mind, then worked slowly through levels of awareness, seeking the chill thread of hostility which could mean danger. But on the level of man, she found only fear, frustration, and pervasive sadness for one who was neither dead nor living. Blindly Selena stood and walked toward the camp.

I stayed to share your grief, Selena.

You knew! You knew and you didn't tell me! Selena's anger burned across Rhanett's defenseless mind, then died as she found only compassion.

Yes, I was spared the telling.

Selena walked mechanically through the meadow until Rhanett's hand pulled her to a stop. Slowly her eyes focused on the obstacle in her path. It was Hugh.

"Where is he?" she said tonelessly.

Hugh looked at her for a long moment before he turned toward a nearby tent.

Selena pressed her hand against the tent and a section rolled upward, revealing a low cot strung with bottles and tubes which bled bright fluids into a still body. A swirling river of memories and dreams buffeted her mind as she sank down beside the cot.

Only part of Mark's face was visible. White dressings covered his dark hair, dipped over one eye. But even the gauze and beard stubble could not conceal the slackness of his lips, nor the blankets the slackness of his body.

". . . was after he'd told the colonists about Tien's betrayal. About ten of them jumped him. He got two, but the rest . . ."

Hugh's words were a galaxy away, fading in and out like a dream. Slowly Selena's fingers traced the edges of Mark's lips, then moved across his cheek to linger over the dark line of eyebrow. Her mind refused the hideous bruise that was Mark's face, remembering only the unexpected beauty of former smiles.

". . . in a coma. Dr. Johnson says we can only wait, but the longer . . ."

Selena felt tears warming her cheeks, but knew they were cold by the time they reached Mark. What good to touch him now; it brought him no pleasure. If he were whole, if strength pulsed again through his body, she would never dare. She lifted her hand from his face and her mind turned back upon her. Mark had been right. She was afraid of trust, of love, of life. Only the certainty of death had unlocked her before, to reach in desperation for warmth, to tremble with love and desire—and then fear, always fear.

Hugh shook her gently. "Selena, he does have a chance. I know . . . I know that you love him."

Selena laughed harshly. "Love him? I don't know how to love. But that is no reason for him to die."

She stood up, startling Hugh.

"Strip away this tent."

"What?"

Selena's eyes flashed. "Remove the tent. I want Mark in the open so that the Changelings can see him."

"But—"

Selena brushed past him and walked outside. As she expected, Lea was waiting.

"Is Dr. Johnson in the camp?" said Selena.

"Yes, he's been—"

"Get him. Tell him I'll need equipment for intravenous feeding. Enough for five if he has it. And pass the word that four Changelings will be here shortly. I don't want some ass to shoot them."

Lea closed her mouth and ran to find Dr. Johnson.

Selena turned back to Hugh, who was approaching her warily.

"The tent," she repeated.

He did not move.

"Mark won't die any sooner for the fresh air, will he?" she said fiercely.

"All right, Selena." He turned and began stripping tent panels from their frame. Selena hesitated, then walked over and touched his shoulder.

"Thank you."

Hugh's hands paused as he stared at Selena. He nodded, then continued working.

Lea returned, dragging Dr. Johnson.

"What's all this about?" he said when he spotted Selena.

"I don't have time to explain. Did you bring the equipment?"

"We only had one more IV setup."

Selena bit her lip. "It'll have to do." She turned to Lea. "Did you warn the camp?"

Lea nodded.

Selena called out to the Changelings. *Shimm, I need the life unit. Will you help me?*

If we can.

You can. Just give me strength.

The Changelings glided into camp like silver ghosts, leaving a wake of startled screams behind them. They formed a half-circle just beyond the skeleton of the tent and waited for Selena's signal.

Rhanett.

Yes, Selena?

I don't want to be disturbed once we're in fusion. But Hugh might try to break us up when he realizes what it could do to me. He must not destroy the fusion.

I understand.

You are a friend, Rhanett. Her mind caressed his briefly, then was gone.

Selena became aware of the concerted stares of Hugh, Lea, and Dr. Johnson. She sighed, then spoke to them.

"I'm going to try to help Mark. It will take a lot of strength. That's what the IV is for." She looked at Dr. Johnson. "Give me whatever is best—joyjuice maybe—anything to keep me going."

"Sounds pretty drastic," he said.

Selena shrugged. "I'll also need all the joyjuice and sustain you can scrounge. Give it to the Changelings as they need it."

"On one condition," said Dr. Johnson. "That you stop before you damage yourself."

Rhanett. Watch Dr. Johnson also.

She felt his assent before she said, "I can't possibly hurt myself. Ask Hugh. He knows I fold before that happens. Right, Hugh?"

"Well—"

"Right," said Selena as she walked over to Mark's cot and sat cross-legged beside it. "Fix the IV."

Selena composed her mind as Dr. Johnson worked over her. She felt a slight sting and knew that fluid was entering her blood.

Selena touched the waiting Changelings' minds, felt them merge, felt her own mind radiate throughout the fusion until the five were one vibrant whole.

They were ready.

Selena slid into Mark's brain, bracing herself against the pain she would find. But pain had congealed into numbness, a distant moan which would not sap her strength. She drifted through his body, assessing damage. His mind, his awareness, was almost totally absent. Only the faintest of energy traces called to her of Mark.

Selena relaxed her driving perception, perplexed by the absence of his awareness. She could heal his body, but what then? Could she bring him back? What had brought her own mind back from searfruit-induced freedom?

She called forth that crescendo of experience climaxed by the eternal moment of . . . was it death? Death in Godhead which could not be Godhead, for omniscience was imcomplete so long as sentience lived and perceived and wore flesh. Flesh, body. Her living body, vessel of perception and growth, demanding unity-balance, clinging to mind. And a giddy slide into life.

First, then, his body.

Changelings, I am ready.

Power coiled within Selena as the fusion melted into her mind. Cells responded to her mindtouch, multiplied to transform gashes into resilient flesh; bruises paled as capillaries sucked dead cells into the bloodstream; torn muscles shivered, stretched, and knit as strength poured into them.

Finally only the head injury remained. Selena probed the brain minutely, searching and at last finding the source of distant agony. A ruptured blood vessel dripped quietly, ceaselessly, increasing pressure by droplets, disrupting the complex flow of nerve information, squeezing, pushing, driving awareness in front of the spreading disruption, drowning humanity in a viscous hardening pool of agony.

Power uncoiled in Selena. Intense, contained energy throbbed briefly. The clot broke apart; the ruptured vessel closed.

Selena felt strength waver, become unfocused, and knew that the Changelings were near exhaustion. For a slashing moment she berated herself for being such a clumsy healer; she had exhausted them needlessly through her own lack of confidence.

Changelings. I must continue. Two of you fuse with me while two rest. Then change off.

Selena felt a shift, then tasted Nova's strength. She returned all of her focus to Mark's mind and discovered erratic awareness. She smothered it easily at first, then found it demanding more and more of her strength, leaving none to finish the healing.

Mark, I want to help you. Don't fight. Trust me.

Fragments of memory beginning nowhere, piecemeal ghost of love, half-aware, Selena . . . yes.

Relief swept over her straining mind as he acceded to her control. Now to take care of those clots. Coaxing, pushing, confining, reducing, she forced the fragments of congealed blood through capillary membrane. Time and energy squandered as she learned when to push and when to wait, when to force and when to ignore. Disentangle and disintegrate. Cell after cell absorbed and captured once again by the network it had escaped. Yet more remained, so many. Too many. Another and another and . . . so tired, too tired, sleep . . . now.

No. More strength, must send all . . . remaining fragments through . . . until they diminished together . . . at the membrane's edge . . . only one group . . . one thought . . . no more . . . blackness.

Rhanett dropped his weapon and carefully straightened Selena's body.

"Well, look at that son of a bitch," said Hugh. "You'd think he cared about her."

"He does," said Dara. "I feel his admiration and sorrow. You can go to her, Dr. Johnson. Rhanett won't stop you now."

"Wish to hell Stan were here," muttered Hugh.

"I'm sorry. I did what I could without knowing his language."

"I know, Dara. You convinced us Rhanett meant business. But I'd like to know what got into him."

"Hugh, get another cot and thermal bag," called Dr. Johnson. "And a fresh IV bag. Yellow tag. Lea, check the Changelings. One of them's stirring."

"What should I do?" she said.

"Put a bucket of Bi-Res under its nose. If it doesn't drink, get a syringe and squirt the fluid in."

Hugh returned with the cot, blankets, and bottle. He wrapped Selena and lifted her carefully onto the cot.

"Jesus. There's hardly anything left of her. She weighs less than Lea."

"The energy had to come from somewhere," said Dr. Johnson. "And she spent the last hour alone."

"Will she be all right?"

"We can hope."

"And Mark?"

The doctor glanced at the other cot. "According to the monitor, he's sleeping like a baby." He straightened and checked Selena's monitor, then shook his head. "Well, we should know by morning, either way."

Both men turned at Lea's startled cry.

"It's getting up!"

They watched as Nova lurched toward the bucket of

Bi-Res. Rhanett left Selena's side to break open a box of sustain. After Nova drained the bucket, Rhanett offered him the wafers while Lea refilled the bucket. Three buckets and four pounds of wafers later, Nova appeared satisfied. He walked over and nudged Shimm into wakefulness, then wrapped his tail around the empty bucket and held it up to Lea.

By nightfall, all Changelings were restored and watching over Selena.

"Do you suppose they can help her?" said Lea.

"I hope so," said Hugh. "They look fit enough now. Let's put the tent back together before it's too dark to see what we're doing."

"What about them?" said Lea. "They might not like being cut off from her."

Hugh glanced at the four Changelings. Blacklighted against the dying sun, they looked uncomfortably like burning guardians of an alien hell.

"We'll have to chance it. Selena's in no shape to spend a night in the open. Nor Mark, for that matter."

Keeping a wary eye on the Changelings, Hugh and Lea resurrected the tent. When the last panel was in place, Shimm shifted uneasily and drew closer.

"Watch out!"

Hugh jumped away from the tent as Shimm's tail slapped against the entrance panel. The panel folded upwards. Shimm looked at the two sleeping forms, then slapped the panels again to close it.

"I'll be damned," whispered Hugh.

Lea laughed.

"What's so funny?" said Dr. Johnson. "I could use a laugh."

"Hugh and I were scared to death of Shimm—at least I think it was her—and all she wanted to do was check on Selena."

"Glad somebody's on our side," he said. "Stan just got back from reconnaissance. He found tracks all over the east ridge. The shuttle brought them in like flies.

Hope they're just colonists coming in for pickup. Rhanett and Stan are setting up a heat sensor perimeter just in case, though. How are the patients?"

"No change," said Hugh.

"I'll take the first watch. Relieve me in about six hours."

"Right. Come on, Lea, let's get some sleep."

When Hugh came to relieve Dr. Johnson, he had to pick his way through a crescent of Changelings. When he opened the panel, one of the Changelings glided up to look inside.

"Best nurses you'll ever find," chuckled Dr. Johnson. "About an hour ago I dozed off. One of them opened the panel, tickled my nose with that damned tail, and then stared at me as if to say, 'Look alive.' "

"Wonder how it knew?"

"The brain gives off a different energy pattern when you sleep. Apparently they sensed it."

"Any change?"

"Mark's EEG readings showed a change from natural sleep to the trance state. Stayed that way for a few minutes, then switched back. He's sleeping now."

"What do you make of that?"

"Ask the Changelings. The second the EEG changed, they opened the flap, stared at him while the EEG went wild, then they closed the flap until an hour ago when one woke me up."

"What about Selena?"

"She isn't responding," Dr. Johnson said bluntly. "Her delta pattern— Oh, oh, they're back."

Hugh looked over his shoulder into a line of eight glowing eyes.

"The monitors!" said Dr. Johnson.

Hugh stared speechlessly as Mark's monitor showed rising pulse and brain activity. Simultaneously Selena's respiration and pulse strengthened and steadied. Color slowly returned to her face as the minutes sped by. Then both monitors showed a drop in activity. The Changelings moved back from the opening and stretched out on the ground. They slept immediately.

"What happened?" whispered Hugh.

"Don't know, but it was good. They're weaker than they were but Selena's stronger." Dr. Johnson looked up from the monitors. "Offhand I'd say that Mark and the Changelings gave back some of what she'd given. Look at her monitor. She's still minimal, but she's going to make it."

"Thank God," said Hugh.

"I'd rather thank the Changelings. Do we have any Bi-Res or sustain left?"

"I'll see what I can find."

"Save some for Selena. She'll need it."

"What about Mark?"

"He'll do fine on regular food, once his stomach gets used to the idea."

"I brought you your breakfast," said Lea, handing Hugh a bulb of emergency rations.

Hugh eyed the bulb distastefully, sighed, and squeezed the contents into his mouth. "Ugh. Tastes worse than it looks."

"Are they both still sleeping?" said Lea.

"Yes. But they're going to be all right."

"I know."

Hugh looked at her in surprise.

"The Changelings are gone," she said simply.

Hugh poked his head out of the tent and looked quickly around. She was right. Not so much as the tip of a tail to be found.

"Where'd they go?" he said.

"The last time I saw them, they were headed toward the rocks south of camp. Rhanett was with them, carrying a silvery fungus-like plant. I think they're still out there."

Hugh shook his head. "I'm beginning to appreciate the meaning of the word alien."

"Alien, but not evil."

Lea and Hugh turned at Mark's words.

Hugh's eyes flicked to the monitor, then back to Mark. "I see you're almost back to normal. How's your head feel?"

"My head feels fine."

Slowly he pulled himself into a sitting position. The room wavered briefly, then settled down. "She did a good job on the rest of me, too." He rubbed his face. "Left the beard, though."

"Lea, get Dr. Johnson," said Hugh.

"That's right," laughed Mark. "It'll take at least three of you to hold me down." He stood up carefully. "Well, maybe just one," he said, lowering himself back onto the cot.

Lea started to leave the tent and bumped into the doctor.

"Oh, I was just going to get you. Mark's awake."

"So I see." Dr. Johnson checked the monitor, then smiled. "Feel like getting up?"

"Yes."

"Good. Give me a hand, Hugh. Let us know if you have any pain. The monitor says your body is completely healed, but I can hardly believe it."

Mark leaned on the other two men for a moment, then waved them off. "The second time is much easier." He walked a few steps in the crowded tent. "Push the cots together so I'll have a place to walk."

They watched as Mark paced the length of the tent several times, then sat on his cot. "I finally figured out what's wrong."

"What's that?" said Dr. Johnson sharply.

Mark smiled drily. "You've been starving me."

"I'll get some food," said Lea.

"What's the matter?" said Mark as he noticed Dr. Johnson shaking his head.

"Nothing," said the doctor as he removed the monitor bands from Mark's chest and head. "That's what bothers me. Intellectually I know you're well. But emotionally—well, I keep expecting to wake up and find a dying man."

"Unless I get some food, you'll get your wish."

"Here it is," said Lea breathlessly. "It's not much, but it will keep you going."

"Thanks." He took three bulbs and rapidly squeezed them dry. "How are the rations doing?"

"Except for Bi-Res and sustain, we've got enough food for a month. More, if we can catch some game," said Hugh.

Mark nodded. "And the shuttle that brought Selena?"

"In the meadow. We've got callers out now."

"Any sign of Tien's men?"

"We're not sure. Stan found some tracks on the east ridge, but he couldn't tell whether they belonged to wandering colonists or guerrillas. We set up the sensor perimeter anyway."

"What about—"

"You're a monster!" said Lea. "Selena nearly killed herself saving your life and you haven't so much as looked at her monitor. I think—"

"You're talking too much," said Hugh. "The only reason Mark hasn't asked about Selena is that he knows. He and the Changelings saw to that last night."

"Oh." Lea blushed and began to apologize.

"Forget it," Mark said. "Selena will probably sleep for another day or two, then be fine." He frowned. "At least, that's what the Changelings told me."

The ceiling of the tent blurred above Selena's unfocused eyes. Colors flowed from brown to green to brown again, spinning gently overhead. The green only, olive green, Mark's eyes looking at her in a soundless fall of color. Her mind was too numb to stop her hands from lifting to touch his marvelously whole face, lingering over the lips which were so close to her own. Sight gave way to other senses, to the warm texture of his mouth and the gentle pressure of his fingers moving through her hair, to the unique scent of his nearness and the litany he made of her name. She clung to him as to a haunting dream at the moment of wakening. Then her body stiffened as habitual fear strove to reassert control of her mind. She fought to bring the dream back, but she was too weak, the fear too close.

Oh, Mark, I'm still afraid. Her thought was a cry of despair.

His answer came not as words but as a rich flow of empathy and love, demanding nothing, bringing peace in the wake of its warmth. With a trembling sigh she slid back into sleep.

The tent panel opened noisily.

"How is the patient?" said Hugh.

"She was awake for a minute."

Hugh looked closely at Mark. "But no *real* change, I suppose. Don't bother to answer; it's written on your face."

Mark turned away from Hugh and stroked Selena's black hair. "She's lived so long with death that she fears life. And when a mind as powerful and stubborn as hers—"

Hugh reached out and spun Mark around. "She wants life or she'd be dead, and she wants you or you'd be dead. But she doesn't know how to go about getting either one. Teach her. That's why she saved your life." Hugh looked at Mark's blazing green eyes and dropped his hand. "I'm sorry. You know that better than anyone. But why in hell can't you use psi to reach her?"

"It's not that easy," said Mark evenly. "She can always refuse. She has in the past."

Hugh smacked his hands together. "Then what can we do?"

Mark smiled crookedly. "Be around when she changes her mind. She's begun to fight fear, and she knows I want her."

The next time Selena awoke, it was to a night filled with urgent whispers and a feeling of controlled haste.

Selena.

"Mark?"

Use mindspeech, he thought swiftly. *Can you ride Shimm?*

Even in my sleep. What's happening?

Mark dropped a bulky pile of clothing next to her cot. He stripped off the thermal bag, ignoring both her nudity and her surprised exclamation. *Don't just lie there,* came his exasperated thought, *help me get you into these clothes.*

Selena stared at him, then snatched the hooded jumpsuit from him and scrambled into it unaided.

The camp is surrounded by guerrillas. You're to ride Shimm out.

What about you?

Nova says I'll be able to ride him if we join minds. I hope he's right.

Take Shimm's harness.

Can you ride without it?

Better than you will with it, thought Selena with amusement.

Mark's silent laughter warmed her mind. *You're probably right. Ready?*

Yes. Selena stood, then reached for Mark as a wave of vertigo swept over her.

Sure you can ride? he thought as she rested against him.

I'll be all right. She straightened and took a few steps. *See? Now what's the plan?*

The camp is divided into four groups. The Changelings will separate and go to the edge of camp, then wait for a signal to run. The simultaneous appearance of four Changelings at four different spots should create enough confusion to allow the groups to slip through the ring. Mark bent over and tucked Selena's hair into the hood. *I wouldn't want all that beautiful hair to make you a target.*

Selena's lips brushed his hand, then she ran from the tent. Shimm and Nova waited outside. Selena took the harness from Shimm and slipped it onto Nova. When she finished, Mark handed her a nerve rod and a set of night lenses. Selena clipped the lenses in place after she got on Shimm.

Where's my pack? asked Selena.

I'm taking both our packs. He felt her unease. *What is it, Selena?*

The Changelings.

Yes?

They're predators.

I know.

Selena watched him mount Nova and felt his mind join with the Changeling's. Shimm and Nova moved noiselessly away in opposite directions.

When Shimm reached a particularly dense stretch of underbrush, she stopped.

We'll wait here for Mark's signal.

Where are the people who are supposed to follow us out?

They're hidden nearby.

Shimm, do you know everyone in camp? Could you tell them from Tien's men?

Don't worry, Selena. None of us will kill except to defend ourselves—or you and Mark.

That's not what I meant. I've seen Changelings when the torlen fly; I know the lust that seizes you. Can you tell human friend from human enemy?

Yes. When the lust flames, our minds are sensitive only to enemies. You were one with us. Did your weapon so much as graze a Changeling's skin?

Selena thought back to the cubs' Season of Becoming and the swarming, swiftly changing melee. Shimm was right—she couldn't possibly have aimed her weapon, yet she had burned torlen off fallen cubs with the sure knowledge that death would fall only where she wished.

Now!

Selena clamped her legs around Shimm as she exploded into a full run. The eerie cry of Changeling battle bloomed from four points of the circle. Brush cracked and split beneath Shimm's driving legs as she swept through the surprised ring of enemies. Her tail lashed out once, twice, and two men dropped to the ground. They were through without a weapon fired. Shimm's claws raked the ground as she swung around to cover the retreat of a group of running figures. A lance of fire seared the brush behind the fleeing colonists. Reflexively, Selena raised her weapon and fired. A truncated scream was proof of her aim.

Selena looked over her shoulder as the last of the group scrambled to the safety of the rocks.

They're safe, Shimm. How about the others?

Dawn and Mist are leading their groups around to the rocks.

Shimm suddenly flattened into a run, but Selena was prepared. She, too, had felt Nova's call for help. A wall of wind-downed trees disappeared beneath Shimm's flying body. Beyond the wall Selena saw Nova and Mark, surrounded by brilliant flashes of death. Mark had his feet jammed through Nova's harness and was firing into a dense stand of trees. Nova's claws tore up great clots of earth as he anticipated and leaped to avoid the lances of light.

Nova gave a short cry of pain as fire scored across his hip. Selena felt Shimm's awful lust break free and merged her mind with the Changeling's to become a harmonious duet of slaughter. Venomous claws and nerve rod flashed in unison as they ripped through the

ambush. Selena felt Nova and Mark join their lust and
the harmony swelled into a quartet of bodies driven by
one mind, one thought, one desire—to kill.

Within minutes, the glade was a pool of silence disturbed only by ripples of heavy breathing and the
crackle of dying flames. Mark and Selena detached
their minds from the Changelings, working through
levels of awareness until they were certain that no threat
remained.

Two still alive in the grove, thought Mark.

Any others?

Not here.

Their minds searched the perimeter together, noting
the dead and the merely unconscious. At last Mark
sighed in relief. *No one from the camp is injured. But
Johnson's going to have his hands full with wounded
guerrillas.*

Selena slumped tiredly in the aftermath of killing as she
entered the tent. She peeled off the protective jumpsuit
and lay on the resilient pad which covered half the
floor—the cots had gone to the wounded. Shadows cast
by the tent light seeped into her thoughts as she turned
from side to back to side to stomach in search of sleep.

But the night was alive with echoes and memories of
screams smothered by death—Tien's people; her parents long dead in a burned-out home; years of living
with death and trading with thieves for life itself; fear
so pervasive she finally accepted it as life, clung to it as
certainty. Yet fear, too, was a kind of death. Then a
stranger who had called to the life hiding within her,
touching her frightened mind before she shut him out.
But she could never quench the resurrected hope which
stubbornly denied fear.

She shifted restlessly to her side. She knew that love
and life waited within Mark—but her parents had given
her love, then abandoned her in death to a hate-filled

world. Love was no guarantee against death; it only made love's loss more terrible, loneliness more grotesque.

Selena forced herself to lie quietly when Mark entered the tent and stretched out on the pad. She shivered as his hand moved bare inches from her shoulder while he rolled over on his side, then on his back. She could tell from his movements that he was stiff from the night's frantic ride. Longing rose in her to soothe away his fatigue and feel again the supple strength of his body.

Selena's hand clenched at her side. To have him so close, to feel his life call to her and yet not to touch that life—loneliness had no agony like this.

Quietly she rolled over to face him. The soft light in the tent dome made long shadows fall from his eyelashes down the hard planes of his cheeks. The shadows stirred, then lifted as he opened his eyes.

You're stiff. Let me rub your back.

Mark smiled. *I'd like that; I can't seem to get comfortable.*

You might try taking off that asbestos underwear. Unless you think we're in for more trouble tonight.

I hope not, he thought as he struggled out of the suit. *Ahh, feels better already. These suits are damned nuisances.*

Better annoyed than burned—ask Nova. Now lie down and tell me where you're sore.

There's an easier way, if you're willing.

Selena hesitated a long moment, then let her tightly held mind merge with his until she felt his body as her own. Her hands moved surely, rubbing, drumming, soothing aching muscles into relaxation. His pleasure filled her mind, and when he was no longer sore her hands lingered that shared pleasure not end. She bent and moved her lips over his shoulder, savoring the supple play of muscle beneath skin.

Selena.

Mmmm?

Would you feel this way—not afraid—without mindtouch?

Does it matter?

It does to me. And it should to you.

Selena's hands moved across his shoulders, traced the ridges of strength which rose on either side of his spine, curled caressingly down until she felt his surge of desire.

It's not this I fear, Mark. What I fear is loving you and losing you to death.

Not if I can help it.

His wry thought made Selena smile. *I know that. And I know that fearing future loss is the same as losing every day. But . . . I've crawled so long I can barely walk, much less fly.*

Mark rolled onto his side and drew Selena into his arms. *I rarely fly, Golden Eyes. I'm not even all that good at walking.*

Selena moved slowly against him, felt his arms tighten and his mouth seek hers. Coherent thought paled beneath the consuming sensation of lips and skin and hands. A flash of fear like lightning against the thunder of his desire, but fear drowned in waves of pleasure. Her soft moan called to him and they came together in a fluid union of mind and body.

X

Selena stirred reluctantly; Shimm's tail was rattling the tent.

Emergency? thought Selena vaguely.

No, responded Shimm. *They're looking for Mark.*

Selena woke fully, acutely conscious of her nakedness. At her sudden movement, Mark's eyes opened and he caught her thought.

"I like you that way," he whispered, pulling her down to him.

"Shimm says they want you."

"What about you?"

There was laughter in his question, but his green eyes searched for her answer.

Selena smiled and opened her mind. He felt the desire which surged through her as she remembered. He couldn't have concealed his response if he had wanted to, but he shared his thoughts anyway.

Shimm's tail rattled the tent mercilessly, but drew no further response. With the Changeling equivalent of a smile, she rippled her tail and lay across the entrance of the tent.

Stan turned to Hugh. "Now what?"

"That's a Do Not Disturb sign if I ever saw one."

"Is Mark all right?"

Hugh suppressed a laugh, then reassured Stan. "If

anything were wrong, Shimm wouldn't just lie there."

"How long will we have to wait?"

"What's the rush? Some people like to wake up gradually. Or something."

In time, the flap rolled up. Shimm moved away to allow Mark passage. Selena followed, moving with a languid sensuality which made Hugh think hungrily of Lea.

Mark yawned and stretched. "What do you want?"

"The callers brought in only twenty colonists. Another six came in when they saw the shuttle. Should we lift or wait for more?"

"Lift, but return the shuttle. Keep the ship in orbit for three days or until we call you, whichever comes first. Then take the colonists you have to Rynlonne."

"Right."

Mark frowned. "More colonists should have answered the signal. How many callers did you drop?"

"Ten. Some must have gone bad, though. Their signals stopped after a few hours."

"Any idea what went wrong?"

"The seven I retrieved worked fine. And three of them had been dumped on rocks, so I don't think being dropped is what put the others out of action. Hell, even if a unit fell into a lake, the call signal would still work."

"Send the scout down. Tell Rhanett to scatter some more callers and report any duds to me. And put the mother ship in deep orbit. I don't want it being spotted by any of Tien's ships."

Stan left hurriedly.

Mark watched him leave, then rubbed his face absently. The unexpected softness of a beard made him smile. Selena had objected to stubble. It was too late to shave, so she had grown him a thick, soft beard.

"You look smug enough to make a psychiatrist cry," said Hugh.

Mark laughed. "I'll have her grow you one."

"No thanks. Beards give me a rash."

"I could fix that, too," said Selena.

"Save your energy."

"But I'm stronger than ever, Hugh. And hungrier."

"Don't look at me that way," laughed Hugh. "The food supplies are in the third tent from the end."

Mark and Selena ate hurriedly, with many grimaces over the tasteless tubes of paste.

"Wretched crap," muttered Selena, squeezing the last viscous bit out of the tube. "Another meal like this and I'm going to turn the Changelings loose on the cook."

"Is their fungus or whatever—"

"Manna."

"—manna any tastier?"

"No. But you don't have to eat as much of it."

"Hope it grows like hell," said Mark feelingly.

Selena rubbed her fingers over the blotchy camouflage fabric of her jumpsuit. "Awful colors, but at least stains won't show." Then. "I think I'll check the wounded."

Mark looked at her in surprise. "Why?"

"I can sense their pain," said Selena simply. "The price of being able to heal, I guess."

"Can you block it out?"

"Why bother? It's not like actually feeling pain. Besides, one of them may feel like talking."

"Doubtful."

"It's worth a try," she insisted.

"All right, but don't go alone."

Selena bristled. "Is that an order?"

"Yes," he said easily, and threw the last tube into a waste sack. "Some of those wounded are damned lively."

"I can take care of myself."

"Fine. Don't go alone."

"Don't think you own me just because—"

"I don't have to," he said. "I'm colony leader in Han's absence."

For a long moment they stared at each other unwaveringly, then Mark decided to try the greater subtlety of mindspeech, where words can be amplified and enriched by emotional imagery.

I don't want to own you, Selena. That is not my idea of loving. But you do have a duty to the colony. Part of that duty is to obey reasonable orders.

The first part of the thought was gentle and sympathetic; the second was unyielding and impersonal.

Since when does every colonist have to have a Changeling guard?

Sarcasm mingled with stubbornness in her thought.

Selena, my order would have been the same to any colonist. No personal control was meant. Even Dr. Johnson does not see the prisoners alone.

Mark did not need mindspeech to tell that Selena was unmoved.

Golden Eyes, why are you fighting me? It's not the order, is it. Are you afraid you have given too much to me, that—

Selena's sudden confusion and instant anger was all the answer he needed. *All right, Selena. Nothing has changed. As a woman you are free to pursue any personal life you desire. As a colonist you are still bound by colony rules.*

Mindtouch ended, leaving Selena very alone. But he would not have the satisfaction of knowing it.

"Yes, Leader, Sir. I'll stay so close to Shimm she'll think she's grown a second skin."

As she swept past him and out the door, he did nothing to stop her; as a man he wanted to, but as colony leader he had to be satisfied with obedience, however unwilling.

Selena moved rapidly away from the mess tent and called Shimm. The Changeling and a cold wind arrived together. Selena shivered until her jumpsuit compensated for the drop in warmth.

Are you cold, Shimm?

Not at all. On Change we don't go into the caverns until manna won't grow.

Selena wondered how cold that was, but had no way of finding out. Earth measures had little meaning for a Changeling. Yet in a few months it would be winter on Paran; in the mountains where they were, winter could come at any moment. She hoped it would not be too cold for the Changelings.

Don't worry. Changelings can sleep on ice and wake up warm. Is that why you wanted me?

No. Curien demands that I have a bodyguard. Can you be it?

As Selena didn't bother to limit her transmission to words alone, Shimm gathered a lot of what had happened.

No Changeling enters a cavern alone; the torlen may not all be sleeping.

Oh, dry up and follow me, returned Selena in exasperation.

Shimm's mind and tail rippled with amusement. *Is that an order?*

Yes. No. Dammit, Shimm, be reasonable.

Ripples again, followed by, *Where are we going?*

To check on the wounded.

Ah, that's why he worries. I will indeed follow you, Selena, but not because I'm reasonable. You are a part of me and I guard myself well.

Selena threw up her hands. *You win.*

We win, corrected Shimm.

Selena was divided between laughter and exasperation as she opened the panel on the first medic tent. Both feelings died as she saw six men and women. She closed the panel that the sight of Shimm not frighten the wounded, though her own mind remained open to the Changeling as well as to the prisoners.

Burns, some deep, some extensive. Bones broken by

whipping Changeling tails or the convulsions caused by nerve rods and venom. Painful, ugly.

The tent was too small for the eight cots. Selena eased her way up the narrow aisle in the center of the tent. One man saw her yellow eyes. He crossed himself and prayed incoherently. Because Selena's mind was open, she for the first time felt the gut fear some normals had of parans. It was a reflex as primitive as breathing, a surge of adrenaline in the face of the unknown, and a consuming admission of helplessness.

But not hatred. No; hatred came later. To some it came naturally, in others it was nurtured, but in all it came after the fear of being hurt.

"I won't hurt you," said Selena gently to the frightened man. "Don't be afraid. What you've been told about parans isn't true. This is what a paran can be."

As she spoke, Selena's hand brushed his cheek. Flesh knit and smoothed, the half-shut eye opened to look again and closely at Selena.

"Yes, I am different from you," she said. "Fire and water are different from each other, but both have use and beauty."

Selena felt his fear giving way to confusion.

"You're in pain," she said. "Your back . . ."

Confusion, then blank hopelessness. He knew he would never walk again.

Shimm.

I'm here. And so are Dawn and Nova. Mist will guard us—and you.

Will you help me? It is easier, much easier to heal now, but I still would enjoy your strength.

Of course, answered all three. Then Dawn alone, *He is afraid. Can you calm him? It would make the healing easier and surer. We'll help.*

Selena suddenly felt again the radiating calm and peace which Shimm had given at their first meeting. Only this time Selena appeared to be the source. Gradually the lines of tension on the prisoner's face faded.

"What is your name?" asked Selena gently.

"Nano Toreh. Tor."

"Tor, you know your back is injured."

"I'm a cripple."

"Now, yes. I hope to change that. As you guessed, I'm a paran. My greatest talent is the ability to heal. I would like to heal your body, but your fear of me will make it very difficult."

He rubbed his healed cheek wordlessly.

"Your cheek wound was superficial; your own body would have healed it within days. Your spine is another matter. To heal it will take strength—and your cooperation."

"What can I do?"

"The body has a great knowledge of itself. This knowledge begins with individual cells, then is transmitted to and stored by the brain. Injury, especially to the spinal column, stops that transmission. But the brain itself 'remembers' what an intact body is. Like a living blueprint, the brain knows what your spine should be like."

Without appearing to, Selena looked closely at Tor. She doubted that he fully understood, but at least he was listening—and very nearly relaxed.

"A healer's job is to bridge the gap between brain and injury. Your brain instructs me and then I tell your injury how to heal. I also provide energy so you heal quickly."

The soothing flow of explanation became an uninterrupted stream of comfort and a subtle suggestion to sleep. Willingly, Tor slept.

Selena and the Changelings began their work. The healing demanded delicacy, but as the injury was essentially simple their work was not exhausting. Under Selena's instructions the pads between spinal discs rebuilt themselves and nerves stretched eagerly to regain former unity.

In a surprisingly short time, Nano Toreh was healed.

Selena stood and smiled at the sleeping Tor. In a few hours he would wake—and walk again.

"You're Selena Christian."

Selena spun to face the voice behind her. She didn't recognize the woman who had spoken.

"Is Tor really in one piece now?"

"Yes."

The woman nodded. "He's a right man. Nasties sent him here cuz he liked a cross better 'n fool's gold."

"Do I know you?" said Selena.

"Nope. Half the world knows you. That trial was a real loop. Screwed business, damn near. No one worked. Every flaming night for three weeks." She laughed suddenly. "You fooled those buggers good."

Selena listened curiously. She could detect no hostility, yet the woman was in the uniform of Tien's guerrillas.

"Why are you—"

"Here? Well, don't know how soft ears might hold my story."

"I grew up in the Pillars—or Piles, as we called it."

"Don't talk like it."

"Thank you. I spent a long time making sure I didn't."

"Yeah. I try, too. Well, I'm here for owning a 'Disorderly House and a House of Ill Re-pute.' Shit," she snorted, "my house was tight as a barracks and better known than any in the city. Only clean boys and girls. Don't have no use for a dirty whore. Paid squeeze on time, didn't 'low slipsnapping, only A type drugs. Christ, I ran that place like an Earther Reunion!"

The woman sighed deeply. "It was politics what got me. Oh, I sit the Nasties meetin' every week, but I didn't let my guts out. I said yessir an nossir an kissassed and—ah, shit. If you lived in Piles you sung the song."

"When the Humanistos—"

"Frigging Nasties," muttered the woman.

"—got the power, they threw jail at you and gave the business to one of their own."

"Dead on. So I was looking at thirty years of metal. Then the Nasties told me if I did their dirt, they'd lose the metal. Now I never sucked the shrill about parans. But I want out. So here I am; bone-busted and lookin' at metal again."

"Do you want to go back to Earth?"

The woman frowned. "Goddamn Nasties would screw me off for the take from a D type fix. But," her mouth turned down, "it's all I got."

Shimm, ask Mark if he will accept defectors.

Prudently, Shimm didn't inquire why she was the messenger.

He will—if you trust them.

"You can join the colony."

"What about them?" said the woman, gesturing to the rest of the sleeping prisoners.

"Are there many like you?"

" 'Cept for that bugger." She gestured to a nearby cot. "He's so Earther he shits dirt."

Selena looked at the man; he seemed to be sleeping. Drugged, probably. Head wound.

"Any who want to join the colony are welcome. Except Earthers. I don't trust fanatics of any stripe."

The woman lifted her good hand to Selena. "Rub skin with Mama Dit. Make that Dit. I'm clean now. But promise I get a piece of the Nasties, first chance."

Selena's laughter woke the sleeping Earther, but she didn't notice it.

"Done. Would tonight be soon enough?"

"You'd heal *me?*"

"Right now. Relax. All you'll notice is a sleepy feeling. Don't fight it. You'll be easier to heal if you're asleep."

Changelings?

Ready.

Dit's injuries took only bare minutes to heal: clean breaks and bruises which her unaided body would have healed, given time. Nonetheless, Selena made sure Dit would sleep for at least two hours more.

Done, thought Selena. *Thank you, Changelings. You make it easy for me.*

Not at all. As the Lucents hoped, Selena, you have become a true Healer. We are honored to share a Healer's mind.

Selena felt vaguely embarrassed by the Changelings' purr of praise, yet not embarrassed enough to conceal a flash of pride. She, too, had felt her skill increase as her mind ceaselessly sorted and digested and learned. Every hour brought new—

A soundless cry of danger yanked Selena to the present. In old reflex, her body assumed a crouched fighting stance, hands stiff and unevenly extended, eyes searching even as her body ducked and wove to meet danger.

Selena felt an arm lock with crushing force across her neck. Even as she choked her heel raked down her assailant's shin and her elbow drove deep into his solar plexus. A fluid twist through his loosened arm and she broke free, right hand raised to chop across the attacker's throat.

Her blow never landed. Mist had slapped open the tent panel as he warned her of danger. Even as her first blow landed, Mist lashed his tail firmly about the prisoner's neck and yanked. The man crashed to the floor between the rows of cots.

Don't kill him!

Oh? I had him measured for a searfruit grotto. If you wish this torlen alive, at least let me teach him the cost of hunting Changelings.

Selena looked into Mist's cold-crystal eyes and shivered inwardly.

Don't worry, my little Healer. I won't—

Whatever Mist wasn't going to do was lost with

Mark's arrival. He pushed unceremoniously through
Changelings and cots until he reached the center aisle.
He bent to examine the prisoner. Mist had loosened his
tail grip enought that the man coughed and whooped
with returning breath. His body writhed with the desire
to reach and kill someone, anyone. Metal flashed in his
hand.

Mark stamped on the man's wrist as though it were
a deadly snake. Simultaneously, the dart on Mist's tail
sank into the Earther's jugular. With a deep convulsion,
the Earther died of Changeling poison.

Mark very carefully picked up the piece of wire which
lay next to the dead man's hand. The wire was thin, yet
rigid enough to be driven deep into flesh. One end was
honed to a needle tip.

"Earther assassin," said Mark. "The tip is poisoned.
If you'd been scratched, you'd be as dead as he is."

Selena felt suddenly weak. She had been so sure that
she could take care of herself. She'd even resented having Mist on guard instead of helping to heal. . . .

Mark's fingers probed gently on her abraded neck.
She braced herself for a round of I-told-you-so. She
had it coming, but she didn't have to like it.

Mark felt her stiffen.

"Sorry. Didn't mean to be so clumsy," he said. "Just
bruised, I think, but have Johnson check it."

Selena felt his concern for her, his relief, his love—
everything but the righteous smugness she had expected. Somewhere in her mind knots loosened. She
stepped into his arms and pressed close to him. Between kisses she murmured, "I was wrong."

Mark held her, savoring the life which surged and
danced and had so nearly died.

Thank you, Mist, he thought as he buried his face
in the black silk fragrance of Selena's hair.

XI

Selena wakened slowly and rolled over to snuggle against Mark. When she realized she was alone, her eyes snapped open. After little more than a week, she was fully accustomed to not sleeping or waking up alone.

Mark?

Her thought carried a sharp edge of unease.

I'm with Stan. Get breakfast and join us.

His thought trailed images of a Rynlon ship, callers, and no colonists.

Selena hurriedly pulled on her jumpsuit. She found the men squatting near the mess tent drawing lines in the dirt. She slipped into the tent for a handful of fruit and nuts, then listened to them while she ate.

"—problem is that, come pickup time, only one out of three callers are still working, and of those, only a few have brought in colonists," said Mark.

"Yeah. Before Rhanett left, he tested all the callers we were going to drop. Mechanically, they tested out fine."

Mark said nothing, but Selena sensed his mind describing, defining and analyzing the problem.

"Selena, have any of the defectors mentioned seeing colonists?"

Selena licked her fingers and rubbed them thoughtfully across the jumpsuit. "Not that I remember. But I haven't really asked. Could Tien's men pick up caller signals?"

Mark looked at Stan.

"Well sure, I guess so," said Stan. "If they had a receiver and were lucky. Besides, if they did pick it up, they wouldn't know what it was. And if they wanted to find out where the signal came from they'd have to be lucky enough to have two receivers within the ten-mile radius of the caller's transmission. Then the guerrillas could triangulate for exact location. Otherwise, they'd spend days crashing around trying to find the signal source."

"Unless," Mark said grimly, "Tien's men have a Rynlon wrist finder, know how to use it, and why."

"Oh Christ," breathed Stan. "If they do, the colonists are sitting ducks."

"Or dead ones. Do you have a map marking where you've dropped callers?"

"Sure, but it's only a rough location."

"How rough?"

"Half-mile radius."

Mark swore. "Better than nothing. Get it. We've got to find out what's wrong with the callers."

As Stan hurried away, Mark turned to Selena. "Do the Changelings have a good sense of smell?"

"I . . . wait a minute."

Mark waited while Selena consulted Shimm.

"Not as good as ours," she said finally. "On Change, there were only a few important smells: water, manna, rock, and torlen. Searfruit in season and, of course, other Changelings. But Changeling minds can discriminate among these things much more rapidly than their noses. Or their eyes. Their vision is good, or they'd kill themselves on the rocks. But ours is better . . . more subtle."

"Damn," said Mark. "We don't have a metal detector in camp. We could spend weeks thrashing the forest for missing callers and never find one."

"What about the scoutship detectors?"

"Callers aren't big enough to register."

"Wish I had the wolves here," said Selena.

"Why? If we had a trail they'd be useful, but I don't see—"

"They can cover a lot of ground in a little time. And they can do it without attracting attention. Give me a shuttle and I'll have them here before dark." Then Selena remembered the energy barrier which surrounded the colony city.

"No problem," said Mark as he intercepted her thought. "I turned your animals loose before the shield went up. There was no reason for them to be at ground zero if Tien drops the big one. They're safe, but they'll be hard to find."

"I'll find them. Do you—"

The sound of shouting from one of the camp patrols came to them. Almost by reflex, Selena and Mark joined minds and probed for danger.

Pain; sharp, piercing even exhaustion, driven by fear and the heavy smell of old death.

As one mind, Mark/Selena saw the injured, exhausted colonist, and knew she was the only survivor out of her group. Like a satellite the colonist's thoughts swung endlessly about a caller, an ambush, near death, and days and nights spent wandering.

Their minds separated.

"Your deep patrols have turned more colonists than the callers," said Selena.

"About three a day. Most exhausted, sick, or injured. Paran is full of food and shelter, but they're too incompetent to find it. Sweet God, they must have slept through their survival courses."

"Stan is coming," Selena said.

"Map?"

"Yes."

Mark waited with concealed impatience while Stan explained the procedure for dropping callers.

"The point," said Mark finally, "is that the guerrillas probably have been on to the callers from the start."

"Right. Some dipshit colonist must have turned over all the plans."

"The woman the patrol just brought in—which drop was she ambushed on?"

Stan was surprised at Mark's knowledge—the woman had been incoherent—but he accepted it. He was getting used to parans. "Near as I can tell it was the first drop. About here," said Stan, pointing to a foothill region of tiny lakes and extensive forest.

"Trying to find a silent caller in that mess will be impossible."

Stan and Selena waited while Mark made a few extrapolations.

"Did the ship's computer finish its weather program?" asked Mark.

"Yeah. You'll love this," said Stan. "Big storm in two-three weeks. Snow down to two thousand feet, melting back to about five. Snowfall varying from two inches to three feet. Maximum depths with increasing elevation, up to—"

"In other words," cut in Selena, "this camp will be under nearly a foot of snow. Half the colonists aren't making it now, when they can literally eat off the nearest bush. What will happen when snow covers their lunch?"

"The colonists were told to stay out of the high areas. No pickup sites for the shuttle up there," said Stan.

"Then why have our patrols turned up twenty-two colonists in the last week? This is supposed to be the only mountain campsite. There shouldn't be a colonist for fifty miles in any direction. They are supposed to stay in the warm, safe foothills, eating fruit and nuts and waiting for pickup!"

"Hunted animals head for high ground," said Stan.

"I hope they freeze their stupid butts off," said Selena.

"Any activity around the colony?" said Mark.

"No. They gave up fast. Probably their pet colonists told them it was useless. A few guards scattered around who test the fence occasionally are all that's left."

"Could you land a shuttle near the river and stay down for awhile without a fight?"

"Probably. Sure I could."

"Good. Take Selena. Land where she tells you—if it's safe, then stand guard while she brings in the wolves. How many can you get, Selena?"

"As many as we can feed here. They won't look for metal if they're hungry for meat."

"You get them working and I'll worry about their bellies."

Selena and Stan paused only long enough to pick up the carcass of one of Paran's deer-like browsers from the hunting camp.

"Someone's gonna be mad when they find their neardeer steaks gone for dog food," said Stan as he and Selena heaved the carcass into the cargo bay of the shuttle.

Selena laughed; the same thought had occurred to her. "Let's go. Mark wants us back by dark."

"He expecting trouble?"

"Don't you?"

Mark barely noticed the shuttle's departure. He and Hugh were trying to figure out a way of calling colonists in without attracting Tien's guerrillas.

"Look," said Hugh. "Why don't we send out some of our patrols to look for colonists?"

"We may have to, but it would be a long, slow, dangerous haul. Hell, it would take years to get all the colonists that way. We don't have that kind of time. But go ahead. Send out Maria's patrol; she's the best tracker we have. Tell her not, repeat not, to fight guerrillas unless she's cornered. Reschedule the other patrols to cover her absence. If anything comes up, you handle it. You have as much information as I do."

"That's goddamn little."

Mark grimaced. "I know."

"Where will you be?"

"Right here, physically. I'm going to see if the Changelings can help our information shortage. Maybe we can find colonists—and guerrillas—without leaving camp or putting out callers. When Selena comes back, she'll have a shuttle full of wolves. She'll handle them; you'll feed them. If Lea isn't assigned, put her with Selena. Someone should be with Selena when the wolves start turning up callers."

"Why?"

"I believe," Mark said tiredly, "that the callers will be surrounded by dead colonists. It won't be pleasant for her."

"Either Lea or I will be with her."

"Thanks." Mark rubbed his forehead distractedly. "Jesus, I wish Han hadn't taken all the working parans with him. We could use them."

"He left the best ones here."

Mark smiled wryly. "All two of us—and the Changelings. Even Dara went with the last ship."

"It wasn't her idea."

"I know. The Rynlon wanted all parans off the planet. Can't blame them; they know they can always start another colony, but they may never find another race of parans they can work with." He shrugged. "Thanks for the crying time, Hugh. Now I'd better get to work."

Mark sent a call to the Changelings and explained what he wanted from them.

Nova responded for them. *We are here to help, but what you want is difficult. One life unit has not the power to sustain dreamwalking in depth, especially without Lucents to direct us. But we will give you all that we have.*

I can't ask for more than that. When can you be ready?

Now. We have eaten and slept well. Have you?

As well as I'm going to.

Come to our manna rocks. It is protected here and comfortable.

For a Changeling it may be comfortable. If you don't mind, I'll stay in my tent on a sleeping pad.

Changeling laughter rippled across his mind. *We are not fond of sleeping on cliffs either. There is a level green place where we all may stretch out. For dreamwalking we prefer flesh contact, or we would not ask you to leave your tent.*

Mark wondered why the Changelings wanted physical touch, but he did not question the need. He had tried to contact colonists on his own, and had gotten nothing but frustration. The unaware mind of the normal colonist was nearly impossible to locate. He could—rarely—sense their presence, but he could not locate them, nor could he communicate with them.

Mark rolled up his sleeping pad and left the tent.

"Quarreling so soon?" teased Lea.

"What?" Then he laughed. "No. I have to work close to the Changelings for a while. Did Hugh tell you about Selena?"

"Yes. When will she be back?"

"Before dark, I hope. If she isn't, come and get me. I'll be at the manna rocks. In fact, why don't you come with me now and bring back some manna for Selena?"

"Does she like it?" said Lea as she fell into step beside Mark.

"Hardly. But she'll need it."

"What is she going to do?"

"You know the problem we're having with the callers?"

"Hugh told me. Are you sure that Tien's men are responsible?"

"Probability is better than eighty percent, but we have to be one hundred percent sure before we abandon them. Stan will take the wolves and leave them near the old drop sites. They'll quarter the area, trying to find the callers or anything else unusual. Selena will . . . guide them. When they find something, she'll know it."

Lea walked silently for a moment, then, "What are our chances?"

"Of finding the callers?"

"Of living," said Lea bluntly. "When you and Selena start grabbing at straws, I get worried."

"Straws?"

"The wolves," said Lea impatiently. "And scattering us across Paran. What good will any of it do? My God, Mark. You couldn't even trust the colonists enough to arm them. One gun for every group! Oh, it all sounded good enough back in the colony, but—Damn it, I have a right to know what our chances are now."

Mark sifted through the feelings which radiated from Lea. Some fear, of course; everyone with the intelligence to count to ten was afraid. Anger, a counterpart of fear. Impatience with not knowing, with being afraid when fear was unnecessary and secure when fear would be the intelligent choice.

Abruptly Mark decided.

"The city was a death trap; perhaps three percent chance of survival. Leaving the city raised our chances seventy percent, if the callers worked and Tien committed less than two thousand people to Paran. The callers don't work; Tien has at least one thousand guerrillas on Paran with more arriving every fourth day. Fortunately, the majority of the guerrillas are no more competent at living off the land than the colonists are. But Tien doesn't care about losses. From what the prisoners say, he's cleaning out Earth's jails and ghettos, putting Earther assassins in charge, and waiting. For Tien, it's a cheap campaign. No supplies, so no supply problem. No prisoners to take care of. No doctors for the wounded. No machines. Nothing but a laser gun and a one-way ticket to Paran. If Tien wins, he gets a planet and a hero's hat. If he loses . . . well, it's a cheap, politically safe way to get rid of malcontents and a corps of deadly fanatics. Win or lose, he consolidates his control at home.

"And right now he has better than a seventy-two percent chance of winning."

"How long do we have?"

Mark shrugged. "Depends on the weather. Two, three months. Maybe as much as five."

Lea looked curiously at the man who walked beside her. For all the emotion in his voice, he might have been discussing protein rations in synthetic foods. Yet for years he had risked his life. . . . She took a deep breath and touched his arm hesitantly. "Thanks. Not knowing was driving me crazy."

"You won't have to worry much longer. I'm ordering the main camp evacuated."

"Why?"

"We were supposed to coordinate the caller pickups. No pickups, no camp."

"What will we do?"

"Whatever the Rynlon tell you."

"You're not going with us."

It was a statement, not a question, and Mark didn't answer.

"The Changelings are here. With manna."

Lea walked up to the Changelings without hesitation. She had lost her initial fear of them quickly; in fact, she was fascinated by them. "Mark, would they mind being touched?"

"Would you?"

Lea smiled and rubbed her hand across Shimm's shoulder. "Just as I thought, halfway between suede and velvet."

Immediately Shimm's tail slipped lightly over Lea's head, ruffling her short dark hair.

"I should have warned you," said Mark. "Our hair intrigues them. There are no textures like it on Change."

"I wish . . ."

"What?"

"I wish I could communicate with them."

"You just did."

"I mean like you or Selena. When Han cracks the searfruit, I'll be first in line."

"Not if I can help it."

Lea looked up, surprised at his harsh tone.

"Searfruit can't do anything for you that training can't—except kill you. If the Rynlon want to fry their brains that's their problem. But if Han starts handing out searfruit to colonists, I will personally see that he gets the first dose."

Lea gathered manna and stuffed it into the many pockets of her jumpsuit. Before she finished, Mark tried to explain.

"Lea, I'm sorry. But if you had felt even a part of Selena's agony . . . and for nothing. Nothing! She could have been taught all that searfruit burned in her. She knows that now. If you don't believe me, ask Selena. And ask Selena if she would do it again."

"I don't have to. She has too much to lose, now." Lea stared at Mark intently, but the tired, lined mask of his face didn't soften. She stowed the last of the manna quickly and hurried back to camp.

With Lea out of range, Shimm switched her attentions to Mark. When he protested having his hair ruffled, she deftly, gently flipped him to the ground.

Shimm, you overgrown torlen bait, I'm here to work, not wrestle.

Mark looked into the changing hues of Shimm's eyes and swore he could hear her laughing. Deliberately, her huge tongue licked over his face.

Shimm! What's gotten into you?

No answer, but another long lick.

Mark sputtered and buried his face in his hands. Shimm began to nibble delicately along his ribs, tickling him unmercifully, and all the while radiating an irresistible invitation to play.

At length, Mark gave in. He peered through his fingers to take a bead on Shimm's tail. When it swept into range, he dove and wrapped his hands around it.

Gotcha! he crowed. He started to tie her tail in a knot, knowing that while he'd never succeed, he'd at least give her something to think about besides nibbling on his ribs.

A throb of approval rose from the watching Changelings as he joined in the play. When it seemed certain that Shimm would soon have Mark pinned and helpless, Nova casually wrapped his tail around Shimm's nearest leg and pulled her off balance. Soon all the Changelings were a swirling, rippling mass of play, yet cautious not to hurt Mark with their own exuberance.

Hints of vulnerable spots surfaced in Mark's mind. He thanked Mist and put an armlock on Shimm's head. With a gleeful laugh he tweaked the corners of her lips. Shimm's neck bulged as she tried to dislodge him, but he hung on until Nova's tail dragged him away.

In a short time Mark was panting and helpless with laughter. The Changelings allowed him to escape, the better to concentrate on each other. Mark watched them leap, turn, and wrestle as though dancing under the direction of a mad choreographer.

In a few minutes Shimm left the melee and offered herself as a backrest. Gratefully, Mark relaxed against her.

It's a miracle Changelings ever reach full growth, thought Mark as he watched the hurtling mass in front of him.

We did not hurt you? thought Shimm anxiously.

Hell no. I only wish Selena could have been here to help me.

Or me! For one so small you are strong.

Mark smiled lazily. *Serves you right. Next time I'll tie a bow with your tail.*

Shimm's laughter was still rippling through his mind

when Nova joined them. Though Mist and Dawn were only minutes behind, Mark barely noticed their arrival. The slow rhythm of Shimm's breathing, the warmth of Paran's sun, and a body relaxed by play combined to make his mind pleasantly stuporous.

Without his conscious awareness, a fusion formed around his floating mind. He felt a buoyant strength he had never known, a delicious ease of purpose. And patience, the patience of iron filings waiting for a magnet. Resting, waiting, eager yet passive.

There, faint currents of sentience in the amorphous sea of life which was Paran. Swiftly the fusion entered the current, slid smoothly to the source of sentience.

Sources. Many minds, smooth as water-rolled pebbles, impermeable as neutron stars.

Carefully, Mark turned the stones over in his mind, discarding those impossible to reach, concentrating on the remaining two. There was a haunting aspect to them, a flavor of familiarity, of—

Hugh and Lea.

With a sigh of apology, the fusion released them from scrutiny and expanded once again into waiting.

At some level Mark sensed time and movement flowing, filings drifting, hoping, waiting, sliding toward new currents of sentience, new stones, impermeable, impossible; movement-waiting-sliding-rejecting, wait-slide-no, wait, wait, wait—

A bold current of sentience broke over the fusion, sucked their waiting minds close, held them, yet drowned their desire to communicate in an outflowing call.

Selena, agreed the fusion.

Impulsively, Mark tried to see. The Changelings responded with more energy.

Ripples of green-gold grass, dark shapes panting, metallic taste of shuttle, a woman whose mind leaped and burned like the sun.

The scene wavered and guttered, a flame in a fitful

breeze. Time and energy flowed as the fusion gained experience in this new way of using their minds to see.

The call stopped, setting them adrift again. As one, Mark and the Changelings made a last effort to see.

Two wolves, running beyond endurance, running toward the call that had stopped.

Abruptly Mark knew what had happened. He abandoned attempts at seeing and focused on Selena. Contact was swift, for her mind was no longer calling.

Mark! What is it?

Two wolves. I don't know how far away, but they're killing themselves to get to you. Can you—

Mark found himself talking to the fusion; Selena was gone. They sensed another call, strong, yet changed. The urgency was gone; in its place was praise and a soothing promise. When the call finally ended in a celebration of greeting, the fusion drifted away.

But there was a difference; where before they had floated buoyantly, almost playfully, now it was an effort. They were sinking gently, inexorably, back to their bodies.

Mark opened his eyes and stretched. The parts of his body which weren't numb were sharp with pain. He rolled away from Shimm and onto his stomach. From the angle of the sun, he knew most of the day had passed.

It had seemed no more than an hour.

Is that how you spend your waiting time in the caverns?

Yes. Dreamwalking and true sleep.

I can understand the sleep. I'm beat. And frustrated.

Mark sensed the Changelings' surprise at his discontent.

But you saw! And you gave us sight. That is a gift the Lucents would envy. The eyes of a human have marvelous subtlety.

Mark mulled over the significance of the Changelings' words. Obviously, an animal which evolved largely in caverns would have little use for sight as humans knew it. The Changelings had vision now, of course; they'd lived aboveground for a long time. And they attached great importance to light, as their names showed. But eyes were still not as important to them as they were to a human.

That's right.

Shimm's lazy thought startled Mark; he hadn't realized he was thinking aloud.

And after searfruit, added Nova, *we had even less need of sight and smell. Even hearing lost its former primacy. We could sense torlen—or any other important object—much sooner with our newly awakened minds than with our eyes or ears. Yet our eviction from the caverns of Change made light—but not sight—the watershed of our species. The Lucents never attempt to see in dreamwalking; sight seems small return for the energy used.*

For our purposes it's damned important, thought Mark wearily. *If I can't mindtalk with the people I find, I have to at least locate them so I can send a patrol or shuttle out.*

We can do nothing now. We are tired and worry makes your mind dense. We must sleep and eat before we dreamwalk again.

And wrestle? thought Mark wryly.

The tip of Shimm's tail ruffled his hair. *Play lightens the mind, little friend. Yours was a heavy stone. Now sleep before I put my tail around your neck and squeeze you into silence.*

The word is strangle.

Shim looped her tail loosely around his neck.

All right, all right. I'll shut up, thought Mark, then he chuckled aloud as Shimm's tail uncoiled and tickled his ear.

The pattern of true sleep, eat, and dreamwalk repeated itself for the next four days. It was frustrating, exhausting work. No matter how he and the Changelings strained, they could not indentify the minds they sensed, much less locate the minds in time and space. On the afternoon of the fourth day, the fusion dissolved.

It is of no use to tire yourself further, Nova told him. *Only Lucents are capable of the kind of dreamwalking you seek.*

Mark's shoulders slumped. If he put callers out blindly, colonists died in ambush. If he didn't put callers out, colonists died of hunger or cold. What he needed was—

Changelings. You need a planet. We're losing this one. If your kind will help, especially the Lucents, you can have Paran as your new home.

The four answered as one. *What would we do with an entire planet? Changelings need manna and rocks. Humans need plants. Give us Paran's deserts, caves, and rocky reaches; keep the soft-tumbling green places as your own.*

You'll get a better deal than that. How many Changelings would be willing to fight for a new home?

Many thousands, if you can reach the caverns of Change.

How many can we feed now?

Up to forty, if we are allowed to hunt. Manna flourishes, even without our encouragement. Within six weeks it can feed us all, human and Changeling.

God, manna will take over the planet!

Mark felt the Changelings' ripple of amusement. *We control it. When it is time, manna will sleep.*

Glad to hear it. I'll tell Rhanett to get the shuttle ready for a run to the ship. You four do whatever is necessary. I'll give you a call when Rhanett is ready to lift for Change.

Only Mist will go. Someone must guard Selena, and you, and the manna.

No argument about the last, thought Mark, with

visions of Paran covered by a six-foot depth of silver manna.

Mark found Rhanett standing watch outside Selena's tent. In the time Mark had spent with the Changelings, Selena had guided the wolves in their search for callers. The results had been unpleasant. Mark put the matter out of his mind and concentrated on Rhanett.

When is the next ship due?

Tonight.

Rhanett's thought was slow, but clear.

That little? Christ, we still have one ship in deep orbit. And not enough live colonists to fill a shuttle.

It grows colder.

Winter is one storm away, agreed Mark. *It will cool off the guerrillas, but it will crucify the more helpless colonists. And every four days one of Tien's ships lands.*

You're sure?

Yes. We can sense them.

Can't an ambush be arranged?

Only if they land close enough. No; as things are now . . . I'm giving orders that the camp be evacuated. Tell the ship that's coming that it is to take everyone in the camp to Rynlonne. You're going to Change with the ship we have now. One of the Changelings will go with you. Pick up every Changeling that the ship can hold and bring them back here. And make it quick. We need them. Now.

Rhanett left to notify Stan and the incoming ship of the changed plans. In his wake Mist moved with incomparable Changeling grace. Mark took over as guard at Selena's tent.

She's awake. Go to her; I'll guard.

Mark jumped at Shimm's unexpected appearance. He was really too tired to be much use.

Selena opened her eyes and smiled wanly as Mark entered the tent.

"Hungry?" he said gently.

"I . . . no. I couldn't eat."

Mark looked more closely and saw the grim lines around her mouth.

"You found the last caller," he said.

She nodded.

Reluctantly he asked, "Any colonists?"

"Ten. All very dead."

Mark drew Selena close to him, hating himself for what he had asked her to do. The last four days had been excruciating for her. Prolonged searches ending always with the sight and smell of death. Even viewing the scenes through the filter of a wolf's mind didn't help; the wolves had a keen sense of smell. Too keen. Many times Selena had come out of trance gagging. He didn't want to ask any more questions, but he had to.

"Know any of them?"

Selena shuddered. "I couldn't tell."

Mark rocked her slowly in his arms. "It's over now, Golden Eyes. It's over. Go to sleep." He held her and murmured until he felt her body relax in sleep. Gradually he eased her onto the sleeping pad, cursing himself for her agony. Only when he was sure she slept did he stretch out beside her and fall into exhausted sleep. Even the sound of the shuttle accelerating through the atmosphere didn't waken them. Shimm lay across the tent entrance, oozing satisfaction that her charges were together. Soon, she, too, slept.

As night deepened, only Nova's unwinking crystal eyes moved in the dark campsite. He sensed the wolves ranging outside the camp, sniffing, prowling, searching for intruders.

But the only intruders were of the mind. Selena thrashed and cried out as a gruesome parade of long dead colonists filled her dreams. Dazed by sleep she yet searched for and found Mark. The touch of living flesh reassured her, and she slept again.

XII

"Have you seen Mark?" said Stan as Selena emerged from the tent.

"No. Can I help?"

"If you could, uh, call him . . ."

Selena yawned indelicately as she sent a questing thought.

"He's with the Rynlon pilot," she said after a moment. "Meet him in the cargo bay."

"Thanks," said Stan and hurried off to the shuttle landing area.

Selena rubbed her eyes and yawned again; one night of broken sleep hardly made up for three days of no sleep. Maybe food would help.

She got to the breakfast tent just as Hugh finished dismantling it.

"What's going on? I come here for breakfast and—"

"Try the blue sack," said Hugh. He telescoped the tent ribs and stowed them in the pockets which were part of the tent.

Selena rummaged in the blue sack. She munched on fruit and neardeer jerky and eyed the fast vanishing camp.

"I have a feeling I slept through something," she said mildly.

"Didn't Mark tell you?" said Hugh as he stacked the tent on top of a pile of camp equipment. "We're evac-

uating. Everyone except Mark and the Changelings."
With the last words Hugh dropped the pretense of being
too busy to talk and waited for Selena's reaction.

He would have enjoyed it, had he been able to inter-
cept it. Her thought brought the three Changelings to
their feet with ululations of surprise.

Mark was not surprised. He excused himself from
the puzzled Rynlon.

It's too dangerous for you to stay.

Had Selena not been so upset, she would have wondered at the lack of vitality in his mindtouch. As it was
she assumed that he was giving her the impersonal
camp-leader routine again. She was still furious, but
damped it nicely.

And what about you? Her thought was redolent of
sweet pliable innocence.

Mark didn't notice. It was as though his mind were
a machine, emotionlessly following its program. *All
superfluous personnel are being evacuated to Rynlonne.*

Superfluous, repeated Selena calmly. Too calmly.

Superfluous, he confirmed. *I've spent the last four
days with the Changelings, trying to contact colonists,
or at least locate them. The only one we could locate
was you.*

His thought warmed perceptibly with the memory,
which only angered Selena more.

*The Changelings said that with more Lucents and
life units, we might succeed,* he continued.

Selena's mind exploded with images of wrath which
leaped like arcs of flame, inchoate.

But Mark caught enough: he was an idiot; an incon-
siderate idiot at that, and above all an arrogant idiot.
Just because he failed was no reason to assume that she
was superfluous. *Did it ever occur to him that he
should go to Rynlonne and let her stay with the
Changelings?*

No. You'll suffer no more for my mistakes.

Mindtouch ended.

Selena's fury crumbled; she hadn't meant . . . he was so bleak, so . . . She worked frantically to disentangle the clot of thought/emotion/innuendo which the few seconds of mindtouch had communicated. He thought that Paran as an Earth colony was dead, and with it the hope of eventually breaking Tien's hold over Earth. Perhaps Paran might be saved for the Changelings; at least they were willing and able to fight for it. He felt responsible for the past deaths—and for the ones which were to come. An implacable determination that Selena should not suffer further and probably die because of his own bungling, his idiot dreams.

And the images cascading—a lifetime of work telescoped into a rude mountain camp melting away before his eyes. The bright burning dream of Earth's children going out to the stars changed to ashes and the taste-foretaste of death, his own.

He had fought too long and too alone.

Selena's face glistened with silent tears. She felt Hugh's arms go around her comfortingly.

"I'm sorry, Selena. I really thought he'd let at least you stay."

"He's sucked dry," she whispered. "And I was the worst."

Hugh made an intuitive leap worthy of his profession. "No, Selena. Mark . . . Mark never had to ask for help, so he never learned how. And the rest of us—well, the rest of us were damn glad to lean on him. You were the only one who gave more than you took. You renewed him."

"I did a shit poor job, then." She rubbed her hands across her eyes impatiently. "But I'm staying. I learned to ask for help; he'll learn, too. Or he'll get it without asking." She smiled crookedly at Hugh. "Don't look so skeptical, Doctor. Remember I once told you that Change was a big planet? So is Paran."

"Lea and I had the same idea. Why don't we just—"

"No, Hugh. Please. Take Lea and get on that ship and help the Rynlon and send your children out to the stars. Then . . . if Earth ever grows up—"

"And what about you? Aren't you planning to be around? Maybe Mark had the right idea. Get everyone the hell off this planet and—"

"You're forgetting the Changelings. They deserve their chance. They, at least, are willing to fight for a new home."

"And you?"

"I'm fighting for Mark." She hugged Hugh suddenly. "Goodbye, Hugh. Tell Lea . . ."

On an impulse, Selena closed her eyes and concentrated on him. A bemused expression came over his face as images of himself and Lea soared like sunrise over clouds of uncertainty and gathered into a blazing disc of life.

By the time Hugh shook off the wonder of mindtouch, Selena was gone.

The last shuttle load of equipment had been lifted. A hushed group of colonists waited for the shuttle to return. Mark looked over the colonists, searching for one person. He had been too rushed to seek her out, and he knew she was angry. His efforts at mindtouch had bounced off her unwillingness like hail off rocks. Yet he hoped that she would yield enough to let him touch her once more . . .

"Looking for someone?" said Hugh.

"Have you seen her?"

"Not since this morning. I was with her when you cut her off."

"When I—"

"Cut her off. Banished her. Told her to get lost so you could suffer in noble solitude. But it doesn't matter; you couldn't have kept her better if you tried."

"What in Christ's name are you talking about?" he said finally.

"Ask Selena."

"I will—as soon as I find her."

"What happened to mindspeech?"

Mark's full lips narrowed to a line, then twisted with something like pain.

Hugh remembered Selena's words and berated himself for kicking a downed man.

"I'm sorry, Mark. You did what you thought was right. Selena disagreed."

"Where is she?" he said tonelessly.

"I don't know. My guess is that she took a walk."

"You let her go off alone! That shuttle going up and down is a goddamn beacon—every guerrilla on the planet will be crawling in this direction." Mark smacked his hands together in frustration. Then apologized wearily. He knew Hugh hadn't "let" Selena do anything; she'd do what she wanted and screw the consequences.

Shimm.

Yes?

Is Selena with you?

Nova and I are guarding her.

Bring her back to camp.

She does not wish it.

Bring her back.

Mark waited impatiently for Shimm's reply. He didn't like it when it came, though Shimm had shifted to a formal, eminently tactful approach.

Selena indicates that the colony has been disbanded; therefore, she is under no obligation to you as colony leader. Should you choose to call upon her admitted personal obligation to you, she would regretfully and with great affection decline.

Let me talk to her.

After the ship has left for Rynlonne, she will be delighted to resume—

Goddamn it, Shimm! I don't want her to die!

Shimm approved of the sentiment, but didn't budge.

And you, Shimm. Do you think I'm wrong, too? he demanded.

I am not human, nor do I understand your relationship. I do understand Selena: she will fight anyone who tells her she cannot live or die with the being she loves. She has a formidable mind. If you choose to convince her of error, we Changelings will not interfere. But as one who considers herself your friend, I would advise you to wait until you are better rested. In your present state of mind—

—I'd get my tail tied in a knot.

Mark frowned and examined the alternatives as rapidly as his fatigue allowed. When he heard the shuttle braking through the atmosphere, he was torn between rage and a relief which only angered him more.

Tell Selena she's won, he thought coldly.

She does not consider it a victory, nor should you consider it a loss.

Mark broke the link, but not before the acid of his rage and frustration seeped through.

Shimm lashed her tail in pain. Hurriedly, Selena apologized for Mark. *He hurts, Shimm; he didn't mean to . . .*

I know. No more than you meant to lash us in your Becoming.

Shimm shook off the last of her headache and turned to practical matters. *We must move further from camp. That's the twelfth shuttle flight today. Even the most stupid torlen head toward an occupied cavern. Send the wolves deep into the mountains. The camp no longer needs guards.*

Shimm ignored Selena's protest by the simple expedient of bounding over rocks and around trees at a dizzying speed.

When the Changeling finally slowed, Selena risked breaking in.

What about Mark?

Nova will bring him after we have found a waiting place. Until then, Dawn guards him like a mate.

"She'd better," muttered Selena to herself as she sent the wolves far from camp. She clung to the harness, for Shimm had increased her speed again in defiance of the rugged country they crossed. Then, the Changeling ran even faster, heedless of the shifting evening light and steep broken country. Selena closed her eyes to slits as the cold wind clawed over her face.

Selena was on the verge of requesting a slower pace when Nova appeared alongside his mate. Shimm made subtle adjustments in her stride until Nova was so close that his bright skin touched Selena's leg. In flawless unison the Changelings leaped, wove and raced in celebration of their skill matched against the intricate land. Selena felt their soaring pleasure in the play of muscle and the rush of blood, sensed a special rapport between them, a communion beyond her understanding or complete sharing. Yet she knew it was good.

Like Shimm lying outside their tent, she approved.

It was a long time before the place slowed.

What's wrong?

We've come to a good waiting place.

Selena unwrapped aching hands from Shimm's harness and looked around. Paran's moons gave enough light for her to see that the rocks of highest elevation had given way to a small grove of trees which grew just inside the head of a steep ravine. A small spring gave water, the trees gave cover, and the surrounding rockfields were proof against any but the most determined guerrillas.

It was indeed a good waiting place.

Selena slid off Shimm, staggered slightly when her numb feet hit the ground.

That was quite a ride, Shimm.

Shimm fairly vibrated with agreement.

Selena stretched and laughed ruefully as her muscles

complained of ill treatment. *Now why don't the two of you run each other's tail off and bring Mark here.*

If I left you alone, Mark would feed me to the torlen.

And I'd help, added Nova.

I'm safe here. I have a gun, and if—

Help me with the harness, was Nova's only response.

Selena took the harness off Shimm and put it on Nova.

Now go to sleep, Selena. If you hope to help your mate, you'll need the strength and patience which rest gives.

Selena shrugged out of her backpack. Nova wasn't the only one worried about Mark. But there was nothing she could do except shake out her sleeping pad and tarp, rub the harness marks off Shimm, and sleep.

When she awoke, it was to sunlight filtering through trees and quiet munching sounds. She looked up and laughed aloud—Shimm looked like she'd suddenly sprouted silver whiskers. With a show of dignity, Shimm licked the vagrant wisps of manna from her lips.

Then Selena remembered.

Where are they?

Safe. Asleep at the other edge of the trees.

Selena crawled out from under the protective tarp. She pulled a handful of manna out of her pack and walked to the moss-bordered spring. She put the manna in the spring, counted fifty, and retrieved her breakfast.

From where she sat, Selena commanded a view of the grove and surrounding rocks. Below her the mountain plunged in furrows of granite and tenacious trees down to a distant, hidden river. The silence was so absolute that her quiet chewing seemed an avalanche of noise.

Delicately, Selena sought the Changelings; as she suspected, they were sleeping. With a smile she left the spring. She tiptoed past Shimm, picked up her distance lenses and gun, and climbed quietly to the rocks above camp. There she hid to watch the approaches to their camp.

Except for a hunting bird, nothing stirred in all the land.

Satisfied, Selena settled back to finish her breakfast. Many hours passed before she spotted the silver shape of a Changeling moving around camp.

Nova, is Mark awake yet?

No.

There was a distinct aura of satisfaction about Nova's thought.

What did you do—rap him on the head with a rock?

Ripples of humor, then, *It is a method we use to control cubs. Far better than rocks.*

Selena was both disappointed and relieved. She really didn't relish facing Mark, yet she hungered for his presence.

We want to search the area for landing sites. Will you be all right until we return? There is no sentient life nearby.

Selena curbed her tart rejoinder and settled for a mild, *Don't break your neck on the rocks.*

She watched the Changelings blend into the rocks to vanish as completely as dew under a hot sun. For exercise, she tried to sift the surrounding ravines for traces of hostility or fear; the Changeling method of standing guard. But it was useless. Unless someone was actively hunting her, she had as much chance of catching their thoughts as catching fish barehanded in a muddy river.

Selena shifted her position. The sun was uncomfortably warm as it reflected off the boulders around her. She gave in and returned to the grove.

The sound of water flowing made her realize she was thirsty; she had left her canteen in the camp. Eagerly she knelt by the tiny creek which flowed from the spring. Though the creek was no wider than her hand, its water was clean and cold enough to make her teeth ache. She drank gratefully, then unzipped her jumpsuit and fanned air across her hot skin. It was hard to believe any danger existed on this still warm autumn day. The sky was a turquoise shout of joy echoed by the umber dance of leaves and magnified by the sparkling air.

Memories of the last few days clashed with the silky moment, filling her with restlessness. She roamed the grove aimlessly, then returned to the spring. Mark had wakened, then slept again. He made no move to contact her. That hurt, but it was the gamble she'd taken when she decided to stay.

Selena pitched pebbles into the tiny spring and tried to control the cold which seeped through her in spite of the warm day. Maybe he had wanted her to leave for other reasons; maybe he was tired of more than fighting; maybe she'd better leave him alone. Maybe—

A handful of pebbles crashed into the spring.

Maybe she had better get it over with. Regardless of how he felt toward her, the Changelings needed both of them.

Selena moved slowly toward the end of the grove where she sensed Mark to be. The slanting light made leaves into serrated orange flames and the stream winked diamonds at her reluctant feet. Everywhere about her drifted the scent of plants spreading and stretching toward the unexpected warmth. For a moment her will faltered—it would be so nice to lie beneath the gentle pressure of sunlight and drink the lyre song of water sliding to a distant sea.

Mark was awake.

In an unconscious reflex she had learned before speech, Selena closed her mind behind an impregnable wall of will; not so much as a flicker of awareness escaped to reach a receptive mind. She knew nothing of her reaction, for all of her attention was on the man who lay at her feet. His eyes were closed, he made no move to acknowledge her, yet she was sure he was awake.

With each breath he drew the sunlight moved softly over his back, defining muscles and turning each hair into a discrete flame.

The chill increased until Selena felt numb. She could not lie down beside him, could not savor the changing textures of his strength, could not so much as whisper her love.

Selena felt suddenly weak. She hadn't meant it to turn out this way, to end as she had begun in numbness and fear. She bent her head and sank soundlessly to her knees, waiting for the strength to escape from this waking nightmare.

Mark's hand closed over hers, pulled it to his lips, caressing. He could not know her thoughts or feelings, for her mind was closed.

"When the Changelings brought me here, they asked me what I would have done if I were you," he said slowly. "They were very tactful, but they wanted to understand why I was angry that you would not leave me. I had to tell them that I would have done exactly as you, and that that was why I was angry. They were kind enough not to laugh in my face. Instead, Nova gently made me sleepy, hoping that I would regain sanity when I woke. I have."

His eyes opened in a jeweled flash of green and he searched her face for a response. "You have every right to shut me out, Selena, but I'd hoped . . ."

He rose and kissed her lips gently, gently, as though she were a fragile crystal which would shatter at a too-insistent touch. His lips told her of longing and loneliness as deep as her own, of needs rooted in the body which flowered in the mind. She returned his light kisses until reality shrank to the movement of his body on hers.

Selena rummaged in Mark's pack until she found two pieces of fruit and a piece of jerky.

"Fruit or jerky?" she said over her shoulder.

"Mmmph."

Selena looked up to discover that Mark was half asleep. She knelt next to him and dropped the fruit on his chest.

"Hey, lazy man. You said you were hungry."

Mark took her hand and nibbled on her fingers.

Selena smiled. "You could get into trouble doing that."

"Really? I thought your name was Selena."

She ruffled his hair and laughed. "You're impossible."

"Nope. I'm very easy."

"Bluff called; and raise you."

"That won't be hard."

"It better be."

Selena awoke in a warm tangle of arms and legs. The late afternoon light winked through the leaves and across her eyes. She turned back and snuggled against Mark's warmth, trying to ignore the insistent noises her stomach made.

Mark chuckled. "There's some fruit around here somewhere."

Selena looked around hopefully, then sighed as she realized it was out of reach.

Mark groaned and got up to retrieve the fruit.

"While you're up," began Selena innocently.

"I know," he laughed. "How do you want your manna—dry or soaked?"

"Soaked, count of fifty."

Selena shivered suddenly. Without Mark, the afternoon wasn't very warm. She found her jumpsuit and put it on hastily.

"Thanks," said Selena as she took the dripping manna from Mark. "I think."

"Wish we could build a fire," muttered Mark as he shrugged into his jumpsuit.

"It was your edict, oh, great leader, that no colonists were to build fires."

"Don't remind me."

"Besides, the Changelings would skin us for advertising," said Selena.

"Where are they?"

"I'm sure at least one is on guard somewhere in the rocks."

"Tactful of them," he said.

"And prudent. They really didn't know what to expect when you woke up."

His slow grin made Selena laugh.

"And," she added, "we haven't exactly encouraged interruptions." She chewed her manna absently. "I suppose we'd better call them in. Nova and Dawn were scouting landing sites this morning, and—"

She stopped as lines of pain drew the peace from Mark's face. She laid her hand gently on his cheek, smiled as his lips touched her wrist.

"The Lucents will help us," she said. "I know they will."

"It's not us I'm worried about," he said wryly. "It's the colonists."

Mark pulled Selena closer to him, kissed her, then said reluctantly, "Yes, we'd better call the Changelings in. Together."

Selena merged her mind once again with his. Each time there was a new beauty, a flower unfolding a few more bright petals of knowledge and love. Their call was redolent of peace and the power of increasing rapport.

Within a few minutes, the Changelings glided into camp, their eyes alight with the pale glow of the setting sun. Shimm's tail looped briefly around Mark and Selena, then the Changelings lay in a triangle around them, as though to warm themselves by a fire.

They are lonely without Mist, thought Mark to Selena. *We were selfish to shut them out.*

Selena rubbed Shimm's head and asked the Changeling.

When Nova and I ran together, were you shut out? responded Shimm.

I shared what I could. For the rest, it was enough that you and Nova were enjoying yourselves.

In that, Changeling and human are alike. We may not understand the full nature of the other's pleasure, but we are pleased nonetheless.

Mark relaxed against Nova's warmth with an unabashed yawn and snuggled Selena against his shoulder. In minutes, all but Dawn were deep in sleep.

On the next day they awoke to a cloud-draped sun. A thin, sharp chill permeated the air.

"So much for summer," said Selena regretfully. Then, "Where are the Changelings?"

"Growing manna. Or rather, keeping it from taking over. The light—or something—at this elevation makes manna go quietly berserk. Thank God it doesn't multiply by spores or seed!"

Selena peered through the trees. Where a few days ago had been only rocks, today was an undulating carpet of manna.

"Mother of us all! Do they need any help?"

"They said no when I asked."

"I hope the manna doesn't get away from them. From here, it looks a good deal less than 'obedient.' "

Mark smiled. "At least we don't have to worry about feeding the Changelings. I'm going to tell Rhanett to bring every Changeling he can get his hands on."

Selena muttered something about mixed blessings and went to dunk her breakfast in the spring.

Later she and Mark explored the field of manna. Close up, they saw that the carpet was by no means solid. Wherever pockets of leaves had been collected by the wind, or lichen clung, or any of the tiny, tight-matted plants flourished, the manna grew no closer than arm's length. Apparently something about organic matter—living or dead—was inimical to manna.

"That's a relief," said Selena finally. "I know the Changelings can control this stuff at home, but I was getting worried about Paran."

Shuttle overhead. Very low.

The Changeling warning sent everyone running for cover. A low shuttle could spot them against the bare rocks. And it was too soon to be a Rynlon shuttle.

"Give me a leg up."

Mark boosted Selena into the branches of a tree. She scrambled higher, braced herself against the swaying tree, and pulled the distances lenses out of her pocket.

"Can't see anyth—there. A shuttle all right. Heading in the direction of the old camp."

"Rynlon?" yelled Mark over the shuttle's booming trail of sound.

Doubt it. Wait ... Shimm says they sense no Changelings. Must be one of Tien's—

Even in their distant mountain camp, Mark and Selena heard the discrete thunder of bombs exploding. Selena mourned for the beautiful valley devastated by unexpected fire.

"I hope to Christ no colonists were nearby," said Mark into the sudden silence.

"The Changelings would have told us; they know when intelligence dies."

"That lets out most of the human race."

Selena ignored his dark humor. "Could we be picked up on an infrared scanner?"

"Hell, yes. But it wouldn't do them any good. How would they know whether we were guerrillas or colonists?"

"Would Tien care?"

"We better pray he does," said Mark as he lifted her out of the branches.

Selena frowned; she and Mark and a few Changelings might be able to elude scanners by staying within the natural heat camouflage of the grove, but there was no way that a large group of Changelings could avoid detection.

"Sorry you stayed?" he said hesitantly.

Selena rubbed her fingers through his unruly hair and kneaded her mouth against his. For a long moment she held him, then laid her lips against his pulsing neck.

"That will give the scanners something to register," she said.

Mark held her even closer until an excited Changeling thought distracted them.

Mist! Mist and Changelings!

How long? thought Mark and Selena simultaneously.

The answer was an image of the sun straight overhead.

So soon? We've got to find a landing site for them.

Nova's response was a mixture of anticipation and laughter. *While you two played, we found three sites.*

"Let's hope the guerrillas dropped all their bombs on the old camp," said Mark for Selena alone.

The Changelings entered the grove in a leaping, racing mass.

"I get the feeling they're happy about something," said Selena innocently.

Mark was too worried to answer. His mind rapidly devised and rejected plans.

"I've got to talk with Rhanett. Help me?" he asked Selena.

Of course, my love.

Together they concentrated on Rhanett. The Changelings sensed the call, and boosted it. Rhanett's surprise and pleasure warmed their minds, but Mark cut the greetings short with an apology.

We've got a problem, Rhanett. The guerrillas are using bombs; they just dropped a load on the meadow camp. How many Changelings do you have?

Twenty-two: four life units and six Lucents.

That many! They must be hanging out of the air-locks.

Not quite, but not far away.

That means at least five shuttle trips, possibly six.

It will be dangerous, but—

But nothing. After the second trip the guerrillas will be over you—and us—like another skin. We have just three sites, and—Rhanett, can you make that shuttle hover close enough to the ground so that the Changelings can jump?

Mark got the impression of difficult, very difficult, but possible. Selena remembered the speed and skill of Rhanett's hands at the shuttle controls. *If anyone can make that hunk of metal dance, it's you.*

Rhanett's response was both laughter and pleasure. *I hope so, beautiful one, I hope so.*

Beautiful one? thought Mark in a swift aside.

Rynlon vision is different from ours.

Not from mine!

Then you'll love their women.

Rhanett felt Mark's laughter even though his thoughts were serious.*If you can hover, then you can deposit each group of Changelings far enough apart to confuse the guerrillas. You won't have to repeat the drop areas even once.*

How will the Changelings find you?

Built-in radar.

Selena amused herself wondering how Rhanett's mind translated Mark's cryptic comment. Apparently there was no difficulty, for Rhanett agreed to the new plan immediately.

Good, thought Mark. *Now, get out your ground map and concentrate on it. More. Harder.*

Selena and the Changelings boosted Rhanett's concentration. A dim picture of the map formed in Mark's mind.

That's it. We're in the twenty-third sector, two-thirds up the highest peak. South side. Got that?

Yes.

Imagine a crescent with the bow of the curve resting near the southern base of the mountain, and the two horns pointing away from us, toward the first camp. Good. Make the first drop at the top of the bow, subsequent drops on alternating sides of the curve. The last Changelings will have further to go, but if the guerrillas catch on, they'll look inside the crescent first. One last thing—are any other Rynlon ships coming here?

Yes. Fhain is bringing one of our biggest ships back. It carries five shuttles, eight scouts, and personnel. Also defensive arms. She should be here before I return from Change.

Is Fhain paran?

More than I, far less than you. Don't worry my friend; mindtouch won't frighten Fhain.

The mindlink dissolved, freeing Rhanett for the delicate work of bringing Changelings close enough to ground to leap safely from a hovering shuttle.

Sooner than expected, Changelings came bounding into camp. The first moments of greeting were uproarious. Selena and Mark waited until things were calmer before ducking through the milling Changelings to add their own welcome to Mist.

Selena didn't recognize the life unit which had followed Mist up the mountain, but she knew from the quality of Shimm's delight that the new Changelings were from Shimm's own cavern, friends since they roamed as cubs over the jagged rocks of Change.

Within an hour, five Lucents silently appeared. Three of them Selena remembered as soon as her mind touched theirs in greeting. Mark joined minds with them tentatively, then with greater reassurance as he felt the case and delicacy of their mindtouch. They had a piercing clarity of mind, like an immense crystal bell ringing in still air.

And you are as the sun rising, radiating power and warmth. Selena is well mated. Together you will light the darkness between the stars.

I'll settle for lighting a fire under Tien's guerrillas.

The Lucents' laughter was as clear as their thoughts. *Mist told us of your problem. When you are ready, we will dreamwalk this new planet together.*

Good. But first eat and rest. Your journey was a strange and crowded passage.

It was all of that, and more.

"What do you think of the Lucents?" said Selena curiously as she watched them leave for the manna field.

"Mindspeech with them is an experience. A pleasure, too. They are unlike mated Changelings. In some ways more powerful, clearer, definitely more precise, yet . . ."

"Less complete?"

"As far as emotions, yes. They don't have the range of a life unit. But now I know how you survived the searfruit. Lucents comprehend death, and in comprehending it, helped you to choose."

"I certainly made them suffer for it."

Mark smiled and put his arm around her shoulders. "They're strong."

"Strong enough to find colonists?"

"I hope so. I'm even beginning to believe it."

It was full darkness, unrelieved by so much as a sliver of moon, before the last Changelings arrived and Mark had a chance to test his hope. Clouds had congealed over the land and the camp braced itself for the birth of winter.

Mark and Selena adjusted their jumpsuits so that only their eyes were unmuffled by the warm cocoon of Rynlon ingenuity. When they were finished, they joined the waiting Changelings.

Six Lucents lay in a crescent before the humans. In back of the Lucents, the five life units lay shoulder to shoulder like a living silver fan set with forty large and flawless diamonds. All the Changelings were well fed, well rested, and in a palpable good humor. Tails slithered and slapped with the passage of unheard jokes. Even the Lucents had a near lilt to their mindtouch.

Mark and Selena lay down in front of the Lucents. The irresistible tide of companionship and humor swept them up until they bobbed like corks on smiling waves of Changeling thought.

The links of mind with mind grew stronger, stronger still. Their bodies, the grove, the rocks, the mountain, all sloughed away, leaving awareness floating free, waiting for the current which would signal their minds.

The difference in sensitivity between four Changelings working with Mark, and twenty-six Changelings working with Selena/Mark was the difference between wood and a tuning fork. Almost immediately they felt the subtle currents of other minds. Swiftly they found the source, examined the impervious shells around the minds, and consulted each other.

This time I know we can reach them, insisted Mark.

Yes, but in what shape will their minds be afterwards? We have the strength to smash their shells, but do we have the skill to leave their minds intact?

So near . . . sighed Mark. *Before, I saw them as pebbles—solid, polished, impossible to reach. Now I know they can be reached, even as the meat of a nut can be reached by breaking the shell.*

Perhaps more Changelings will give us the ability to crack these shells delicately. I would prefer that to smash-and-pray.

You're right . . . We'll have to do it the hard way for now.

They merged again, and willed sight.

Like ghosts seen through rippling water, a group of humans appeared.

Selena/Mark concentrated, drew strength from the Changelings, and willed.

The surface of the water calmed, the figures solidified into a group of ten colonists. They were obviously hungry, cold, exhausted, and discouraged, huddled together in the chill comfort of the lost.

As though the sight of them triggered something deep within Selena, her mind stretched even further. Something drew her to three of them, something impersonal yet familiar, compelling.

Pain.

One colonist's hand had been badly burned by a forbidden campfire. Another hobbled on makeshift crutches, trying to relieve his swollen ankle. The third, in haste to drink from a stream, had taken a shortcut through a patch of nettles; her face and hands were swollen large by poison.

Almost reflexively, Selena healed each injury in the act of cataloguing it. The colonists' surprise was surpassed by Mark's.

How in God's name can you heal a mind you can't even reach?

Healing has little to do with their minds. It is a matter between brain and body. And their brain is accessible to a Healer.

Fine for them but not very helpful to us. Short of visually backtracking from them to us, how can we locate the colonists for shuttle pickup?

Ask the Changelings; they have a rapport with the land which is beyond ours.

Mark asked. The answer was simple—and frustrating: like visual backtracking, it could be done, but only at great cost. In the end, it would barely be more efficient than sending out patrols on foot. It would be better to seek less impervious minds, or wait until more

Changelings arrived; then more minds would be accessible.

Until then, let's continue dreamwalking, thought Selena. *At least we can heal the injured.*

Only after we look at them, insisted Mark. *Goddamned if I waste energy on guerrillas.*

And so they continued floating, sliding, probing shells in the increasingly forlorn hope of reaching the mind inside, willing sight, and healing until their own bodies could no longer be ignored.

Selena's eyes opened to a world of moving, sifting white. The rocky folds of the surrounding ravine broke the force of the storm, but they could hear its distant scream over the exposed flank of the mountain.

"We're going to be buried," said Selena as she watched the snow patiently envelop leaves and small plants.

"No help for it. I hope the Changelings will be all right."

"Shimm once told me that a Changeling could sleep on ice and wake up warm. She'll get the chance to prove it."

Mark smiled crookedly, but was obviously lost in thought. "Something bothering?" said Selena.

"Yes. How could the Changelings nudge a very distant, alien race into roaming the galaxy, while we can't even reach the minds of our own kind on our own planet?"

"Was there a difference between four Changelings and twenty-six?"

"Yes. More range and power."

"Six times more?"

"At least."

"Then imagine many, many thousands of Changelings interlocked in dreamwalking."

"I can't," he said bluntly. "But I'd give my arm to walk with them."

"I have a better use for that arm," laughed Selena. "Now let's eat and sleep. There are more luckless colonists to heal tomorrow."

They awakened at noon to a clear, wind-bright sky. Yesterday's snow stirred wetly beneath the pressing wind. Had the snow been lighter it would have quickly buried the camp in drifts. As it was, Selena and Mark had to dig their breakfast our from under a foot of clinging snow. They ate their frigid manna to the accompaniment of erratic plops of snow slipping from heavily burdened trees.

"Looks like the weather computer missed," said Selena. "It's already thawing."

"Good. I don't like the idea of tracking colonists through snowdrifts."

"Giving up on dreamwalking?"

"Not yet. But I still haven't worked out a good way to locate the colonists well enough to send a shuttle after them."

"The colonists aren't completely helpless. They have eyes enough to spot mountains and to see where the sun rises and sets and maybe even where the moons are. If they can tell us that, Rhanett can get a shuttle to them. Besides, don't the wrist finders have a compass?"

"Nothing so primitive," said Mark wryly.

Selena exhaled a long plume of white air. "Well, one thing has worked out," she said.

"What's that?"

"Manna." Her hand traced an arc over the rockfields dotted with feeding Changelings. "Even the snow didn't discourage it. But," she grimaced, "why does manna have to have the taste and texture of freeze-dried kelp?"

"The Changelings don't seem to mind."

"I am not a Changeling," she said firmly. "But if I eat much more manna I just might grow a long tail."

"Your tail is pretty nice as is."

"Just pretty nice?" she said threateningly and dove at

his chest. Mark grabbed her and they rolled laughing and grappling into a nearby snowdrift.

They had forgotten that Changelings find wrestling irresistible. Within seconds, sixteen Changelings had joined the fracas. It wasn't long before Mark and Selena were helpless with laughter. The Changelings then ignored them in favor of more active quarry and treated the humans to the sight of four life units spraying arcs of glittering snow as they raced and leaped in unison over the rocks.

As before, play merged imperceptibly with dreamwalking. Interlocked minds searched and healed and hoped and days passed in an unheralded flow of light and dark until a ship from Change arrived.

It was Fhain who responded to their mindtouch.

Can you really feed all the Changelings we Rynlon bring?

Yes.

Then we will empty every cavern on that hell planet.

Fhain's skill with the shuttle proved a match for the rugged terrain. By fours and fives Changelings leaped from shuttle to ground and began the steep journey which would unite them with their waiting kin. They ate, slept, and joined the dreamwalkers. Seeing became easier with each shipload of Changelings, but weeks of effort brought little reward. The results of mindtouch with the few reachable colonists were frustrating.

The colonists refused to believe the messages of their own minds. Hunger, fatigue, hallucination, all were used to rationalize away the unprecedented contact. And the few who did believe were functionally useless. They had neither talent nor knowledge in the ways of mindtouch. The one or two who could convey simple sun positions could not convince their friends that a shuttle would arrive when no caller summoned it. No one would leave a safe campsite for the open spaces where a shuttle could land, especially when the shuttle was obviously the creation of a tired, frightened imagination.

The tempo of Rynlon ship arrivals increased. Now every second day a ship arrived packed with Changelings. The distance of the drop sites from the mountain camp increased, yet the Changelings found their silent way up the mountain, rested, and poured their strength into dreamwalking.

Rest, came Selena's firm thought. *I'll direct the dreamwalking for awhile.*

Mark separated his mind from the Changelings, relinquishing to her the focal point of Changeling strength. Immediately Selena was swept from her body into the massed awareness of the Changelings. At almost the same moment, twenty Lucents entered camp and immediately interlocked with the dreamwalkers.

As though a critical mass had been reached, Selena felt the nearest group of colonists with microscopic clarity. What had been first impermeable rocks of awareness, then hard shells enclosing minds, now appeared as fragile, imperfect shells through which delicate tentacles of mindtouch could reach.

The first message was as simple and profound as warm arms cradling a newborn baby. It was a message of love and care, a message to quiet the leaping fear of the unknown.

With breathless care they waited for a response. It came as a soundless cry of confusion and hope—and pain.

As one, the life units withheld their strength, then patiently increased it by increments to the threshold of their contact's pain. Selena surrendered the focal point to the Lucents, who had greater experience with bringing minds into full awareness.

She watched their thoughts surround the nascent mind like a jeweled spiral. There they waited for an unknown signal. Selena sensed the colonist's acquiescence, his tremulous feeling of hope and wonder, and the Lucents' calm reassurance that they would press no further than he desired, would teach no more than he wished to learn.

Selena followed the intricate, subtle shifts of light which flowed erratically up the spiral. Gradually she sensed a pattern in the seemingly random surges of light. The pattern became more than intriguing; it became a hypnotic, compelling dance of minds. She opened herself to its rhythm and took her inevitable place.

A new, jeweled center of light blazed on the spiral, coaxing, encouraging, praising the mind which cautiously tested the strength of the sustaining spiral. With increasing confidence the mind reached and twined itself along the rising curves. Further and higher it wound, until half the spiral radiated the mind's emergent presence. Yet more jewels shimmered above, glowing curves receding to infinity. Mind stretched and longed, but could not reach.

The spiral flashed out of existence, leaving no memory of itself to haunt the colonist with unattainable heights. It was enough, and more, that a new mind touched theirs freely where before had been only a defensive shell.

Will he be all right? asked Selena anxiously, remembering her own terrible confusion when she awoke from the searfruit.

We are not searfruit; we did not claw his mind unwilling from its cavern. He stretched as far as desire and ability allowed. He is changed, yes, but not helpless.

Good, thought Selena tiredly. *We haven't the time to nurse him.* Her candor did not shock the Lucents; in their own manner they were supreme pragmatists. In silent agreement, Lucents and Selena concentrated on another colonist. The spiral grew and died twice more before Mark's insistent thoughts pulled Selena away.

You're supposed to be asleep, Mark. What's wrong?

I rarely sleep for a day, unless Nova decides I'm in need of a rest cure.

A day? It seemed no more than an hour or two . . .

The vitality and crispness of his mindtouch made her realize how ragged her own was.

How do the Changelings do it? Weeks, months, a whole incredible winter of this.

Selena's plaintive thought made him chuckle. *I doubt that what you've been doing is ordinary dreamwalking. And in spite of all the manna we've consumed, we lack the Changeling metabolism. Or haven't you noticed that we actually eat more than the Changelings?*

But Selena was far too tired for a discussion of metabolic differences. With a grateful sigh she gave herself up to sleep.

Mark joined the Changelings. Though somewhat prepared by the images which had seeped past Selena's words, he was still shocked by the quantum leap in power of the interlocked minds. It was like going to sleep by a stream and waking by a river in flood. Tentatively, then with surging delight, his mind drank the river of strength. As Selena had, he watched, learned, and participated as minds stretched to awareness, slept, then joined their recent teachers to touch new minds. Each awakened colonist poured strength into the river, adding depth and savor to its flow.

Time was measured not by cycles of light and darkness, but by fluctuations in the river's power as Changelings and humans withdrew for rest and food. New snows came and went, dusting motionless bodies with the bold crystals of winter until the grove resembled a white sheet lumped and wrinkled where Changelings lay beneath.

Only once did the river falter. A second sun rose briefly and died over Paran's first city. The anguish of three minds torn from flesh flamed over the river of minds, disturbing its flow, rippling it with discrete drops of individual thought.

The city.

Gone.

Small bomb.

Enough.

Scanners. Another bomb?

The river turned, redirected its flow, deliberately sought a hostile mind. Hunted, pursued the mind relentlessly, and the result was an Earther assassin.

The Lucents separated, washed over the mind, examined it minutely.

This one will never know the spiral.

Mark/Selena agreed. *He would die first. Or we may have to kill him ourselves. But now we must see.*

A campsite. Tired men and women sleeping, their assassin leader on guard. No shuttle, nor sign of one.

Selena reached out and brushed the assassin's brain. With a surprised look the Earther slumped into unexpected sleep.

The river withdrew, sought other hostility, pursued, and examined. Another assassin slept, and the hunt passed on, relentless. At last an assassin was found who piloted a shuttle.

They killed her without warning.

And continued to hunt. When four shuttle pilots lay dead, Mark/Selena withdrew. But not before the Lucents' compassionate thoughts reached Selena.

It is difficult for a Healer to bring death. We have had to kill our own children. We know. Take what comfort you can with the knowledge that four deaths ensured a thousand lives.

Selena thanked them, but their words could not remove the sickness which permeated her. Mark wrapped her body and mind in love, was close while the sickness raged, comforted her when the sickness slacked.

I've killed before, came her weak thought, *but never like that, so . . . dying and dying and . . .* Her thought ended with broken laughter. *You were right, Mark. The Lucents understand death. They ought to. They . . . I don't know why I'm . . . I'd kill as many as I have to . . . I want to live and be free with you . . . The Changelings need . . .*

Mark merged his mind with hers, gathered her lashing thoughts, shared their pain, and accepted her. When he felt her strength return, he sifted her thoughts for self-hatred, but found none. If he could accept and love what she was, she could also.

We must go back, he thought reluctantly. *It's not finished.*

Will it ever be?

The river grew without regard to sun or darkness, stillness or storm. It flowed ceaselessly, absorbed tributary Changelings, flowed swift and deep and potent to an unknown end. In the river's backwash and eddies, guerrillas and colonists alike surfaced to a different reality. Some left the river and met Rynlon shuttles. Others waited, floated, then plunged their new awareness back into the current. Changeling and human interlocked with increasing skill and strength beyond measure.

Yet for all its awesome power, the river of minds was gentle. It beckoned, rather than demanded; desired, rather than forced. When the river's course brought it to minds which refused or were incapable of change, the river flowed on with neither retribution nor regret.

Inflowing minds grew from a trickle to a stream increasing. The river and time flowed ever faster, wider, draining the continent of willing minds, gliding people to safety, isolating others on self-built islands of hatred, until finally no new minds remained.

A change came over the river; power became latent,

current relaxed; the river paused and rested, and murmured to itself.

Over?

Yes.

No. Tien.

Other ships? Other shuttles?

Of course.

Now or future.

Inevitable.

Yes.

The river of minds reached and currents tightened, surged between closing banks of Lucent will, raced white with energy.

Now.

Mark/Selena dammed the river, rode the curling, climbing white energy, drank its power, led it through ebony cold to the light of another sun.

Tien was in his conference room, glaring at the Ear who sat transfixed in her chair.

"What is it, Ciral?" he snapped.

"Paran," she whispered. "My God . . . can it be like that?"

"Speak up! Is there a traitor here?" he said, staring at the suddenly pale men and women which lined the conference table.

But Ciral didn't answer immediately.

Tien looked at her staring, sightless eyes, and felt cold currents over his spine. He reached out and slapped her once, twice, until she remembered where she was.

"Is there a traitor here?" he demanded again.

"None of these people. They refuse to be reached, as you do. But I can't help it; I'm a receiver."

Ciral trembled, whether in fear or some other emotion. Tien neither knew nor cared. He shook her roughly.

"Tell me!"

"I have a message for you," she said dully. "A shipload of Earther assassins will arrive within a week. Paran doesn't want them."

"What?"

"They say Earth should eat the fruits of its own hatred."

"They? Who are they?"

"Many minds, so many."

"Aliens?" he demanded with rising voice.

"I . . . The word has no meaning. Mind is universal."

Tien swore obscenely, but Ciral continued as though she hadn't heard.

"They say you will cease all attempts to attack Paran. Immediately. You will cease persecuting parans on Earth. Immediately. You will cease propagandizing against so-called aliens. Immediately."

Tien's laughter was as brittle as thin ice.

"You'd like that, wouldn't you, Ciral? Now, if your silly little act is over—"

"Or die."

Tien's hand closed into a fist, but before he could lash out he found himself falling helplessly to the floor, paralyzed. When the other council members would have rushed to his aid, they, too, were felled by paralysis.

In the sudden silence, Ciral's words came with unflinching clarity.

"Your paralysis is temporary. It could be permanent. Or fatal. The choice is yours.

"You, Tien, are a demagogue. In as much as a single person can be held responsible for mass actions, you are blamed. From you we take the power of speech.

"From the others we take nothing. They have merely licked the feet of power; they would lick ours, could they reach us. It is their nature.

"Do not fear for your power, Tien. We will not claw Earth unwilling into our future. Nor will we permit you to claw it into your past. If you are wise, you will readjust your power base, find something other than hatred to bind your organization. If you are unwise, if you continue to use your power against us, we will take that power from you, and with it your life.

"Choose."

Tien was released from his paralysis. His pale lips formed words, but no sound followed. In despair he nodded his head.

With a soundless ingathering of will, the river returned to its source.

Mark and Selena awoke to a grove changed almost out of recognition. Humans and Changelings lay asleep on the snow, numbers beyond their desire to count. As they watched, seeming snowdrifts stirred, then exploded as the Changelings beneath rose in search of food. Other humps of snow exhaled plumes of white air; the Changelings beneath slept comfortably, as impervious to cold as the humans in their Rynlon jumpsuits.

"Sleep on ice and wake up warm," she murmured.

"But stiff," came Mark's rueful reply.

Selena smiled invisibly behind her enveloping clothes. Only her eyes were uncovered. With a quick motion she peeled the protective mask back and shook her hair free.

"Ahh, that feels better," she said as the cold air freshened her skin.

"Much," agreed Mark, removing his own mask. "Now I can give you a proper good morning."

Selena returned his kiss, and laughed when his beard tickled her lips. They lay against each other in long embrace, savoring being close and safe.

"For now," qualified Selena. "Earth remains; even dreamwalkers cannot reverse decades of hatred and fear."

"Not all at once; in time Earth will change. We made a good beginning."

Memories of the river of minds flowed from him, and

of the rich haven the river had won for human and Changeling alike. His lips brushed hers, his breath warm and sweet on her mouth.

"A good beginning indeed," she murmured as she drew Mark down to her.

FUN AND LOVE!